THE TRUTH WE TELL

NIKKI LEE TAYLOR

Magpie

Magpie Creative Media

Published by Magpie Creative Media

ISBN 978-0-6484406-4-2

nikkileetaylor.com.au

THE TRUTH WE TELL

BOOK TWO

This book is dedicated to all the incredible women who have walked beside me over the years. Those we have lost along the way, those who live incredible lives in faraway places, and those who I am lucky enough to see every day. None of you are relatives, but all of you have been my sisters.

Foreword

This book contains limited material relating to suicide and self-harm. While there are no deaths relating to self-harm included in this book, should it raise issues for you please contact a mental health services provider in your local area.

If this book raises issues for you, please contact your nearest mental health provider. In Australia call **Beyond Blue on 1300 223 636** or **Lifeline on 13 11 14**.

Chapter One
HARLOW

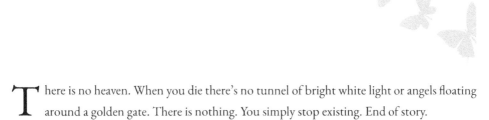

There is no heaven. When you die there's no tunnel of bright white light or angels floating around a golden gate. There is nothing. You simply stop existing. End of story.

A lot of people have argued with me about this, mostly because they're scared and sometimes because they think I'm just a dumb seventeen-year-old. Like what do I know, right? But in the end, I always win the debate. And why shouldn't I? I'm the only one who's ever been dead.

I was eleven when it happened. A car accident. Well, a kidnapping and attempted murder if we're being honest, but the medical report called it a car accident. I was officially dead for three minutes before they managed to restart my heart. Apparently, that's the longest your heart can stop pumping blood and oxygen before you begin to suffer irreparable brain damage.

Everyone expected me to be traumatized by what happened, maybe suffer post-traumatic stress disorder having *died* so young and all. But for me, the experience was nothing short of cathartic. When my injuries healed, I left the hospital knowing exactly what I wanted. To be free of my fame-seeking mother, the infamous Madelyn-May Marozzi, parental blogging queen of North America. I wanted, no, I *needed*, to be free of her. I felt as though my second chance at life depended on it.

Not long after I was released from hospital, my parents and brother Harry moved to Australia to start over. Much to my mother's disgust, I stayed here in Philly with my best friend Kempsey and her parents Steve and Rhonda who were more than willing to become my official guardians until I come of age.

For so long, I thought of the day I moved in with them as my rebirth. The day I got to *choose* my family. Since then, I have lived a quiet, reserved life, away from the spotlight forced on me by my mother. For six years it's been a wonderful life in a lovely home surrounded by warm and caring people. If only things could have stayed that way.

Chapter Two

SOPHIE

Poppy was born at one minute past two at the University of Maryland Harford Memorial Hospital, and to everyone's surprise, she came out with an extra thumb. According to the doctors it wasn't that uncommon. But lying there in the birthing suite, my hair wet and my skin slick with sweat, I felt as though I failed my daughter before she even took her first breath. In terms of natural childbirth, at age thirty-five I was considered geriatric. I knew without a doubt that it was my aging body that let her down. I hated myself but the doctors were adamant. There were no signs of congenital defects or issues of concern, other than the thumb. To them, she was perfect.

Because Poppy arrived right on my due date, I took it as a sign she might be an easy baby. I hoped it meant she had some in-built understanding that the world of adults was ruled by dates and times. That she would work in with my plans. But she didn't.

As the weeks turned into months and months turned into years, Poppy became a tired and irritable child. I was sure she slept and cried more than any normal baby should. More than Josh had.

By the time she was three, we were regulars at the Westbrook Family Medical Clinic, but no matter how many times I pleaded for him to look harder, Dr Martin Havinack remained adamant that she was fine. She was just '*one of those children who needs a little extra love and attention*', he would say. But deep in my heart, I knew something was wrong. I just didn't know what it was.

By the time she was four, five separate psychologists had assured me it was normal to be overcautious. To not just think the worst but to expect it. My son Josh died when he was six, not because I missed the signs of an underlying health condition, but because a drunk driver killed him and my husband in a car wreck. They told me again about survivor's guilt, post-traumatic stress disorder, and all the other conditions grief can create. They willed me to believe that it was fear not fact when I told them something was wrong with Poppy. They said my ongoing anxiety, coupled with the fact that I randomly uprooted my life and moved to Havre De Grace, was proof enough that I was the one who needed medicating. I hoped they were right, but I also knew they were wrong. My move to Havre De Grace was not random. It had been very much on purpose.

"Now you be careful," I tell Poppy, my face pressed gently against her tiny button nose. "Some of those kids are bigger than you."

"Come on, Mom," she whines. "I'm up next."

I zip up her hot pink parka and say a silent prayer. She's five. It's March and still cold out. Our school has a team in the local social baseball competition for under-eights. The team is a mix of boys and girls and at the end of the season, the winning team gets to host an all-expenses-paid day at the Fun Factory, a popular kids' game and pizza place just off Main Street. All the teams in the league attend, so no matter how good or bad the kids play, everyone gets a prize at the end of the season.

"Are you sure about this?" I ask again.

"I want to play," she says, her tiny hands clenched into determined fists at her sides. "Please, Mommy, I want to play."

"Alright, okay." I tuck her long ponytail into the back of her parka so none of the other kids accidentally pull on her hair. "Come straight back if you feel puffed out or tired. I'll be right here."

She runs off and I pull myself up, my stomach twisting. Since the day she was born, I feel like I've been waiting, side-stepping the inevitable.

Beside me, my golden retriever Miss Molly doesn't bother to get up. She was a rescue so it's hard to know her exact age but if I had to guess I'd say she's around ten years old. Her bones creak and her gait is slow, but she never leaves my side. It's been that way since the day I brought her home. I give her a smile and a scratch behind the ear then glance out over the field.

Poppy is up on the plate, bat in hand. She swings and the bat connects. She is off, running toward first base, her ponytail already untucked and flapping around like a happy dog's tail. When she trips and falls, I take a nervous step forward, hand on my chest, silently willing her to get up. One. Two. Three...

As I am about to run forward, her giggle carries on the breeze and she gets to her feet.

See, you're being ridiculous. She's fine.

Feeling silly, I sneak a glance at the other parents. Did anyone see me lurch forward, eyes wide with panic? Do they think I'm a helicopter parent? Or worse, do they think I know something is wrong and am letting her play anyway? I'm so concerned with deciding if other people are staring at me that I don't see her fall the second time.

"Sophie," one of the other parents says, an edge of concern pitching her voice higher. "Is Poppy okay?"

I snap my head back and peer out over the field. A tiny shape wrapped in hot pink is lying motionless on the ground. From the edges of the field parents slowly start to move in, their steps hesitant, not wanting to believe that something is wrong. The referee blows his whistle and hurries toward her. I can't feel my legs but I'm already running, the freezing wind slicing my cheeks.

"Poppy! Poppy!" My cries echo and I can't tell if it's me screaming or one of the other parents. "Poppy!" When I reach her, I throw myself down and push the hair back from her face. Two ribbons of bright red blood trickle from her nose and her eyes are closed. "Poppy, wake up! Wake up!" The crowd is closing in on me. The weight of their fear is palpable. "Poppy!"

"I've called 911," A male voice says. "They're coming but - "

"But what?"

"They have to come from another call. They're fifteen minutes out."

I rest my hand on Poppy's forehead because I don't know what else to do. Her skin is slick and too hot for such a cold afternoon. When I finally look up at the sea of faces staring back at me, some are familiar and others I've never seen before but the one thing they share is the look in their eyes— fear.

I scoop her tiny body up into my arms and cradle her against my chest. The bottom half of her face is stained red from the blood running out of her nose. As I wipe at it with my sleeve and hate myself for every minute I've wasted doing anything other than learning how to save my child's life.

If she dies this will be my fault.

"I'll take you to the hospital." A burly man wearing a Havre de Grace Warriors windbreaker is suddenly standing in front of me, keys in hand. "Do you need to call her father?"

"There's... there's no father," I mutter. "It's just me."

"Right. Let's go then."

People jump out of our way as we run single file toward the carpark. Their faces are a blur, and no one speaks as we pass. A woman in jeans and a windbreaker clutches at her chest as we race by. Next to them a man and woman pull their small son between them, closing ranks. I know they're worried, but I also know a tiny part of them is relieved it's me racing against time and not them.

The dusty carpark is only meters away, but Poppy's lips are blue. She's gone still in my arms.

"I think she's stopped breathing!" I scream. "What do I do?"

The man stops abruptly and turns back, his brow pulled into a tight frown. "Put her down."

"What? No, I don't know CPR... I can't - "

"We need to find someone who knows how to do it while we wait for the ambulance."

"We can't," I shout back, my voice breaking. "We have to go. They won't get here in time!"

An icy wind whips across the back of my neck as I readjust my grip on her tiny body.

He steps in close. "What's your name?"

"Sophie," I sob. "My name is Sophie."

"Sophie, once we get into my truck there's no one to help us. She won't make it without CPR. If we can keep her breathing the ambulance might get here in time. There's still hope."

I stare at him, willing his words back down his throat. She's heavy in my arms, gravity pulling her down and away from me. "Goddamn it!" I scream as loud as I can. "Help me! Anyone! Help me, please!"

Screams scrape against the tightness of my throat. As each second passes, I feel her slipping away as though a light is slowly dimming inside me. If she dies, every spark of joy will be extinguished from my life. If she dies, I will die with her. Maybe not my body, but my soul, my love, my will.

"I'll find someone," he calls, already running back toward the field. "Stay there, Sophie. I'll find someone! I'll find someone!"

I fall to my knees and fold my daughter's lifeless body across my lap. Her skin is translucent, clouds of gray gathering at her temples. A storm about to break.

"Don't you leave me, Poppy," I whisper. "Don't you leave me."

Seconds feel like hours as I gently rock her back and forth in my arms. I knew this. I knew something was wrong and I didn't prepare myself. All I had to do was take a CPR class. One stupid class. That's all I had to do.

"Lay her down on the ground," someone shouts at me from across the carpark. It's a woman's voice, strong but breathless. She's been running. "Quickly dear, there's no time."

When I look up, I register that the woman is older than me, maybe in her sixties. She has a short bob of gray hair and deep lines etched around her eyes. The rest is a blur.

"Roll her onto her back," she tells me, as I slide Poppy gently onto the ground. "What happened?"

"I... I don't know. She was running. I looked away for just a second." I glance desperately at the man who was going to drive us to the hospital. "Did you see what happened? Was there a collision?"

He is down on one knee. His cheeks are scarlet. His chest is heaving. "Beats me. Best I can tell she was just running and then…" he draws another deep breath, "…down she went. I didn't see any other kids near her."

"Does she have a health condition?" the woman asks.

I note she has the efficiency and tone of someone who knows what they're doing. "Are you a doctor?"

"No, but I was a nurse for thirty-two years. She's very pale. Is she anemic?"

"Anemic? No… I… I've taken her to doctors before. They never found anything like that."

The woman crosses her hands over my daughter's tiny chest and begins compression. "But you thought otherwise?"

I nod quickly not wanting to believe I might have been right. "Please," I whisper to the sky as I watch her tiny chest rise and fall, "not again."

"Where's the damned ambulance?" the man curses, getting back to his feet and looking out toward the road.

"We can't wait," the woman says. "We need to go."

"Are you sure?" I have no control over my daughter's life. I don't know how to help her and will have to rely on this woman, this stranger, to make a choice that will decide whether she lives or dies.

"I've got a faint rhythm," she says. "I'll continue chest compressions in the car. But we've got to move. Now!"

I gather Poppy up off the ground and together we run toward the man's truck. With every step and every breath, I beg. I beg the power of the universe. I beg God, even though I have always been one of the faithless. I beg anyone and anything to take my life and give it to Poppy instead. I silently apologize for what I did, for having her without telling Bastian. I apologize for having slept with another woman's husband. I apologize for thinking I deserved a second chance, and for daring to try and be a mother again. I apologize for everything I can think of. But most of all I apologize for once again failing a child whose only flaw was to depend on me.

"Please, you have to get us there in time," I say, as I slide Poppy onto the dirty back seat of the truck. "She's so little… she's…"

He nods and starts the engine. Beside me, the woman immediately starts compression on Poppy's tiny bird-like chest. But as we reverse, the man catches my eye in the rear-view mirror and it's hard to miss his look of panic. As we race toward the hospital the car is silent. No one dares to speak but if we did, we would all say the same thing - *If we make it, it will be a miracle.*

Chapter Three
HARLOW

It's the pain that wakes me. A dull, throbbing ache that immediately settles into my bones. Spiderwebs of lingering sleep cling to me and I wonder if I'm back in the hospital. If perhaps the past six years have been nothing more than a dream.

But as I open my eyes, I'm greeted by soft light falling in through cream curtains and the delicate chirp of birds in the tree outside. I'm safe beneath my lemon and white comforter and up on the wall hangs a familiar abstract painting, its warm pastel hues reminding me of a sunrise.

This time I have not been kidnapped or almost killed in a car crash, but as I reach up and touch my lip, there is no doubt in my mind that I'm injured. I can feel it. Split and swollen.

What the hell happened?

My head throbs, and when I push back the comforter, I see deep scratches running from my shoulder to my elbow. I try to pull myself up, but the room swims in and out of focus. A choking rush of bile burns the back of my throat and I battle to swallow so I don't throw up all over the bed.

'You're awake,' Rhonda says, striding in without knocking, the usual warmth missing from her voice.

"If you could call it that," I manage.

"Well, you have to get up, Harlow. We need to talk."

I squint as Rhonda tears back the curtains and bright sunlight assaults my eyes. "What time is it?"

"It's just after one o'clock in the afternoon." She doesn't look at me and instead picks my clothes up off the floor and folds them over her arm. There's dried blood on the sleeve of my shirt.

"Is that..." I peer in closer.

"Now, Harlow. I'll meet you downstairs."

She's gone before I have a chance to respond or ask about the stain on my clothes. It also occurs to me she didn't bother to ask if I was okay. Confused, I cast my mind back to last night and feel a sudden jolt of fear when I realize that I can't remember how we got home.

In my ensuite bathroom, I'm horrified at the disheveled girl looking back at me in the mirror. My hair is mattered with lumps of dried blood. The right side of my lip is swollen, an angry split running from top to bottom. On my forehead, is a lump the size of a potato.

"Jesus…" I breathe, forcing myself to lean in and evaluate the damage. "What the hell happened last night?"

Carefully I pull my nightgown up and over my head, mindful not to bump my lip or the lump on my forehead. When the hot water hits my scalp, I close my eyes and let it wash over me. At my feet, the water turns a bloody mix of red and brown as it circles the drain.

When I eventually make my way downstairs, Rhonda is sitting stiff and stern at the formal dining table. Beside her is Kempsey, both their faces are blank and cold, and I shiver despite the warmth of the fire crackling in the hearth.

"Harlow, come and take a seat." Rhonda gestures to a leather chair directly across from her and it strikes me that we've never sat in this room the entire time I've lived here. Beside her Kempsey's head is down and she's pulling at one of her fingernails, something I know she does when she's nervous.

"I'm so confused about last night," I begin. "How did I end up with all these cuts and bruises?"

Finally, Kempsey looks up and when she does, I cannot hide my shock. Her right eye is swollen shut, an angry purple bruise stretching from the rise of her cheekbone up to her eyebrow.

"Kempsey, oh my God, are you alright?" I reach across the table, but she pulls away before my fingers reach her.

"Harlow, what you did last night is beyond words," Rhonda begins. "I don't even know where to start."

"What I *did*?" I repeat. "I can't remember anything about last night."

Kempsey huffs and looks away. "As if."

"No really," I try. "I can't remember anything. What happened to us?"

"To *us*?" Kempsey snaps. "You. You are what happened to us. You freaked out at the club and started acting like a crazy person."

"The club?" I close my eyes and brush through the spiderwebs trying to remember.

"Yes," Rhonda says. Her tone is sharp. Her lips are tight. "You are both seventeen years old. Too young to be out in a nightclub with boys."

"It wasn't a nightclub, Mom," Kempsey says with a sigh. "It was just a beer garden."

"At night with boys."

"I remember sitting with Darcy," I mumble. "He and I were talking and then we came back to the table. I felt dizzy and then - "

"- you climbed up onto a table and flashed your boobs at everyone. You were yelling and shouting like a maniac," Kempsey finishes.

"No," I quickly shake my head. "I would never - "

"Ah, yeah... you would," she assures me. "Then you started making out with some old dudes letting them feel you up and shit. It was, like, so gross."

"Kempsey, no. I wouldn't... I didn't..." I trail off and feel like I'm going to be sick.

I would never do that... would I?

"Then, after you saw Darcy and me together you went ballistic." She points to her black eye. "Security tried to throw you out, but you made such a scene you ended up falling and smashing your head on the gutter outside."

I push back against the chair desperate to get some distance from the things coming out of Kempsey's mouth. It can't be true. I would never dream of acting like that. But my physical pain is real, and it's clear from Kempsey's bruises and the look in her eye, that hers is too. I glance at Rhonda hoping for some explanation, a solution, anything, but she just stares back stony-faced.

"So, what do you have to say for yourself, Harlow?"

"I... I don't know. I don't remember any of this."

"Did you take something?"

"Did I take something?" I glance at Kempsey, but she quickly swallows and drops her eyes. Through the fog, I begin to remember that she was the person who brought over my final drink. "Kempsey did you - "

"Don't try and blame this on me!" she snaps before I can finish. "You're the one who got wasted and freaked out."

"I only had two drinks. After the second, I... everything is a blur."

Rhonda rests her palms out on the table and glares at me. "Neither of you should have been drinking at a club. But Harlow, you hurt my daughter. I can't have that."

My heart pounds against my ribs and I begin to panic. I'm being accused of things I can't remember. "If I did then I didn't mean it," I begin, my words rambling. "I would never intentionally hurt Kempsey. Please, you must know that."

Rhonda closes her eyes and slowly shakes her head. "I need to think this through."

"Someone must have drugged me." I glance at Kempsey, but she refuses to meet my eye. "They must have. Rhonda, you know me. I would never act like that."

"I can't have drugs here, Harlow."

"But I'm not on drugs!" I get to my feet, my eyes brimming with tears. "I would never take drugs. I don't... I don't want drama in my life... not after everything, you know that. That's why I stayed here. I don't - "

"Then I wouldn't go back to school on Monday," Kempsey tells me with a dramatic roll of her eyes. "Because there's definitely going to be drama."

"Why? Did everyone see what I did?"

"Everyone? Yes, Harlow, *everyone* saw what you did."

"What does that mean?"

"It means your little show went viral. You're all over socials."

I clutch at my chest as the air disappears from the room. "You filmed it?"

"Not me, but pretty much everyone else. I'm surprised you haven't seen it."

I rub my forehead as the room swims around me. "But I... I don't even have socials. You know I hate that stuff."

Kempsey exchanges a look with Rhonda then slides her phone toward me. "Here, but don't say I didn't warn you."

My skin goes cold as I watch the disaster play out on a video posted to Kempsey's social media account. My soft pale breasts are exposed. The fly on my jeans is unzipped. I'm up on a table holding a glass of beer over my head like a trophy. The light is dim but two men I've never seen before, both much older than me, are clearly groping and clutching handfuls of my bare skin. One has a dirty-looking beard and red-rimmed eyes. He squeezes my nipple between his fingers and slurs something to the camera that I can't understand. The other looks just as drunk. He has my left breast cupped in one hand and is taking a selfie with the other. But the most humiliating part of it is that I'm laughing. I look so joyful, so carefree. I swallow hard and close my eyes.

Did I like it? Why didn't I try and stop them?

When I look back at the screen, the camera phone is following me. I climb down from the table and stumble toward two people kissing in a darkened corner of the beer garden. Through vacant eyes, I glance back at whoever is filming. Dried spittle hangs from my lip and my hair is a mess.

"Whoa... you are wa-sted," a male voice sings from behind the camera. "This is going to be a-ma-zing."

When the two people on screen break apart, to my surprise it's Kempsey and Darcy who were kissing. I glance up from the phone and stare at her in shock. "You kissed him?"

She shrugs and pushes the phone a little closer. "Keep watching."

Suddenly onscreen, I raise a chair up over my head and hurl it at my best friend's face. She screams and Darcy shouts out. The video falls out of focus and disembodied voices yell to call an ambulance. I hear myself sobbing and it's hard to tell whether the sound is coming from the past or present.

"Kempsey, I... I don't know what to say," I tell her, pushing the phone away from me. "Someone put something in my drink. They must have. You know I would never act like that on my own... even though you were kissing Darcy."

But again, Kempsey just shrugs and then pushes the phone back into her pocket. "I don't know why you even care that we were kissing. It's not like you guys were dating. You liked him. No one ever said it was mutual."

"I never said I liked him. "

"Oh, please..."

"Girls," Rhonda says, her arms stretched out toward us. "Forget about the boy. This is serious. We have to meet with the school on Monday. Let's see what they have to say and we'll take it from there."

"I don't use drugs. You both know that," I plead. "You gave me a home when I wanted to stay, and I'll always be grateful for that. I would never try to hurt you Kempsey, not on purpose. I don't know what I would do without you guys."

"Well, you could consider going to live with your *actual* family," Kempsey suggests, her tone making it clear she's still furious.

"Is that really what you want me to do?"

"Just... do whatever you want, Harlow. But I really like Darcy so since you messed that up for yourself, don't go messing it up for me too."

"Sure." I force a smile. "Of course not."

She nods and pushes back from the table. "I'm going over to Laura's. Darcy's coming to meet us. Obviously, you're not invited, Harlow. Sorry not sorry, you know?"

I glance at Rhonda, but she doesn't meet my eye. Instead, she gets to her feet and disappears toward the kitchen leaving me to sit alone at the table.

When they're gone, I rest my head in my hands and try to think. One of the last things I remember is Kempsey bringing two beers over to Darcy and me. But what happened after that?

I think hard, trying to remember every detail but my head is throbbing and the best I can conjure are blurry visions of people moving in slow motion. Did she drug me? The thought seems impossible. She took pity on me after the accident and when the truth about my mother came out, she convinced her parents to be my guardians so I wouldn't have to move overseas.

She always liked Darcy and I know deep down it bothered her to think he might be interested in me – her weird little introverted sidekick, but to drug me? I don't want to believe she would be capable of doing something like that, of putting me in danger, especially over a boy. But I also learned a long time ago that the people who love you are usually the ones who end up hurting you the most.

Chapter Four

SOPHIE

F lanked by the man and woman who helped get us here, I run as best I can toward the hospital's emergency department, Poppy's lifeless body hanging from my arms like a rag doll.

"Help me!" I scream, my voice almost incomprehensible. "My daughter! Help me!"

Instantly men and women in teal scrubs run at us from every angle. People who were slumped across seats in the waiting area are up on their feet, brows knotted, and a woman tucks her small daughter in closer.

A middle-aged woman with cropped red hair and a stethoscope around her neck takes Poppy from my arms and places her gently onto a gurney. Relinquishing her to a stranger is like taking my heart and willingly placing it in the cupped palms of someone I have never met.

"What happened?" she asks, her eyes trained on Poppy as she takes her vitals.

"I... she fell. I don't..."

She leans over Poppy but looks up and meets my eye. "I need you to take a breath and tell me exactly what happened."

"She was playing Little League Baseball," I manage between sobs. "She fell but it didn't seem like she was hurt. I think she fell because..."

"...because what?"

"Because something is wrong. I've felt it ever since she was born. Something isn't right."

She holds my gaze, clearly assessing my mental state versus the strength of a mother's intuition.

"Prep for an MRI and full bloods," she barks at two of the nurses watching on. "Now!"

As they turn and wheel Poppy toward a set of plastic double doors, I gather my bag and begin to follow but a young female nurse wearing so much mascara it has congealed on her lashes, steps in front of me. "We'll need you to stay here and fill out her insurance and medical details."

"But I -"

"She's in very capable hands."

The woman looks too young to even work at a hospital and I panic at the idea of Poppy being taken somewhere I can't see her. "Are you sure? I mean…"

Can I trust these strangers with my baby?

"Doctor Yates is incredible," she assures me. "Your daughter will get the best care possible."

I watch after them as Poppy's tiny shape is swallowed up by a pair of double doors.

"Can you follow me please?" she asks again.

I turn to the man and woman from the field. "I don't know how to thank you both," I say, as a bewildered fog falls over my brain. "I don't even know your names."

"I'm Martha," the woman smiles, "and there's no need for thanks. I'm just glad we made it."

"Agreed," the man says with a nod. "I'm Barry. Baz."

Around us, people slowly fold themselves back into their chairs and slump their chins against balled-up palms.

"I don't understand what happened," I mumble half to them and half to the air around me. "She just fell and -"

"I really need you to come with me," the mascara nurse tells me again. "We need your daughter's details."

"Alright, Christ!" I snap, stress breaking through the fog and catching me unaware. "Oh shit, I'm sorry," I apologize immediately. "I didn't mean that. It's just…"

She nods and opens one arm ready to guide me toward wherever it is I need to go.

"We'll wait over here," Martha offers, but there is a question mark in her tone. She probably has somewhere else to be.

"No, don't be silly," I tell her. "You've both done everything you can. Go on back. I'll be fine."

"You're sure?" Baz asks, awkwardly rubbing the back of his neck. "I'd stay, it's just my son is back at the field."

"No, I mean it. Please, you've both done everything you can."

Finally, much to Mascara's delight I take a seat in an uncomfortable orange chair and begin to fill out Poppy's details. When I'm done, they direct me to a small white waiting room with sparse furniture and a wooden coffee table adorned with biscuits in small plastic wrappers.

Unable to even think about eating, I pull out my phone and call to check that Miss Molly is safe. She won't understand being left behind and I hate that I couldn't bring her with me. I scan through the school phone tree and find Delilah's mother saved under her actual name, Julia.

"Julia," I sigh when she answers, "it's Sophie. I was hoping you took Miss Molly from the field?"

"She's here at home with us," Julia says, and my shoulders sag with relief. "She's quite happy and snoozing by the fire with our dog Bosco."

"Thank you so much. I'm sorry to burden you."

She dismisses my apology and asks how Poppy is doing. I tell her all that I can, which is nothing, and then hang up and wait.

After a few minutes, a tired-looking man who looks like he hasn't slept in days shuffles in and folds himself into the seat across from me. Our eyes meet, he nods in recognition and then looks down at the ground. He doesn't speak and either do I. Neither of us wants to give life to the only words there are to say. *I hope. If only. Please, no.*

Together we wait in silence, the wall clock ticking down the moments that will determine the rest of our lives. Eventually, the woman with the red hair who took Poppy away appears in the doorway and gestures for me to follow her.

"How is she? Do you know what happened? Is she alright?" I feel like I'm barking at her and purposely lower the volume of my voice. "Can I take her home?"

"She's resting."

"Oh..." My palm comes up to my collar bone and I let out a long breath. "So, she's alright?"

What I want is for her to smile and tell me that of course, she's alright. It was nothing. She tripped and bumped her nose. Don't be silly. You can take her home right now. But she doesn't.

"Ms Miller -"

Oh, God.

"It's Sophie, please."

She nods and swallows, her neck muscles constricting for the most fleeting of seconds. It is a tiny gesture but one that sends a shock wave of panic from the top of my head down and into my toes. Pins and needles sting at my face and for the first time in years, my heart beats out of rhythm. The first sign of a panic attack.

"Sophie - "

"I... I think I'm going to have a panic attack," I manage. "I used to have them, not in years, but I can feel - "

She stops where we are and eases me into one of the chairs along the wall of the corridor. "Just breathe. Slow and deep, Sophie. In through your nose, out through your mouth."

The smell of antiseptic and fear flood my nose as I inhale deeply, searching for a stable breath. Beside me, the doctor pulls out a cell phone and asks someone to bring two milligrams of Valium.

"Keep breathing, Sophie. In and out." She leans in and wraps her fingers around my wrist to check my pulse. "You're doing great."

"What's wrong with my daughter?"

"Let's just get you calm and breathing properly then we can discuss Poppy's condition."

"Condition? What condition?"

A male nurse who looks young enough to still be in school approaches us carrying a small cup of water and a plastic thimble containing a small white tablet.

Valium, Xanex, Prozac. None are strangers to me. After my husband and son were killed it was years before I could function without some form of medication. For years my anxiety and I lived a very small life, not leaving the house, each day spent chained to a pillar of guilt and remorse.

Get it together. This is not like that. Fear, not fact.

I take the tablet and scold myself. Indulging in fear and panic is selfish. Poppy needs me. I have no right to escape into a panic attack. Somewhere in this building, my daughter is scared and alone. I have no right.

"I want to see my daughter," I say, finally finding an even tone for my voice. "I'll be fine. Please, just take me to her and tell me what's going on."

The doctor nods and I pull myself up and follow her. We turn left, then right, take an elevator up one floor, and memories of Josh's accident flood my mind. In a hospital just like this one, my family was identified and autopsied. He looked so tiny lying still and silent on the gurney, like his body had contracted around the empty space his soul once took up.

"We have her here in the pediatric wing," the doctor says, interrupting my memory. "We'll keep her here tonight. I'd like to monitor her and run some more tests."

When the elevator doors open, sterile white walls are replaced with lashings of bright color and cartoon animals. Instead of looking cheerful, they strike me as garish.

"But you know what happened?"

"I think so, yes."

I hold my breath and wait for her to elaborate.

"I can't be one hundred percent certain until we do more tests, but your daughter is displaying signs that align with something called Fanconi Anemia."

Oh, thank God.

"Anemia, yes," I gush, instantly relieved. "The woman who helped me get her here, she was a nurse and mentioned something about anemia."

The word anemia feels so benign compared to the atrocities I had been imagining. Lymphoma. Brain tumor. Leukemia.

"Poppy's been to see our local doctor several times though," I tell her. "He never said anything about anemia. But that's good, right? Anemia? I mean, it's treatable."

"I noticed a small scar on her hand," the doctor says, ignoring my questions. "Did she have a birth defect? An extra digit?"

"Yes, an extra thumb but the doctors said it was nothing to be concerned about."

"Mm-hmm."

"You don't agree?"

"Let me run a few more tests. For now, you can go and see your daughter. I'll be back when I have more information."

"But she's going to be alright?"

"For now, she's alright and she's asking for you. I'll update you as soon as I can. She's down the end in bed seven."

As I make my way through the ward, I try not to look at the other children or worried parents hovering over them. Instead, I try to make sense of what the doctor has told me. All I know about anemia is that it has something to do with red blood cells and feeling fatigued which makes sense because Poppy has always been a tired child. Perhaps she'll need supplements, or we'll have to look at her diet, maybe add more red meat. Something about needing iron also rings a bell.

There is a curtain around her bed, and I pause for a moment before pulling it back. I don't want her to see that I've been crying, especially not when a hamburger and some vitamins might be all she needs to get back on her feet.

I force a smile onto my face and push my fears down as deep as they will go. "Hi sweetheart," I chime, as I pull back the curtain and walk toward her tiny shape tucked up in the hospital bed. "How are you feeling?"

She shrugs and yawns, pulling a teddy I've never seen before tighter into her chest.

"Who's your new friend?"

"He's from here," she tells me. "I don't know his name."

I smile and smooth an invisible crease from the sheet that's covering her. "Well, you know what? I bet he'd love it if you gave him a name."

She glances down at the teddy but again just shrugs and looks disinterested. I remind myself they think it's anemia, something that is treatable. Poppy will be okay.

Fear, not fact.

"What's wrong with me, Mommy?"

Her voice is fragile and tiny and yet the impact is powerful enough to tear apart even the hardest of hearts. I swallow and command myself to find a voice that will calm her.

"You, my sweet girl, haven't been taking your vitamins." I give her my best smile and hide my trembling hands where she cannot see them. "And, I think that when the doctor is finished checking on you the first thing we have to do is get you a big hamburger. How does that sound?"

"Can Miss Molly have one too?"

"She sure can," I tell her. "She'll be so happy to see you."

Poppy finally smiles and I tell myself that as soon as they're done I'll take her home and we can fix this. That everything will be alright - because it has to be.

Chapter Five

HARLOW

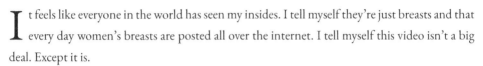

I t feels like everyone in the world has seen my insides. I tell myself they're just breasts and that every day women's breasts are posted all over the internet. I tell myself this video isn't a big deal. Except it is.

When my family packed up and moved to Australia, I promised myself that staying here in Philadelphia, more than ten thousand miles away from my mother, meant I could start over. I thought that when she was gone, with time her lies about my birth would go with her. I thought that all the online attention would be gone. I thought that after everything that happened, her *Love, Mommy* blog with its millions of followers would fracture and fall like a defeated empire. And it had. But now this video of me with its thousands of views is making me feel like instead, I have just taken her place.

For the past six years, I've avoided social media. I don't have any accounts. I don't read blogs and I only use Google when I absolutely have to. Kempsey calls me a recluse and an introvert. She makes fun of how much I love reading paperbacks, the way I cherish the feel of a book in my hand, the musty scent of time trapped within its pages. She could never understand what it feels like to be second best to a computer screen, to be a cog in the wheel of your mother's savage pursuit of success. I know my mother had her reasons. She grew up in a trailer park and when she met my father, a successful publisher, it must have felt like all her dreams had come true. To keep him she lied about not being able to fall pregnant and instead used an egg donor to try and hide her past. I was eleven when I found out another woman provided an egg so that I could be born. But by the time I knew the truth the woman had moved away with no forwarding address. I didn't hate my mother for using an egg donor. I hated her for lying and treating us like vessels to a better life, one where she could present herself to the world as the perfect mother adored by millions.

I sink down into the bed and close my eyes. This morning I went to school but left an hour after I arrived. Everywhere I looked kids were laughing and whispering, their eyes trained on me like recording devices. I'm a joke and a laughing stock. I have never even kissed a guy and now there's footage out there of me laughing as two grown men grope and fondle my breasts.

I close my eyes as a single tear slips over my cheekbone. It's just a video and they're only my breasts, I remind myself again. But the gritty feeling of being exposed won't stop itching at my skin. It claws at me, creeping up my legs, scratching to be let in. They saw me. Watched me. Their eyes and their phones forever capturing the moment I was stripped bare.

I swallow hard and try to stay calm. Eventually, they will move on to the next thing. They will forget about me and move on; just like my family did. A fresh start will come and until it does, I will stay here in this room and never ever come out.

"Harlow, are you in there?" Rhonda knocks at the door. "You need to come out. We have to talk."

So much for that idea.

I gingerly open the door and peek out leaving a gap no wider than a couple of inches.

"Can you come downstairs, please? I need to talk to you."

I nod and reluctantly follow Rhonda into the kitchen. The setting is less formal than the last conversation we had and I hope it means I won't be getting kicked out.

"Harlow, I spoke with your guidance counselor and the principal this afternoon. They agree what happened at the club was out of character. You have a 4.0 GPA and an unblemished record."

I intend to say something like thank you but instead, just feel myself nodding.

"Based on your grades and record of good behavior we all believe that you are telling the truth about being drugged. That said, we'd like you to consent to a blood test so we can get to the bottom of all this."

"Of course, Rhonda, thank you." A long sigh of relief escapes my lips. "I would never - "

"You will still have to deal with Kempsey though. She's not happy."

"I know."

"Well..." Rhonda's eyes are softer, almost tender, "if you can work things out with my daughter, I don't see any reason for you to leave us. Things tend to happen when you're a teenager, but Harlow, they are things that can usually be avoided. You have to make better choices."

I nod and let my eyes fall to the table. "I know and I'm sorry. It won't happen again. Not ever. You have my word."

Chapter Six
SOPHIE

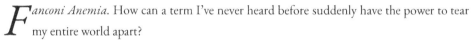

Fanconi Anemia. How can a term I've never heard before suddenly have the power to tear my entire world apart?

When Poppy's tests came back it was confirmed and at first, I had been relieved. Anemia was manageable, or so I thought. Anemia as I knew it, was a condition that makes a person feel tired and weak. I've since learned that's due to the body's lack of ability to produce enough healthy red blood cells. It can be treated with iron supplements and diet. That's what I thought we were looking at. I had no idea how wrong I was.

"Fanconi Anemia is a congenital blood disorder," Doctor Mary Yates, explains in hushed tones in the hall outside Poppy's ward. "It means your daughter's bone marrow isn't making enough blood cells."

"So, what do we do?" I ask. "Add more red meat to her diet? Get supplements?"

When she shifts her weight from one foot to the other and looks away, I immediately know in the deepest part of me that something terrible is about to happen.

"It's not that simple, Sophie," she says. "Our bone marrow is responsible for producing both red and white blood cells and what we call platelets. We need to continually be creating all of these in order to stay alive. At the moment, Poppy's body isn't doing that. Not properly anyway."

My brain absorbs the information. It's my heart that refuses to listen. "So, how do we fix it?"

"Sophie..."

"No, just tell me. Is it surgery? Medication? What?"

Fact, not fear. I just need the facts.

As I wait for her to answer, my entire being splits into two. There is half of me that is angry and impatient. It wants facts and figures and answers and strategies. But there is also another half. One that has already buried a child. That half of me is already coiled up in the dark and refusing to come out.

"Sophie, please understand we will do everything we can," she tries, "but Poppy is already showing symptoms of Stage One acute myeloid leukemia. It's a common complication of her condition."

"Leukemia?"

"Sophie - "

"No, you're wrong," I tell her, my voice venomous. "She's been to the doctor several times. He would have known... he would have... No, I'm taking her home. You don't know what you're talking about. Sign the forms or whatever you have to do but I'm taking her."

"That's not a wise idea."

"I'm not leaving my child here with a bunch of incompetent people who clearly have no idea what they're talking about." I'm desperate to believe that I'm right. But even as I shout at her there is a part of me that knows Poppy is dying. There is a part of me that's always known.

"Sophie, there is one way to treat her."

And then suddenly I'm in free fall and someone has opened a parachute.

She can fix this.

A rush of hope pulses through my body and I wonder if my legs will hold me. She can fix this and has waited until this point in the conversation to mention it. Why?

"Then fix it. What are we waiting for?" I burst. "If it's about money I'll find it, I'll..."

I have no money. Not real money. My savings account holds around $10,000 that I keep for emergencies, but I know it won't be anywhere near enough for whatever procedure they think might save my daughter. But no matter how much it is I will find it - somehow.

"Sophie -"

"I'll find it," I assure her. "Whatever it takes."

"It's not just about money. Poppy would require a bone marrow transplant and even if we found a match and the procedure was successful there is still a high rate of relapse after only a few years."

"Then let's do it. Let's give her every chance at beating this," I gush, my words tripping over each other. "I don't understand what you're waiting for?"

And that's when it happens. She asks the one question I have been dreading since the day my daughter was born.

"Are you able to contact Poppy's biological father?"

Chapter Seven

HARLOW

For the past week, Kempsey has been giving me the cold shoulder. At school, I'm not allowed to sit at her table during lunch and at home, she takes every opportunity to say something nasty or hurtful as I go by. I know she needs time. I hurt her, physically and emotionally, and I get it. She's the type of person who will only feel better once the appropriate punishment has been handed down and endured by the perpetrator - me.

What she doesn't understand is that her version of hell, of being made to feel invisible and obsolete, is exactly what I need. Unlike Kempsey's public display of hurt, my anger and rage are silent. They don't shout or lash out. Instead, they tangle and taunt, holding me down in the dark where no one can reach me.

In the days since the video was posted, resentment and anger have slowly started to asphyxiate me. Every breath tastes sour. Every smile is forced.

Until now I have been able to keep a lid on the anger I feel toward my mother and what happened to me out on that freeway. Having a new family allowed me to breathe, to push my resentment down to the darkest depths. But this video, this new betrayal, has brought everything bubbling back to the surface.

I close my eyes and let the quiet of the room wrap around me. Kempsey, the one person I trusted, put pills in my drink. Now that I've had time to think about it, there is no doubt in my mind. She was jealous that Darcy found my introverted, lack of interest in him appealing in some way. While every other girl tried to impress him, the school's star quarterback with his sweep of sun-kissed hair and tanned arms, I had kept to myself, the chance of him sidestepping my walls all but impossible. It had intrigued him. And Kempsey had hated it. Now she is back where she thinks she belongs – in the center of everything, the rest of the school orbiting around her. All is right with the world, and for the most part, I couldn't agree more. But she hurt me more than she can imagine.

My phone vibrates with a text alert. No one has spoken to me for a week, so I can't imagine who would be sending me a message. I pick up the phone and am shocked to see Darcy's name on the screen.

Darcy: *Hey not sure if you saw the vid but it's on Kaleidoscope now. I know that's not who you are Harlow. Sorry it happened to you.*

Kaleidoscope is a local news and gossip site. If the video of me is really on there, everyone in Philadelphia will have seen it by now. I quickly thumb his message into the background and open the app.

"No, no, no...please," I whisper as I scroll the homepage, praying he's wrong.

But there it is.

My chest falls still, and no air moves through my lungs. There's a video thumbnail and above it, a headline that reads Teen Daughter of Shamed *Love, Mummy* Blogger Bares All.

"No, no, no..."

I scroll down and gasp at my mother Madelyn-May's angelic face smiling back at me, her hair glossy blond hair, and teeth perfect white.

"This can't be happening, it can't..."

I scroll back up to the top and begin to read.

> *Harlow Marozzi, the seventeen-year-old daughter of shamed Love, Mommy parenting blogger Madelyn-May Marozzi was recently caught on camera at a local nightclub topless and more than a little tipsy. Seen partying with friends in the beer garden, the underage teen queen left nothing to the imagination as several men took the opportunity to...*

"No...." I manage, as tears sting my eyes. "This can't be happening."

I scroll down further and keep reading.

> *Kaleidoscope understands Harlow stayed in America with friends after her mother Madelyn-May and the rest of her family fled the country after an attempted kidnapping that resulted in a sensational car accident almost claiming the life of the then eleven-year-old. It was later revealed the perpetrator was none other than Madelyn-May's own mother, Lacy Myers*

sparking questions over the blogging queen's past and her involvement in the murder of her own father in a Californian trailer park when she was fifteen.

The phone drops from my hand and I squeeze my eyes closed. By the end of the day, the video of me standing topless in a nightclub and laughing as strange men grab and squeeze my breasts will be all over the country thanks to my mother's notoriety.

When Rhonda comes in, she doesn't speak. Instead, she closes the blinds, crawls up onto the bed, and pulls me into her chest. This cannot be fixed and we both know it. There is nothing she can say that will take the video off the site. Nothing that will take away the humiliation that is quickly consuming me. My head falls against her chest and I long to sob and let it all out, but I can't. I am numb from the inside out. No pain or sadness. My heart isn't pounding wildly. And I swear there is no sensation in either my arms or legs.

"Everyone will see it," I whisper eventually.

"By tomorrow everyone will have moved on to something else. You'll see."

"She did this to me."

Rhonda's hand stops stroking my arm and the air thickens around us. "Your mother?"

"Kempsey," I correct her. "She drugged me."

"You don't know that," Rhonda tells me quietly.

I close my eyes and try to lose myself in the darkness. But no matter how hard I try, I cannot silence the voice in my head that won't stop screaming, *but I do know that. I do.*

Chapter Eight

SOPHIE

He knew me. Really knew me. He knew what made me laugh, what made me cry, and usually what I was about to say even before I spoke. Bastian. He was never mine to love but it happened anyway. A powerful and consuming love, strong enough to have saved my life.

After the accident stole my husband and son, Bastian was there for me. It's a cliché to say he was my boss and had an obligation to check on me from time to time, that those welfare checks had turned into friendship, and that friendship into love. Even more of a cliché that he was unhappily married, that he had a wife who *didn't understand him*.

Back then, as I huddled in my home, anxiety and post-traumatic stress crippling me, it was Bastian who took my arm and helped me up. Together, he and Miss Molly had been a lifesaving team. Without them I would still be wandering in the darkness, pushing through fog and ghosts trying to find my way home.

Now, as I feel myself plummeting back toward the murky depths, once again it is he I reach for, not as a lifeline this time, but as Poppy's father. The only problem is - he doesn't know she exists.

When he picks up the phone I am immediately struck by the warmth and familiarity of his voice. Even after all these years, it has a timbre all its own, one that reaches in and wraps around my heart.

"Bastian, it's Sophie." The line goes quiet and my heart sinks at the idea he may have hung up. But eventually, he answers. "Sophie? Is it really you?"

His tone carries a mix of surprise and what I think sounds like relief. I wonder if he, like me, has been holding his breath since the afternoon I drove away. "Bastian, I need to talk to you."

"Alright, well I'm still in Australia. Is everything okay?"

I gather myself and try to speak, but nerves get the better of me and I jumble the words.

"Sophie, just breathe," he tells me. "Is it Miss Molly? Is she alright?"

"She's fine. It's not that, it's..."

"I want to help you Soph, but you need to tell me what's going on. Whatever it is, you can tell me. You know that."

I do know that. But I didn't.

There's a part of me that wants to pretend he already knows about Poppy. After his wife Madelyn-May and I were in the car accident trying to save Harlow and her brother Harry from being kidnapped, I blacked out and one of the emergency officers asked if I was pregnant. It was a simple question, nothing more than procedure, but Madelyn-May had overheard. Before I moved away, Bastian mentioned it to me. I had told him not to be silly, that it was nothing. But inside me, our tiny life had already started growing.

"Bastian, when I left it was because I wanted to do the right thing for both of us," I begin. "You were trying to work things out with Madelyn-May and I... I just needed a fresh start."

"Alright."

"I came to Havre de Grace."

"Sophie, that's lovely but you didn't call me after all these years, and at what must be three in the morning your time, to tell me you moved to Maryland. What's going on? You're scaring me."

I take a deep breath and steady myself. "Bastian, when I left Philadelphia I was pregnant." Again, the line falls silent and I hear only my own breathing echoed back at me. "Bastian?"

"I'm here."

"Can you say something?"

"Why are you telling me this now?" he asks, but then as usual says my words for me. "Is our child sick?"

I can no longer hold back the tears. I'm beside myself over Poppy but it's more than that. Left to my own devices I would have held it together, for her, I would have. I'm all she has. But hearing his voice, knowing there's a person out there who has cradled my heart in his hands, I let myself fall.

And without question, he catches me. "Sophie, tell me what you need."

I tell him about Poppy and her condition. I explain to him that she needs a bone marrow transplant and finally that if she doesn't find a donor match soon, she could die.

"I'll be there by tomorrow," he tells me. "I'll hang up and book the first flight out of Sydney."

"Wait. Bastian, the doctor said there was a better chance of a sibling being a match. Do you think Harlow and Harry would come out? It's a long trip and a hell of a lot to take in, but -"

"Sophie, Harlow never left America."

His words catch me off guard and it takes a moment to sink in. "Harlow is still here?"

"She stayed in Philly with her best friend's family." He pauses and I hear him take a breath. "She and Madelyn-May, they didn't get past what happened. Harlow blamed her for the accident and everything leading up to it. She barely communicates with us, but she's there."

"Does she know?"

"About you?"

"About the whole situation. That I'm her..."

"She knows there was a donor, but she doesn't know who you are."

Finding out I was the egg donor of Bastian's twins had tormented me. As much as I tried to stay away, it had been beyond me not to see them at least once. When Madelyn-May brought them to meet me, even though it had been with the intention of making me stay away I was captivated by both of them, Harlow in particular. Her hair was exactly like mine, her eyes Bastian's. She had been eleven then, clueless as to why she was there and completely unaware of the impact her presence had on me.

"She must be seventeen now."

"She is."

"I'm sorry, Bastian," I tell him. "And I know sorry is an incredibly small word considering the circumstances. I just don't know what else to say."

"I'll call Harlow," he says, ignoring my attempts to apologize. "Maybe she can get there right away. Either way, I'll book Harry and me on the next flight. One way or another we'll fix this, Soph. I promise."

"You're not mad?"

"That you never told me about Poppy?"

I let my silence answer.

"What do you want me to say? It's done and she needs our help. Let's just deal with that first."

I nod silently as a single tear of gratitude slips over my cheek. He doesn't need a verbal response to understand that once again he is saving my life. It's Bastian and me. And for us, explanations have never been required.

Chapter Nine

HARLOW

Kempsey drugged me. I have no real proof, but she was the last one to hand me a drink and she hated that Darcy had the nerve to like me instead of her. She did it. That much I know, but despite everything, I made a promise to myself not to confront her.

Now, watching her across the quadrangle holding court with Darcy on her arm and a gaggle of girls hanging on her every word, it's making me sick. She was my best friend. I told her everything. I let her really know me, even the stuff about my mom. In return, she's made me the laughing stock of Philadelphia.

She catches me looking, holds my gaze, and then deliberately pulls Darcy into a long, lingering kiss. As I watch, she pulls away and whispers something into the ear of her offsider, head cheerleader Amber Sherlock. They look at me and together begin to laugh. Beside her Darcy glances in my direction and the only word I can use to describe his expression is pity.

He never knew that I liked him too. I couldn't bring myself to open up, to give him the chance to get close enough to hurt me. Maybe if I hadn't been so shut down, I could have let him know how I felt but instead I wore my anger like a shield. I had been determined never to let anyone hurt me again. But the pain spreading across my chest is proof that my armor has a chink - and her name is Kempsey.

Over at their table, Samantha Sutton leans in. She whispers something that makes everyone, even Darcy, laugh and it's the last straw. Without thinking, I get up from the bench, hitch my bag over my shoulder, and stride across the yard, my eyes fixed on Kempsey.

"Stop!" I shout as I get closer. "Just stop it, Kempsey! Haven't you done enough to me?"

"Watch out everyone, it's unhinged Harlow," Samantha says in a snide tone. "We may have to call security - again."

"Oh, shut up, Samantha," I spit. "You don't know a thing about me."

"Well I do," Kempsey announces stepping away from Darcy. "And you've been broken inside ever since the accident. Just admit it, Harlow, you were never quite right after that, were you?"

She is so close that I can smell her perfume. I drop my eyes and see that her left hand is trembling. For her, this is everything. This confrontation is a direct threat to her position. If she shows compassion or fear it will be seen as weakness by the others. That's the law of the jungle and high school isn't much different.

"I'm fine, Kempsey," I tell her, hands planted on my hips. "At least I was until you drugged me. But I guess that's the only way you could get Darcy's attention, wasn't it? By getting rid of me, which is pretty sad."

"Whatever bitch."

Around us, the other students start to gather in a semi-circle.

"I'm a bitch?" I say, my brow raised. "Did you not hear what I said? You *drugged* me Kempsey. Over a guy."

Darcy snaps a look at Kempsey and I can see his mind racing, thinking back.

"You brought Darcy and me those drinks," I continue. "You handed me the glass Kempsey. That's not a coincidence."

"Stop lying, Harlow. I let you live in my house and this is the thanks I get? Being accused of drugging you?" She rolls her eyes and throws up her arms grandstanding for the crowd. "Do you really think I'd need to drug you of all people, the little weirdo who follows me around, to have a chance with Darcy? Like, *actually*?"

I hold her gaze. A current of adrenaline, hurt, and pent-up anger pulses through me. "Yes Kempsey, I do, *actually*."

The circle of students tightens around us like a fist and the quadrangle heaves. Someone behind Kempsey shoves her and she trips forward falling against me. They are gagging for a fight. I push her off and look around expecting to see the flushed, eager faces of pent-up teenagers but all I see are camera phones pointing at me. Behind the screens they're cheering, pushing for Kempsey to hit me, to start something they can post.

I scan the crowd one last time and see the only person not holding up a phone is Darcy. Instead, his icy blue eyes are looking right at me, willing me to stop. I swallow hard and think of all the times I could have reacted to his attention. All the times he sought me out and I ignored him.

For the first time, I gather the courage to hold his gaze and give a slight nod. Without another word, I withdraw and turn away, their accusations and abuse ricocheting off me as I retreat across the yard, their cameras catching nothing but my back.

Chapter Ten

SOPHIE

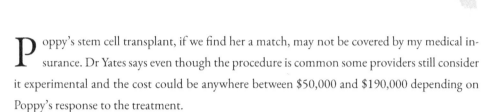

Poppy's stem cell transplant, if we find her a match, may not be covered by my medical insurance. Dr Yates says even though the procedure is common some providers still consider it experimental and the cost could be anywhere between $50,000 and $190,000 depending on Poppy's response to the treatment.

I haven't found the courage to tell Dr Yates that I don't have that kind of money. I did some calculating and if I sell the house, once the mortgage is deducted I might have around $90,000 left, $100,000 with my savings added, so there is some hope. If the bill is on the lower end, I can pay it. It will mean renting for the rest of our lives but that matters little. If it's more, then all I can hope is that Bastian might be willing to help.

The chair beside Poppy's bed is hard and uncomfortable. My back aches and my butt has been numb for the past two hours but I don't dare leave. Somewhere in this hospital Dr Yates and her team are putting together a treatment plan for Poppy while we search for a donor. Until then I will be here by her side.

As I watch her sleeping, I try to wrap my mind around what's happening. My body created and carried her, yet when she needs me most my biology is misaligned with hers. I have already been tested and told that I'm not a match. She is part of me, and I am part of her, and yet I have never felt more useless than I do right now.

Last night when the other children in the ward were asleep, I rested my hands on her chest, closed my eyes, and prayed. I don't believe in God or the Bible or any of that, so it wasn't a prayer to Jesus or Mary or Joseph. Instead, it was to the universe, the elements, and the energy that flows through all things. I asked the universe to harness my love, my light, my energy, and transfer it to her. I begged and pleaded to any power listening to take my life and give it to my child. After a few minutes, my hands grew hot and tingly. I told myself that it was working, that I was giving my life to her, and that she would heal. I wanted to believe it so much that when I felt light-headed, I took it as one more sign the universe was listening. But then a nurse came in to take Poppy's vitals. She told me that Poppy was stable and fighting but it was taking a lot out of her. She was running a fever. Out of the nurse's line of sight, I wiped my sweaty palms along the leg of my jeans and cursed myself for being so stupid. If I couldn't surgically give her part of my body to mend what was broken, how did I think resting my hands on her tiny burning chest would fix anything? I was desperate and delusional to think I could cure her. A mother's love is strong. Strong enough to lift cars and battle the demons that dwell within, but it cannot harness the universe. And in that moment, I also had no choice but to accept that it cannot cure cancer.

Chapter Eleven
HARLOW

In the two days since it was posted, the video of me on *Kaleidoscope* has had almost a million views. Almost a million people have watched a stranger's fingers squeezing my breasts while I laugh. My nipple is pixelated but it's not hard to see what's going on. I click the button to *watch again*, and for the twenty-eighth time let the tragedy play out across my phone screen. When it's done, I scroll down and read the comments.

jojo_brown21: *What a slut. She loves it*

jason_sporto_hudson: *Her Mom must be SOOOOO proud*

phillyflava_tamara: *Guess the Love, Mommy expert was a fail*

brianna_inthehood33: *Mommy's girl for sure*

lolaRifkin: *Heard she was drugged*

peel.jessie21: *Stop slut-shaming you don't even know what happened*

martykegs: *Her tits are shit*

suzie_phillyfan: *What do you expect. Her mother is trailer trash*

ranimarsh: *Hey guys take it easy*

flyersboi: *DM me for her address*

My eyes catch on the final comment and I stop scrolling. My address? The name on the account doesn't look familiar and the profile picture is of a football player I've seen on the news. When I click on the profile it tells me the account is private but when I scroll through the updates, I eventually find a profile picture from six months ago and it's Jason Beckford. He was two years ahead of us at school making him a sophomore now. He was always a loud-mouthed, self-entitled jock. Worst of all he is the type of person who would totally give a stranger my address without a second thought just to entertain himself.

My heart races so hard I can feel it in my throat. I start writing him a message to stop being an arsehole and putting me and Kempsey's family in danger. But before I get past the second sentence Rhonda comes in and once again, says we need to talk.

"Harlow, sweetheart, I am so sorry for everything that's happening to you," she begins. "How are you holding up?"

I put the phone down and nod, willing myself not to crumble.

"This situation is getting very complicated," she continues. "Kempsey says some boy is giving out our address on social media and that at school today you tried to attack her."

"What? No, I didn't," I protest. "I asked her to stop tormenting me. It was the other kids who pushed her into me trying to start a fight."

Rhonda sighs and I notice dark shadows beneath her eyes that I've never seen before. "Harlow, I'm going to call your mother."

"You're what?" My body stiffens and pins and needles sting at my face.

"I think with everything that's going on it's best for you to go to Australia. I really think a fresh start is what you need, somewhere away from all this drama. It's no good for anyone, especially you."

"It's no good for Kempsey is what you really mean."

She reaches out and gently rests her palm on my leg. "No, sweetheart, I mean for everyone. In Australia, you could start over. No one will have seen the video and maybe you could work on things with your mother. I know she'd like to try."

"Oh, she'd like to try?" I manage, my voice breaking. "So, you spoke to her already?"

"We talk every so often. She misses you, Harlow. She likes to know you're alright. Your dad too."

"So, you're doing this for her?"

She gives me a half-hearted smile, part pity, part defeat. "Like I said, it's for the best. For everyone."

Her eyes are gentle, caring. She thinks she's doing the right thing. What she doesn't realize is that she's sending me straight to hell. "It's a done deal then? There's nothing I can do to change your mind?"

"I'm going to call her tonight and make the arrangements. I'm sorry, Harlow. Honestly, I am."

When she leaves me alone, I look around and take in every aspect of the room I've called my own for the past six years. This is my home and I thought Kempsey was my friend. For as long as I can remember my entire life feels like it's been under the control of other people. Since I was born our mother used me and my brother Harry to make people think she was the perfect parent. My grandmother tried to take me against my will. Kempsey has humiliated me, and now Rhonda is casting me out. For seventeen years, I've had no say in my own life. Well, that ends right now.

I throw my legs off the side of the bed and waste no time rummaging through the closet for a duffle bag. As I search, tears well and fall, dripping from my cheeks but I'm too angry to notice. This is so unfair. I hate Kempsey for doing this to me. I hate her. I hate her. A rush of blood and rage pulses through me as I blindly throw things across the room searching for the bag. Everyone knows. Everyone saw me on that video. Everyone has an opinion. My chest heaves as I swallow down the pain. Worse still, everyone has something to say – and a place to say it.

Finally, I see the bag squashed down in the back corner of the closet and I drag at it with all my strength. It catches on something but determined, I pull at it, again and again, until my arms burn. With one final pull my pain, shame, and anger erupts as I reef the strap toward me. The bag comes free and I fall back, the side of my face whacking against the edge of my desk chair.

"Damn it! Stupid fucking chair."

When I slowly pull myself up, my head pounds as I shuffle into the bathroom. There's a trickle of blood on my arm and a bruise already showing on my temple. It's only been a week since the last round of cuts and bruises. With so many injuries, I look like I've been to war, and right now, it feels like a battle that's only just beginning.

If Madelyn-May thinks I'm traveling to Australia so we can all start over she's got another thing coming. For once in my life, I'm going to take control. I am going to decide what happens in my life. I gaze into the bathroom mirror, the hazel and gold flecks of my eyes staring back. This is it. This is the defining moment when I decide who I want to be and what happens next. I've had enough. And if anyone gets in my way they better watch out.

Chapter Twelve

VALENTINE

Teenage boys are such idiots. A fake social media profile, a few direct messages pretending to be some hard-dicked sophomore from another campus, and minutes later the address dropped into my inbox. It was so easy I almost couldn't believe it. I say almost because people are so stupid that nothing they do really surprises me, but this was like taking candy from a baby and the prize is going to taste just as sweet.

For six long years, she has plagued my thoughts, interrupted my dreams, and burned in my veins. Madelyn-May. The one that got away. If Lacy hadn't been so useless the plan we had to kidnap Harlow would have punished her, maybe evened the score. Making her reap the pain of losing someone she loved, the same pain she caused me, might have provided some satisfaction but I made a mistake. Lacy owed me and so I left the task to her. I won't be making the same mistake twice.

All this time I thought Harlow was long gone, whisked off to Australia with Madelyn-May and her perfect little family when all the while she was right under my nose, growing and blooming, just waiting to be plucked.

I look at the address one more time and a smile tugs at the corner of my lip.

I hope you're ready Harlow because this time I'm coming for you myself.

I adjust the butterfly pendant around my neck and settle back into my seat as the pilot makes his announcement. *"Welcome aboard your flight from Los Angeles to Philadelphia. The duration of the flight will be approximately five hours..."*

I ignore the rest of his spiel and motion to a flight attendant to bring me a drink. Vodka, plenty of ice.

Beside me sits a man with pock-marked skin and hair that's graying at the temples. I can smell the heavy scent of his cologne and the cheap fabric of his suit shouts that it's clearly off the rack. When he clears his throat and turns to me I immediately hold my hand up to his face.

"Let me stop you there," I say before he gets the first word out. "Do us both a favor and save it."

"I was just going to say that you have striking eyes," he continues, despite my objections. "I can't say I've ever seen someone with eyes so blue."

Why don't men ever just take no for an answer?

I sigh, stop looking through my bag, and turn to him. "I have my father's eyes. They're beautiful, aren't they?"

"Yes, they are." His hungry gaze falls from my eyes and settles firmly on my lips.

"They run in the family," I tell him. My grandfather, my father, and now me."

"How extraordinary." He sits back deeper into his seat. He thinks he's won me over.

"Well, not that extraordinary," I continue, taking my drink from the flight attendant. "My grandfather and my father are the same person, so..."

I sip my drink and hold his gaze as he mentally does the math. I watch him closely, waiting for the moment he figures it out.

"You mean..."

"Yes." The plane takes off and the ice clinks in my glass.

As he stares at me, eyes wide and lips ajar, I take half a Xanax, drain my glass, and sit back. Men are so boring. I just don't have time for their bullshit right now. All I have are five hours. Five hours to sit here and rest before we land in Philly and all hell breaks loose.

Chapter Thirteen

HARLOW

I'm halfway down the stairs, duffle bag slung over my shoulder when I hear a key turn in the front door. Rhonda is home early. I freeze where I am, my right foot suspended mid-air. When she opens the door and sees me on the stairs, her expression rests somewhere between shocked, hurt, and angry. Her eyes are wide, but her brow is stitched. Her feet are rooted to the spot but her shoulders sag.

"Harlow? Where are you going?"

"Rhonda," I begin, "I'm sorry but I can't go and live with her. I told you that."

"So, what do you plan to do?" she asks, finally stepping inside and closing the door with a firm thud. As far as she's concerned, I'm not going anywhere.

"Honestly, I have no idea. I just know I can't go to Australia. Not now and not ever."

"So, you're going to live on the streets? In a shelter? What?"

I shrug and let my gaze fall. The idea of running off had seemed gallant a few moments ago, taking control of my life and relying on myself. Now, under her gaze, I feel childish and stupid.

"Do you even have any money?"

"Some."

"Enough for a motel?"

"Depends," I mumble. "There's always shelters like you said."

"Shelters?" she repeats the word as though it tastes bitter on her tongue. "You won't be sleeping in any shelters."

"Well, I'm not going with Madelyn-May."

"Harlow, your father and brother are already on a flight to come here and collect you." She drops her keys into a bowl on the side table and sighs. "You need to talk about this with your family. There's really nothing else I can do."

Before I can answer, the front door opens again and this time her husband Steve comes in, a leather satchel slung over his shoulder.

"Steve, thank God," Rhonda says with a long exhale. "Harlow says she's leaving to go and sleep in a shelter. Bastian and his son are already on a flight out of Sydney. I could really use some help here."

"You know that I'm standing right here," I remind her. "I can hear everything you're saying."

Steve glances at me then nods and slowly removes the satchel from his shoulder. He places it down on the carpet and stretches his arms out toward me. He wants me to think he comes in peace. "Harlow, we can work this out. You just need to stay calm."

"I am calm," I tell him. "I'm just not going to Australia."

He whispers something to Rhonda that's too quiet for me to hear and she nods and hurries off toward the kitchen.

"Harlow, your dad is on his way. We promised to keep you safe until he gets here, which will be..." he glances at his watch, "in just under twelve hours."

Rhonda returns, gives her husband a quick nod and they both stare up at me.

"What's going on?" I ask. "You can't make me stay here if I don't want to."

"Harlow, just try to stay calm." Steve stretches his arms out even further toward me. "We need you to go back to your room and wait until your dad gets here."

"No, I already told you. I'm not going. You can't make me."

"You'll have everything you need in your room," Rhonda adds. "But we can't let you go running off to who knows where. It's not safe, Harlow. You could get yourself killed, or worse."

"Or worse?"

"You know what I mean."

"The only thing worse is being made to go back to Australia to live with *her*. You can't seriously mean to keep me in a room for twelve hours."

Together they slowly move toward me, their arms outstretched like two zookeepers trying to trap an escaped animal. I step back up the stairs one at a time. I need to figure out how to get past them before we get too high up. If they edge me to the top of the stairs, it's only a few steps to the bedroom door.

"Harlow, it's just for a few hours." Rhonda takes a small silver key from her pocket and positions it between her fingers. "You know I don't want to do this but the way you're acting... you're leaving me no choice."

"You're going to lock me in?" I ask, my eyes wide.

"It's for your own good. We care about you. You've been like a daughter to us - you must know that. If you could have just waited for your dad to arrive none of this would have to happen."

"That's illegal!" I shriek. "You can't imprison me in a locked room."

"Like I said, it's just until your dad gets here, I promise. I'm sorry Harlow, really. I just want to keep you safe."

"No, I'm calling the police." I grab my phone from the back pocket of my jeans. But in the second it takes me to glance at the screen, Steve runs at me taking the stairs two at a time. He grips me around the waist, knocking my phone and bag to the ground.

"Steve, be careful," Rhonda shouts. "Don't hurt her."

"Get your hands off me!" I scream as he tries to fold his arms around me. "Stop it! Let me go!"

I try to fight him off as Rhonda runs past us. Behind me, I hear the bedroom door open.

"Hurry, Steve," Rhonda says, her tone urgent. "I can't stand this."

I struggle against his embrace, my feet kicking out wildly but finding only air.

"Stop fighting me," he hisses. "It's for your own good."

"Let me go!" I scream, this time my voice so loud it cracks like lightning striking metal.

"Harlow, stop it!"

"Let. Me. Go!" I dig my nails into the back of his hands and he shouts out in pain. Three thin trails of blood spill across his skin as he hauls me up and over the last three steps on the staircase.

"No!" I thrash around in his arms but no matter how loud or how many times I scream they pay no attention to me.

His hands curl under my armpits and he pulls me backwards down the hall. My heart bashes against my ribs. Adrenaline rushes along my arms and legs as every cell in my body fills with the urge to flee. As we approach the bedroom, the heels of my boots scrape against the carpet so heavy that leather marks transfer onto the fibers giving the impression there's been a drag race down the hallway.

At the open door, Rhonda is standing ready, key in hand and a grim look on her face.

"You can't do this," I shout at her, as he drags me inside the room. "You can't!"

I scream and kick out at her but she refuses to meet my eye. When my boot catches her ankle she shouts out in pain.

"Damn it, Harlow," she curses. "Just do as your told."

"I'm seventeen!"

"Yes, and you're a minor. We have to do what's best for you."

With one final grunt, Steve twists his body and throws me down onto the carpet. I desperately try to scramble to my feet but it's too late. As the door closes, I hurl myself against it but the sound of the lock clicking seals my fate. I pound against the wood and scream for them to let me out but deep down I know they've already walked away. They think they've saved me. They think I'll be safe here in this room. They have no idea what they have just done.

Chapter Fourteen

SOPHIE

Over the past five years, I've spent countless hours imagining what I would say and how I would act if I ever saw Bastian again. I've rehearsed speeches about why I didn't tell him about Poppy. I've thought about what clothes I would wear and how I would style my hair. I've pictured us meeting on the beach, in a warm café, and at a fancy restaurant. Often my eyes well with tears as I imagine him taking me in his arms and whispering that it's okay, that he can't wait to meet his daughter. He explains how he and Madelyn-May are divorcing, and says he's never stopped loving me. But never, in all the times I've imagined our reunion was it in a hospital as our daughter lay dying and the only thing I could say to him was that I'm sorry.

As Bastian comes down the hall, Harry loping along beside him head down and hands shoved into his pockets, it strikes me that they are almost the same height. The last time I saw Harry he was eleven years old with gangly legs and a fringe that covered his eyes. But now he is leaner, lankier, and while he doesn't walk with the same confident posture as his father their similarity is striking.

I focus on Harry because I don't have the courage to meet Bastian's eye. From the glance I stole, I could see he has gray around his temples now and a tightness to his jaw I don't recall ever seeing before. But the past six years have done nothing to diminish the effect he has on me and my stomach tightens as he gets closer.

As he closes the distance between us he doesn't speak and instead scoops me into an embrace, the warmth of his body instantly melting my pain.

"Thank you for coming," I whisper into his neck. "I'm so glad you're here."

Beside us, Harry absently kicks at the gray linoleum floor. I can't imagine what he must be thinking, and I wonder how much Bastian has told him.

"Hello, Harry," I say, as Bastian releases me from his arms. "You've certainly grown."

He nods and shrugs but doesn't look up. Unsure of how much or what I should say, I look to Bastian for guidance, but he shrugs it off and asks me to tell him everything I know about Poppy's condition and what Harry needs to do to find out if he's a match.

When I've told them all I know, I turn to Harry and force a smile that I hope looks reassuring. "I had the test already," I begin, "so I can tell you exactly what happens, Harry. It's really easy and not painful at all."

Finally, he stops kicking at the floor and looks up at me. His eyes are hooded, resentful. It's clear he doesn't want to be here, and that Bastian has made him come.

"I'm so sorry about all of this," I try. "You don't know me and you've never met Poppy. It's a lot to take in and you don't have to do the test if you don't want to."

He takes a moment and I wonder what he's thinking. It felt like the right thing to say that he doesn't have to take the test but if I'm honest, there's nothing I won't do to change his mind if he says no. Poppy needs this and even though Harlow is still here in America, two options are better than one.

"So, you're my real mother then?" he asks, catching me off guard. "That's why you saved me from the car accident that day?"

"Oh, sweetheart, no. Your mom is your real mom." I glance at Bastian and he pats Harry on the shoulder.

"We went through this on the plane buddy," he says. "Sophie was an egg donor, but your mom carried you, gave birth to you, and raised you. Genetically you and Sophie are linked but that's all. She's not your mom."

Even though it's true, the words sting and I remind myself not to confuse my role in Harry or Harlow's life. Like Bastian says, I'm not their mom. I was an egg donor and nothing more. But his proximity to me and the way light catches the chestnut flecks of his hair the same way it did with Josh has me struggling not to pull him in and never let go.

"This is such bullshit!" he huffs, his face thunderous. "Where's Harlow? Why can't she do it?"

"She's going to buddy."

"And then what? We're going to drag her kicking and screaming back home?"

Bastian catches my eye and raises his brow, an indication the move to Australia has done little to improve the strain on Madelyn-May's relationship with her daughter.

"Harry, if it's alright with you a nurse will come and take a cheek swab to see if you are a match for Poppy," I tell him, desperate to keep him focused on why he's here. "If you are, then you're the best chance we have for saving her life."

He looks from me to Bastian and then back again. "So, you're not my mom but Poppy's my sister?"

"I know it's a lot," I tell him. "And I'm sorry for all of this."

He shakes his head and rolls his eyes to the ceiling. "This is what I'm talking about, Dad. Mom did this. She lied to us our whole lives and now look at the shit it's caused. I have some sister I've never met whose dying and now this woman whose apparently not my mom but actually is. It's bullshit. I hate it. You know what, fuck this. I'm out of here." He turns and strides down the hall shaking his head and mumbling something we can no longer hear.

"I'm so sorry, Bastian," I try again. "I just didn't know what else to do. If it's too much…"

"He'll do it," he assures me. "He's just… trying to get his head around it. It was a long flight, he's probably tired."

I nod and force myself not to push. All I want is for Harry to take the test, but if I push him and he refuses I will never forgive myself. "Bastian, what if you take the test then go back to the hotel and you both get some rest. Come back this afternoon and maybe he'll be a little more open to it."

"And you'd be alright with that?" He rests his hands on my shoulders and looks deep into my eyes.

There's no point trying to lie. "No, but I'd rather wait until this afternoon than risk him saying no completely."

Bastian's lips pull into a tight line that's probably the best version of a smile he can manage. "Is there any chance I could be a match?"

"About one percent. That's what they told me when I took the test but at this stage, anything is worth a shot."

"Can I meet her?"

They are the words I've replayed in my mind a thousand times over. Hearing Bastian ask to meet his daughter – our daughter. Technically Harlow is our daughter too, but Poppy is different. We conceived her, his body intertwined with mine, a rush of love bringing her to life.

"Of course, you can. Just let me talk to her first. She knows she has a daddy who lives in another country, but I didn't want to say more until you were here. Not with everything she's already going through."

"Did you think there was a chance I wouldn't come?" He steps back and pushes one hand into his jeans pocket. It's obvious the very idea has offended him and I chastise myself for choosing my words so poorly.

"I knew you'd come, Bastian, that's not what I meant. It's just a lot for a little girl to take in. I thought it would be better to tell her when she could meet you right away rather than making her wait until you arrived."

He nods and looks embarrassed. "Sorry, Soph. This is a lot for all of us I think."

"And Madelyn-May? How did she take it?"

He rubs at the back of his neck and looks absently out the window. "We got a call just before I left. Harlow's in some strife. I've got to take her back with us when we leave."

"I kinda got that impression from Harry. So, Harlow knows you're here. Does she know about Poppy?"

"No, I haven't spoken to her. I wanted to come straight here. I figured if Harry was a match I could save her the hassle of going through all this."

This time it is me who steps back, his words stabbing at my heart. "The *hassle*?"

"Not the *hassle* Soph, shit. That's not what I meant." He sighs and lets his head fall backward. "Harlow was drugged at some club. There's a video of her topless, I don't know. The family she lives with wants her to move out, come back to Australia, but she's refusing."

"Is she alright?"

"I don't know. Madelyn-May wants her home but bringing her back against her will is the last thing we need. Things aren't..." he briefly meets my gaze then looks away, "they're not great between Madelyn-May and me."

For a moment we stand in silence. I want to pull him to me, to tell him I love him, that I've always loved him. But instead, I stare down at my canvas runners and remind myself now is not the time.

"Mr Marozzi?"

We both look up to see Dr Yates walking toward us, clipboard in hand.

"Yes, that's me."

"Has Sophie explained to you about taking the test?"

"Yes, I know the odds of being a match are low but I'd like to try anyway. My son is... still coming to terms with the whole thing. I'd like to bring him back this afternoon if that's alright?"

She glances at me, the look of concern on her face undeniable. "Sophie, I don't need to remind you that we are on the clock here."

"I know, but he needs time. He's a teenage boy. They had a long flight and it's a lot for him to take in."

She tilts her head briefly to the left, makes a note on the clipboard, then looks back at Bastian. "Come with me please."

I watch him walk off down the corridor, his height dwarfing Dr Yates' tiny frame. In my heart, I know Bastian won't be a match for our daughter, but he's here in America and so are Harry and Harlow. For now, that will have to be hope enough.

Chapter Fifteen
VALENTINE

I was nine the day I found my mother's body. Cold and pale, lying tits out on the floor of our trailer, her eyes wide with surprise as though an overdose was the last thing she expected. It's hard to imagine why death had come as such as shock to her. The needle was still hanging out of her arm.

They called it an intentional drug overdose due to the amount of heroin in her system. Nothing out of the ordinary for a down-and-out user who lived in a trailer park. She was a victim of incest with nothing to live for, so why not go out with a bang? That's what they all said, but I knew better. My mom had her struggles. Our whole family did. But she wouldn't have left me, not on purpose. She was probably half out of it on Xanex or Quaaludes, anything to take the edge off while she waited to score. Then when it came, she took it too far. The day I found her was a week before her twenty-fifth birthday. Guess she'd celebrated early.

I don't have any checked luggage so as soon as they let us off the plane I head into a bathroom stall and unzip my small carry-on.

The last time I came to Philly was to visit my grandmother Lacy at the State Correctional Institution at Muncy. It wasn't so much a visit as an opportunity to ask what the hell happened the day she bungled our plan to kidnap Harlow. What she did accomplish though was drawing the attention of the entire FBI.

I remove the auburn wig I wore on the plane and replace it with a razor-cut blonde bob. I change my black thigh-high dress for tight blue jeans and a white button-up shirt to cover the flutter of blue-inked butterflies along my arm. Using a small compact mirror balanced in my lap, I change my eyes from their natural brilliant blue to chocolate brown contacts. Now that I'm back I'm not taking any chances of being identified as an associate of my imprisoned grandmother. I've got shit to do and no time for hassles with the FBI.

Satisfied with the transition, I open a small leather wallet and choose a Philadelphian driver's license that shows the name Pamela Stevens. According to the card, I live just outside the city and have a birthday two weeks from today. The photo shows me as I look now with the blonde wig and brown eyes and was made by one of the most talented forgers in California. It's one of five that I keep handy. This way no one ever sees me coming and that's exactly how I like it.

Outside, I climb into a taxi and give the address of a modest hotel in Center City. I settle back into the seat and as we speed over a bridge that crosses the Schuylkill River it strikes me how much Lacy would love a visit. The prison is just a three-hour drive from Philly. It would be easy to make the trip and she'd get such a kick out of knowing I was about to finish what we started six years ago. I imagine her shuffling out to the visitor's room, confined to prison overalls, her eyes lighting up when she sees me sitting there. My smile deepens at the rush that comes from knowing I will never go there, and she will never feel the happiness of seeing me in that room waiting for her. Giving others pleasure is not something I do. Pain on the other hand, well... that's another story.

Chapter Sixteen

HARLOW

The room is silent. Outside my window twilight swallows up the day and now it's just a waiting game. A few hours ago, I heard Steve and Rhonda drive out of the garage, probably tired of my shouting, and Kempsey must be out with friends. I considered climbing out the window, kicking down the door, or waiting until someone came in so I could overpower them like they do in the movies. In the end, the window seemed like the easiest escape route but as I hoisted it up and peered down at the ground below, Rhonda's words echoed in my ear. *"So, you're going to live on the streets? In a shelter? What?"*

Working at the local library on weekends helped me save about $250 but I have no way of making any more money. My parents provide Rhonda with enough for everything I need but I don't have access to any cash. Even though I'm furious they locked me in I'm not about to try and steal from them or go rummaging through their drawers, even if I could find a way out of this room. Until now they've been good to me and deep down I know locking me in here is their misdirected attempt at keeping me safe.

I consider turning on the television but can't be bothered. I don't even feel like reading. There is no escaping this situation, physically or mentally. So instead, I pick up the phone and am surprised to see another message from Darcy.

Sorry to hear you're moving back to Australia. That sucks.

Tell me about it, I think as I start to text back but then change my mind. What's the point? Within hours my dad will be here to take me away and besides, Darcy is with Kempsey now. I missed my opportunity and it's something I'll have to live with.

It's been almost a week since the video was posted and I wonder to myself if the comments on *Kaleidoscope* have stopped. Knowing I shouldn't, but with nothing better to do, I click back to the story.

When I scroll down, I see the post has been updated to include screenshots of social media comments as well. To my horror, most of the accounts belong to kids at school.

@thereal_jethro: Can't believe I actually have to share a classroom with this ho

@dreamweaverrain1: I know for a fact she's been taking drugs for years

@callismith101: Calling bullshit on being drugged. I know this chick. Total slut

@samsutton_cheer: Heard she trained eight guys in the shitter last summer

@cheerbabe689: Loves posting pics of her tits all over socials

@amber_sherlock: Probably a prosty on weekends

@kkarrigan_cheerstar: She should just go kill herself

The world stops. The final comment is from Kempsey. *She should just go kill herself.*

I drop the phone and clutch at my chest. There's no air. I can't breathe. I can't... Why would she write that? Does she hate me so much that she wishes I was dead?

Comments from strangers online were one thing, but these are so much worse. They're from people who actually know me. My mind spins as I try to unravel the hate-fueled comments. I can't decide if this is what they really think or whether they are just writing it to be cruel.

I've never touched drugs in my life. I'm still a virgin and yet the comments are so humiliating, so degrading, and disgusting. Why would they want to hurt me so much?

I pad into the bathroom and stare at myself in the mirror. Am I really as disgusting as everyone says? Unable to tolerate my own reflection for another moment, I collapse onto the tiles and start to cry. It takes just minutes, maybe even seconds, for me to convince myself that those comments are what they really think of me. They all saw men grabbing my breasts as I laughed and enjoyed it. Maybe they're right. Maybe I am a slut. It's right there on video.

I pull my knees up to my chest. My mother lived in a trailer park and my grandmother is in jail. I know I'm the result of some other woman's egg, but Madelyn-May carried me. It's her trailer park blood running through my veins. It would make sense that I'm damaged, that I'm all the things they're saying. Maybe they know me better than I know myself. All those comments. I know those things didn't actually happen but maybe deep down I want them to. Maybe that's why I let those men touch me - because that's who I really am. Maybe I really am my mother's daughter.

She should just go kill herself.

The words attach themselves to me like barbs.

She should just go kill herself.

Everyone hates me.

She should just go kill herself.

I have no place to go.

Then suddenly it's so simple that I don't know why I didn't think of it before. There is one escape. The only escape. I'd never have to see my mother, or Kempsey, or anyone else ever again.

She should just go kill herself.

I wipe away my tears and get to my feet. Yes, I think to myself as the pain quickly begins to subside. She should.

Chapter Seventeen
VALENTINE

I slide into a corner booth as near to the back as possible. The suburban bar is dingy and dark. It reeks of stale beer and damp carpet. The perfect place for me to go unnoticed.

After checking into a hotel under the name Pamela Stevens, I took off my blonde wig and brown contacts, pulled my natural ebony hair back into a tight ponytail and tucked it up under a tan baseball cap. Next stop was a shitty car yard run by an overweight, rhinoceros of a man where I paid cash for an even shittier piece of crap car that no one would ever look twice at.

Now, tucked away in the corner of this suburban bar I order a vodka straight up and remind myself that what I'm about to do is the right thing. Sure, Harlow's just a teenager but I'm doing her a favor. In my experience, blood is blood and it's our poison that runs through her veins. She was stained at conception. We all were, and I saw that video. At seventeen, dirt and pain are already oozing from her pores like tiny maggots. A human body can only carry so much infection before it starts to break open - before rot finds its way to the surface. In that stinking Californian trailer filled with sweat and semen, my grandfather killed us all before we were even born, infecting us with his unrelenting, unrequited version of love. Death will save her from a life filled with misery and hate. And in the process, Madelyn-May will finally find out what it feels like to have her beating heart shredded to pieces.

Eventually, I slip a couple of banknotes under the empty glass and make my way toward the exit. Overhead, a bell chimes as I push through the front door and step out into the crisp night air. The night sky will provide a perfect cover for me to investigate access points to the house where Harlow lives, how close the neighbors are, and how best to leave without drawing attention.

My boots crunch in the gravel as I make my way back toward the shit box car I parked in the back of the lot. I dig into my pocket for the keys, my mind already running over the logistics of my plan when somewhere in the dark I hear a woman's voice say, '*Take your hands off me. I said no*'.

I stop and scan the darkened lot. There are no security lights, only the sliver of a slowly rising moon to help me see. Finally, standing against the outside wall of the bar I catch sight of two shapes, and it doesn't take long to see that one of them is pinned.

I remind myself that whatever is happening over there doesn't concern me. The last thing I need is to get involved in anything that will draw attention to me. Deciding to let it be, I turn and head back toward the car. But as I take another step, once again her voice cuts through the stillness of the night. *'I said, no'.*

I stop mid-step and take a deep breath. This is a bad idea.

But shoulders back, I turn and stride across the carpark. As I close the distance between me and the couple, their faces slowly begin to appear through the dark. A very drunk, very skinny girl who can't be more than twenty-two is standing with her back to the wall, her arms pinned at the wrists. Towering over her is a bald man with thick shoulders and completely inked arms. He is twice her size and not taking no for an answer. I glance around and breathe a sigh of relief. No security cameras. Must be my lucky night.

"Hey, fuckhead," I call out. "She said no."

He turns to me, not bothering to unwrap his fleshy fingers from her wrists. "Fuck off bitch and mind your own business."

Thankfully my hair is pulled up inside the baseball cap and won't get in my way. "I'm not telling you again. Let her go."

Finally, he lets go of her wrists and she slumps over rubbing at them with her palms.

"You're *telling* me?" he repeats, his neck jutting forward. It's a challenge and one that I'm happy to accept.

I get my footing. Stabilize my balance. "Do yourself a favor. Walk away."

"Or what, huh?" He spreads his arms wide and steps toward me. "What the fuck are *you* going to do about it?"

"Come and find out."

This wasn't part of my plan and defending weak women is not something I do out of the goodness of my heart. But men like this who think they can do whatever they want because they have a dick, well that's just not okay with me.

"You asked for it bitch," he says with a wide grin. "Let's dance, sweetheart."

He lunges toward me with his right fist just like I knew he would. When he was holding her against the wall all his weight rested on the right side of his body. His dominant side. Idiot. This was going to be too easy.

THE TRUTH WE TELL

Instead of blocking his swing I instantly drop into a squat. His fist goes over my head and I punch him straight in the balls. A guttural growl finds its way from his stomach, up along his throat, and eventually escapes his lips. He clutches his crotch as his eyes roll back.

If I were a better person I would walk over, help the woman back inside, and leave this prick out here gasping in agony. But I'm not a better person. I'm a much worse person. So instead, I throw a second punch that lands right on his jaw. As he stumbles, I kick him in the stomach hard enough to send him falling back against the wall. When he crumbles and slides down, his body folding over on the ground, I pull out a small knife I like to keep in my back pocket and hold it to his throat. His eyes follow my lips as I crouch down and lean in close.

"A woman will always let you know when she wants to be fucked," I whisper into his ear. "And that woman over there, she didn't."

Less than a meter away, the drunk woman tries clambering to her feet but stumbles and falls backward onto her bottom.

"Look at her," I tell him. "She can't even stand up for fuck's sake."

"I thought she wanted it," he mumbles, blood mixing with spittle.

"No, you thought you could take it. But guess what?" I draw up the knife and then quickly stab it as hard and deep as I can into his thigh. "You're the only one getting penetrated tonight, sweetheart."

He howls and grabs at the wound. "You're a fucking psycho."

"Oh, you have no idea." I wipe each side of the blade against my jeans and get to my feet. "I'd call an ambulance if I was you. You don't want that femoral artery bleeding out. I'd say you have about five minutes. If you're lucky."

Knowing it's time to go, I walk over to the woman and crouch down beside her. "You alright?" She sways from side to side and tries to focus her eyes. There's a stain down the leg of her jeans and she reeks of stale beer and urine. "You're so drunk you pissed yourself. What did you expect coming out here with a guy like that?"

She shrugs and looks as though she's about to vomit. Not expecting an answer, I sigh and turn away.

"Don't slut shame me for being out here," she slurs. "That's *so* not cool."

I look back at her, unable to believe my ears. "It's not *cool*?"

"No man. I can do what I want. I don't need you being all judgy and shit." She pulls herself half up but then topples down again. "You got any smokes?"

"Stupid bitch," I swear under my breath. "Why did I even waste my time."

"The fuck did you say?" she manages. "You calling me a bitch... bitch?"

Before she realizes what's happening, I crouch down and throw a punch that connects directly with her cheekbone. She falls back, arms flailed out beside her.

"You're a fucking lunatic," the man, now a ghastly shade of gray, mumbles. "What the fuck is wrong with you?"

"So many things," I tell him, as I lean over feeling for anything in her pockets. To my surprise, I find a purse with $70 in it. I take the money and get to my feet. "So many that you'd be dead by the time I got to the end of the list."

I turn to walk away but then stop and let out a frustrated sigh. If I leave her here with no money, she'll be stranded. "You're lucky I'm not an arsehole," I say under my breath, tucking a $20 note back into her jeans pocket. "You get home safe now, *bitch*."

Chapter Eighteen

HARLOW

The chill of the blade is something I didn't expect. Frigid against the tender skin on the inside of my wrist, I flinch and let the knife fall away. I catch my eye in the mirror and ask myself, *are you sure you want to do this?*

Two weeks ago, the thought would have never crossed my mind. I was happy. I had plans, abstract but peppered with hope. Going to Brown University. An obligatory year spent in Europe. Writing my first novel. Maybe even love someday. I look down at the knife in my hand, its sharp edge ready to cut all those dreams short.

Before the video was posted online, I knew who I was but now it's almost impossible to navigate the tangle of everyone's opinion. They all seem so sure of who I am. They claim to see me so clearly and yet all I see are fragments. The flash of a memory. The hint of an idea. A rush of hope for what could be. I am seventeen and trapped in the purgatory of innocence lost. Afraid to move forward, and unable to go back.

She should just go kill herself.

I steel myself and press the knife back against my wrist. The cold spreads and this time finds its way toward the inside of my elbow. It's easier this way. I don't want to start over. Wherever I am that video will find me. My mother's notoriety will make sure of it. Even if I travel to Australia, start a new school and make new friends, one day when I least expect it I will arrive to find their heads huddled over phone screens, laughing and snickering. The slut shaming will start all over again and I'll be right back where I am now. Everyone makes mistakes. I know that. But thanks to the internet, now they last forever.

I take a deep breath and press the tip of the blade into pale skin. Beneath the surface, a labyrinth of green and purple veins pulse, rising and falling in time with my heart. I wince as the first drop of blood breaks the surface, bright and garish. It holds for a moment then slowly trickles down toward the crook of my elbow.

She should just go kill herself.

Are you sure you want to do this?

Darcy's smile flashes through my mind. Kempsey's frown. Rhonda's pity. It's better this way, I remind myself. Once it's done the pain will stop and I'll be free.

I begin to drag the knife through my skin. It's tougher than I imagined, jagged and sinewy. I wince and clench my teeth. I thought it would be like slicing through butter, but my body is resisting. The chill of the blade quickly turns to fire, metallic and hot, and a searing pain tears through my wrist. I feel the twist of the blade deep in my gut and my entire body clenches. Tears stream down my cheeks and I tell myself that I need to keep going. I channel the pain and embrace the hate that rises from somewhere deep inside. I hate Kempsey for doing this to me. I hate Darcy for kissing her. I hate Rhonda for making me leave. I hate the kids at school for writing those comments. I hate my mother for ruining my life. But most of all I hate myself for even existing.

She should just go kill herself.

Are you sure you want to do this?

As the blade goes deeper, I'm finally sure. There's nothing worth staying for. No one who could change my mind. I close my eyes and mentally psych myself. I need to do this. There's no other way. The knife cuts deeper and longer. I tighten my grip on the handle until my knuckles turn white.

But suddenly, light spills in through the crack beneath my bedroom door and I catch my breath. Someone is home.

"Shit." My grip loosens and the knife drops away.

I didn't hear a car or the front door open, but perhaps I was too distracted. Reluctantly, I rest the knife on the bathroom vanity and wrap a towel around my wrist. The cut isn't deep enough or long enough to do any real damage, but it won't stop bleeding. When I try the handle of my bedroom door it's still locked but I can hear someone downstairs in the kitchen. Maybe it's my dad, I think to myself. Despite the hate and confusion swirling inside me, the tiniest tingle of hope sparks at the thought of seeing him. Maybe I don't need to end my life just yet. Maybe I could stay a little longer just to see him.

"Hello?" I call out. "Dad, is that you? If it is please unlock this door. I'm not going to run I swear."

Instantly the house falls silent and the hair along the back of my neck prickles. Something isn't right. I can feel it.

"Who's there?" I call out again. "Kempsey, is that you?"

No one answers and I press my ear against the door. There's a soft footfall on the stairs and my heart quickens.

"Rhonda?" I call, but my voice is quieter this time. Unsure. "Who's there?"

The footsteps stop outside my bedroom and a shadow falls over the gap between the door and the carpet. I step back and hold my breath. The shadow holds. I take another step back as goosebumps run the length of my arms. Slowly, the handle turns, and I hold my breath.

"I'm calling the police," I tell whoever is out there.

I have no phone, but they don't know that. "I'm dialing right now. Hello, there's an intruder in our house. The address is 29 Poppy Place Chester Hill. Please hurry."

I finish my fake 911 spiel then listen and hope my bag and phone are no longer sitting on the stairs where I dropped them. When the shadow moves away from the door, I sigh with relief. They believed me. I squint and press my ear against the door as faint footsteps head down the stairs. It must have been some idiot who got our address from Jason Beckford and thought they could trash the place when no one was home.

When the lights of a car flash in the driveway I rush to the window but whoever has come home is already in the garage. Not enough time has passed for the intruder to have left. I hurry back to the locked door and press my ear against the wood. I count one, two, three, four, then comes the sound of a door opening downstairs. I wait, straining to hear anything in the silence of the house. And then suddenly Kempsey screams.

"Kempsey!" I pound my fist on the door. "Kempsey there's someone in the house!"

Something smashes. She screams again and I kick at the door. "Kempsey!"

When the door doesn't budge, I run to the other side of the room and haul open the window. I stoop and duck my head through the opening as another crash echoes up from downstairs. I slip one leg over the window sill then stop when I realize behind me everything has fallen silent. I pause and try to hear something, anything, but am met with just the quiet, stillness of the house. I slip my bottom onto the window sill and prepare to jump when from behind me comes the sound of a key turning in the lock. I gauge the distance. I'll have time to run next door before the intruder can get back downstairs and out the front door, but there's a part of me that hesitates. I need to see who it is. I swallow hard and hold my breath as the door handle turns. Blood leaks from my wrist as I press down with all my weight ready to spring from the window. I brace myself, ready to see the face of whoever has forced their way into the house, but to my surprise, the handle stops turning. Outside the window, the front light of our neighbors Mr and Mrs Healy illuminates the dark and I hear him call out.

"Everything okay in there?"

I want to shout back, that no it's not, to call the police, but my lips refuse to move. I can't take my eyes off the handle as I wait to see who is about to come through the door.

"I heard screaming," he shouts again. "I'm calling 911."

Then from the corner of my eye, I catch sight of a figure moving in the yard below. I squint trying to make out who it is but it's almost impossible to see through the shadow of the trees. Suddenly the dark figure stops, turns, and looks up at me. I don't dare to breathe. I can't see their face, but I can feel their eyes on me. The figure looks too small to be a college football player. Perhaps a boy or a woman. We stare at each other through the darkness then finally, the figure turns and disappears into the street.

"Kempsey," I breathe. "Please be okay. Please…"

I let myself out of the room and even though I saw the intruder leave, I hesitate at the top of the stairs. The house is silent, but light is spilling out from the kitchen below. Taking one step at a time, I make my way downstairs, carefully tiptoeing through the living room. I pause just before the corner of the kitchen.

"Kempsey, are you alright?" I whisper, too scared to go in. "Are you there?"

Met with silence, I count to three and then step around the corner.

"Kempsey…"

Blood drips slowly from my wrist and begins to pool on the tiles. My stomach churns and without warning, I turn and throw up on the floor. I wipe my mouth with the back of my hand, spittle hanging from my lip as I stare at her. She is on the floor staring back at me, her eyes wide and wild. I step forward but quickly pull my leg back as though I've been stung. I want to reach out but don't dare. She is in the room, but I am alone. She is here, but she is gone. Her vacant eyes stare into mine and yet she sees nothing.

Chapter Nineteen

VALENTINE

I hadn't planned to go inside but when I got there everything was dark. I figured no one was home and I'd have the perfect opportunity to do some recon of the house. I've never met Harlow, never heard her voice, but the moment someone started calling out from upstairs I knew it was her. I have no idea why she was locked in a bedroom, but I couldn't believe my luck. She was a sitting duck, home alone and locked in a room. It was going to be like shooting fish in a barrel. But then that girl came home.

I start the car engine and pull away from the curb. I parked three blocks away from the house and despite being in peak physical shape my heart is still racing. I don't like being caught unawares and it was my own fault. What had I been thinking going upstairs with no way out and no idea when someone would be back? *Stupid.*

I think back to Lacy's mistake and realize I have done exactly the same thing. Taking opportunities instead of being strategic and patient. It's not like me. I don't make mistakes but for some reason, this girl and my need for revenge have me unhinged.

After driving for fifteen minutes, I find a quiet street and pull over to clean up. My hands and shirt are covered in that girl's blood. When she came in through the kitchen, I had no choice but to improvise. The first thing I saw was a metal fire stoker. And maybe it was better this way. It looked exactly like what it was - an unplanned attack, just like what might happen if two friends got into a heated argument.

Clearly, something was wrong in that house for Harlow to have been locked upstairs. Eventually, I found the key in a dish on the mantle and a bag with her wallet, phone, and a bunch of clothes propped against the bottom step. She had called out, *I'm not going to run.*

If Harlow was locked in that room it meant there was conflict in the house, and if there was conflict, there was motive. That busybody neighbor may have ruined my chance to kill her, but despite my mistake, I've accomplished the next best thing. There is a dead girl on the kitchen floor and Harlow was the only one home. To the rest of the world, she just became a murderer.

Chapter Twenty
SOPHIE

I was right. Neither Bastian nor I are a match for Poppy, but I expected as much. What I didn't expect was Harry's test to come back negative for a match as well. That only leaves Harlow and given the strain on her relationship with Bastian and Madelyn-May I have no idea if she'll even consider taking the test.

"She'll do it," Bastian assures me, but the words provide little comfort.

"How do you know that?"

"Because I know who she is."

Bastian nods to himself and sips coffee from a Styrofoam cup. Within hours of arriving at the hospital dark circles have formed beneath his eyes and his brow looks permanently strained. It could be fatigue from the flight, but I doubt it. He's never met Poppy, but she is his blood. Her pain is his pain, just like it is mine.

"I don't mean to be cynical, Bastian, but how long has it been since you actually spoke to Harlow? People can change, especially teenagers."

"It'll be fine."

"Are you even on speaking terms?" When he doesn't answer my heart sinks. "She won't even talk to you?"

"It's a technicality," he replies. "Behavior can change. Hearts don't."

He meets my gaze and I know he's right. Hearts don't change. Once you've loved with your whole heart it's a love that lasts forever. That's just the way it is. Always between a parent and their child. Sometimes between a man and a woman. And forever between Bastian and me.

I nod and take his hand. "You're right. In the meantime, would you like to come and meet your daughter?"

Since she was admitted, Poppy has been moved to a private room. As we head out of the waiting room, behind us a television up on the wall announces breaking news that a teenage girl identified as Harlow Marozzi is a suspect in the murder of Kempsey Karrigan, a teenager whose body was found in the kitchen of her Chestnut Hill home earlier in the evening.

Bastian's hand immediately pulls from mine and he strides up to the television set where a journalist is standing outside a house buzzing with police.

'A nationwide manhunt is now underway for seventeen-year-old Harlow Marozzi, believed to have fled the scene after murdering her housemate and friend in cold blood. Sources say there was conflict between the two girls after a video showing Harlow drunk and topless in a local bar went viral.'

Bastian interlocks his fingers behind his head as his entire body sags forward. "What the hell?"

"Bastian, there must be some mistake," I try. "That can't be right."

An image of Harlow smiling, her arm slung around her now-dead friend's shoulders, flashes up on the screen and I catch my breath. "You don't think..."

He spins around and stares at me wild-eyed. "...that my daughter is a murderer?"

"I didn't mean that."

"No I don't, Sophie. Jesus!" He presses his fingers to his temples, scrunches his face, then turns to me. "I have to find her. Wherever she is, I have to find her. Will you help me?"

"Help you?" I repeat. "You mean, leave Poppy?"

Despite what I said to Harry earlier, that I am not his mother, the truth is he and Harlow are my children. We share the same genes, the same DNA. They wouldn't exist if it wasn't for me. Now, Harlow is out there somewhere, alone, terrified, and accused of murder. She's also the only chance I have of saving Poppy's life. But to help Bastian means leaving my daughter alone in a hospital full of strangers.

"Sophie, will you help me?" he repeats. "I need you."

I gaze down the corridor and then back to Bastian. There's no time and he's asking me to make an impossible choice.

Chapter Twenty-One

HARLOW

Two blocks away I crouch behind a weathered garden pergola and rummage through my bag. My heart is crashing into my ribs and my legs are jelly. I hadn't meant to run. I'm covered in Kempsey's blood and back in the kitchen, my own blood and footprints are all around her body. I should have stayed and called the police but without thinking I picked up the fire poker next to her body. Clearly the murder weapon, it was lying beside her, the sharp end dripping blood onto the kitchen tiles. What the hell was I thinking? I touched the murder weapon. My blood and prints are all around her body. Now I've taken off.

Knowing I can't be out on the street in blood-stained clothes, I struggle into a clean pair of jeans and a black hooded sweater, my hands trembling and clumsy in the dark. When I'm dressed and my old clothes are shoved to the bottom of the rucksack, I take a breath and consider going back. Maybe it's not too late. If I go back now no one will ever know I left. I can explain what happened. A stranger broke into the house, killed Kempsey, unlocked my bedroom door, and fled.

Next door a dog barks and I leap and clutch at my chest. It was public knowledge Kempsey and I had been fighting. I was being kicked out of the house because of what she did. There is a knife upstairs with my blood on it. Once Rhonda tells the police I was locked in a room waiting to be forced onto a plane they'll know I was trying to kill myself, that I was mentally and emotionally unstable. Out of my mind even. They'll think Kempsey came home and I convinced her to unlock the door. They'll think I went down to the kitchen and we got into a fight. They'll think I became overwhelmed with anger and resentment, grabbed the fire poker, and stabbed it into her neck.

In the distance, a police siren screams through the night. They're coming. If I go back now, I'll be arrested for the murder of my best friend. No one will understand. They'll never believe me because what really happened makes no sense. There was no reason for the intruder to unlock the door and then just walk away. Even I know that. Pennsylvania still has the death penalty. If I go back, I will be trialed and convicted of murder in the first degree. They'll strap me to a gurney and force a needle into my arm. If I go back, a curtain will open and a group of strangers with blank expressions will watch me die from a row of shitty plastic chairs.

I wrap my arms around myself and shiver from the cold. Just hours ago, I was willing to take my own life. It seemed like the easy way out, but as the sirens get louder and death creeps closer, I am no longer so sure I want to die.

I feel around in the bottom of the rucksack. The last time I used the bag was on a writer's retreat at Cape May last summer. It doesn't take long to feel the familiar shape of a pen caught between my bloody clothes and a toiletry bag. From my phone, I copy two numbers onto the inside of my arm. One belongs to my dad, who will have landed by now, and the other number is Darcy's. I have no idea if he will be willing to help me, but I know he can get fake IDs from his older brother like the ones we used to go to the bar the night this all started. If I have any chance of getting out of here, I'm going to need one.

When I get to a corner store four blocks from the house, I steel myself and push open the door. I need to buy another phone before the police have my picture plastered across every television screen and newspaper in Philadelphia.

Adrenaline courses through me as I approach the counter and try to keep my head down. I can feel the clerk's eyes boring into me as he takes my money for a pre-paid phone, a bottle of water, black hair dye, and pair of scissors. To me, the items scream that I just killed my friend and am on the run. Any moment I expect him to come out from the counter and place me under citizen's arrest, but instead, he pushes the bag toward me and says, *'have a good night'*. I nod and hurry out the door, hoping the hood of my sweater has concealed my face from any cameras that might have been inside.

Just like in the thriller novels I love to read, my plan is to change my appearance, get a fake ID from Darcy, some money from my father, and go someplace no one has ever heard of Harlow Marozzi. I will get a simple job, rent a basic room, and eventually, none of this will have ever happened. I might only be seventeen, but the truth is I have been alone for a long time. I can do this. It's a story line I've read so many times that I know it by heart. Go to a small town, live a quiet life, and don't make contact with anyone from the past. If my life is going to end, either physically or emotionally, it will be on my terms, not in front of a room full of strangers for something I didn't do. Kempsey's death has no rhyme or reason. There is no way of explaining what happened. All I can do now is run.

Chapter Twenty-Two
VALENTINE

"Well, this is interesting," I say out loud, as images of police setting up roadblocks flash across the television screen.

So, the kid ran. Good for her. As much as I hate to admit it, I admire her spirit. I expected her to crumble and cave. Seeing her dead friend's body sprawled out across the kitchen floor, those wide vacant eyes staring into oblivion should have broken her. It would be enough to send most people into a spiral, their minds fracturing and their hearts breaking. I had been relishing the moment the cameras captured Harlow's dirty, tear-stained face as they led her out to a waiting police car. Savoring the very thought of her red-rimmed eyes meeting mine through the screen. But choosing to run has denied me that satisfaction - for now.

I pour another glass of wine and sit back against the pillows of the bed in my hotel room. The police will catch her. She's a seventeen-year-old kid. In the next few hours, she'll call mommy and daddy from her cell phone and it will all be over. Until then, there's nothing else to do but sit back and watch the show.

Chapter Twenty-Three

HARLOW

As I let myself into the library, the eyes of thousands of people trapped within the pages of books watch my every move. I quickly punch in the security code and lock the door behind me. For the past year, most Saturday mornings I open up for head librarian Marta Kormish. To me, there is nothing more peaceful or sublime than those first few hours in the library when I am the only living soul in a room full of ghosts. But tonight, the room is different. I feel watched. Haunted.

My skin prickles and I glance back over my shoulder one last time before pushing open the door to the lady's bathroom. Above me, the fluorescent tube light flickers casting a macabre tinge of green and yellow across my face. It highlights hollows that have formed beneath my eyes and casts a reflection that already belongs to a stranger.

As the dark hair dye slowly suffocates the chestnut highlights of my hair, I take a deep breath and dial Darcy's number.

"I don't usually answer private numbers so whoever this is, make it good," he says.

"Darcy... it's Harlow. Please don't hang up."

"Harlow, what the fuck?" he replies. "Kempsey's dead."

"I know, but it wasn't me." I pace the length of the bathroom and try to find the right words to make him believe me. "The whole thing makes no sense Darcy, but I didn't kill her I swear."

"Then who did?" His voice is hard, accusational.

"I don't know. There was an intruder. I heard them. They were outside my room. I thought it was something to do with Jason Beckford putting our address online, some stupid college football prank to scare us. But then Kempsey came home. Whoever it was must have..."

"Did you see them?"

"No, I was locked in my room. My dad was flying over to get me. I didn't want to go and so -"

"Then how did you run?"

I swallow hard and pray that what I am about to say comes out better than it sounds in my head. "Whoever it was unlocked the bedroom door." The line goes silent and I know he doesn't believe me because who would? "Darcy, I know how it sounds but I didn't kill her. Despite what happened she was my best friend. She…"

Until now I have been running on pure adrenaline. Strategizing and trying to figure out how to escape but saying the words out loud triggers something inside of me. The enormity of what happened, of what I saw, suddenly crashes over me. Kempsey is dead. Her vacant eyes flash through my mind and I catch my breath. The gaping wound in her neck. The kitchen tiles stained with her blood. "Darcy, oh my God," I cry. "She's really dead."

"Harlow, I'm not gonna lie," he replies, ignoring my sobs. "It looks bad."

"I know," I manage, trying to catch my breath, "and I don't understand any of it. It couldn't have been a college kid. They killed her Darcy. I think they were coming upstairs to kill me next but our neighbor came out into his front yard. He shouted about calling 911 just as they unlocked the door. It must have spooked them."

"You keep saying *them*. Was there more than one?"

I think back and am certain there was only one person in the house. "No, I saw someone outside on the front lawn. It was just a dark shape but whoever it was stopped and looked up at me. They looked…. small. Like, it wasn't a man."

"Someone our age then?" he asks. "Shit do you think it was someone from school? Like, because of all that shit getting posted online?"

"No, I think it was a woman."

"A woman?" He pauses and then adds, "Like the woman who tried to kidnap you when you were a kid?"

The bathroom spins and I reach out for the sink to steady myself. I hadn't even considered that the break-in could have been about me. Lacy is still in prison and besides, that was six years ago. She'd be at least seventy by now. It couldn't be. *Could it?*

"Harlow? Are you there?"

I take a long deep breath. "I'm here."

"Do you think it was related to your accident?"

"It can't be. She'd be too old and I'm sure she's still in prison."

"Maybe she sent someone."

My mind folds in on itself as I consider the possibility that my own grandmother has sent someone to hurt me. I didn't kill her, but could it still be my fault that Kempsey is dead?

"But why now?" I ask. "She's had all this time. She's never even tried to contact me."

The line falls silent as we mentally work it through. Then suddenly Darcy shouts out. "Holy shit, Harlow, the video. It's the video. That college fucker online giving out your address. Don't you see? That woman, your grandmother, would have thought you went to Australia with your folks then all of a sudden, you're all over the internet. She knows you're here. That's why someone came to the house, Harlow. They were after you."

A cold shiver runs through my body. It's the only thing that makes sense. "Okay, but why didn't they kill me?"

"Kempsey came home. You said a neighbor shouted about calling 911. It all started to go sideways," he explains. "Harlow, if you really didn't kill her that has to be what happened."

"Then that means... someone is still after me."

For a moment neither of us speaks and the gravity of the situation weighs heavy. It's not just the police who are after me. There's also someone out there who wants me dead.

"Harlow, this is serious. You need to go to the police, like right now."

"No, I ran. They'll think I killed her."

"Not if you explain it like I just did."

"I can't," I sob. "I'm such an idiot. I picked up the poker. The one used to kill Kempsey. I moved it away from her, Darcy. My fingerprints are on it. My footprints are in the blood around her body. If it really was a professional, they would have worn gloves which means my prints are the only ones they'll find."

"Shit, Harlow," he says with a sigh. "That's messed up."

"I need an ID like the ones you got us to go out," I tell him, my voice, rambling with panic. "I have to get out of here. I have to go away. I can't let them catch me. It's the death penalty. It's -"

"But even with a different name, they'll still recognize you, Harlow. That won't work."

I glance at my reflection in the mirror. The hair dye has taken effect and my chestnut hair is long gone. "No, they won't," I tell him. "In fact, I can hardly even recognize myself."

Chapter Twenty-Four
SOPHIE

Poppy looks up at me and it breaks my heart to consider leaving her, even for a couple of days. She won't understand. All she knows is that she's sick and Mommy would be leaving her alone in a scary place full of people she doesn't know.

"Sweetheart, Mommy might have to go away for just a couple of days to get your medicine," I begin. "It's very important."

She looks so tiny in the bed. The pillows are too big, dwarfing her face and no matter how many times I straighten out the sheets they always seem to creep up around her neck.

"No, Mommy." She wraps her fingers around my wrist and doesn't let go. "I don't want to stay here. It smells funny."

I will myself not to be visibly upset. If she sees me cry, she'll know something is wrong. "The doctors and nurses will take such good care of you, sweetheart, and you know what? When I get back maybe Miss Molly can come for a visit. How would that be?"

"I want to see Miss Molly," she says. "But why do you have to go? Don't they have medicine here?"

I want to shield her. It's not fair she has to deal with what's happening but it's also not fair to lie. Despite her age, she's incredibly smart and can obviously see right through my attempts at sidestepping the truth. I take both her hands in mine and look her right in the eye.

"Sweetheart, to get better you need something called bone marrow," I explain. "Everyone has it but not everyone has the same kind. Mommy did a test, but I'm not a match so I can't give you mine. But there's a girl out there who might be. She's seventeen and there's a very good chance that you and she have the same bone marrow which means she can give you some of hers and you'll get better."

Poppy searches my eyes and I wonder if any of this is making sense to her.

"But doesn't she need hers?"

I swallow down the lump in my throat and manage a smile. "Well, sweetheart, when you're healthy your body can make as much as you need. Her body will make more and she'll be just fine."

She looks down at herself and her shoulders slump. "But my body's not healthy."

"Not right now, but it will be. That's why Mommy needs to go. To help you get better. Do you understand?"

She nods but doesn't look at me. I lean in to tuck her hair back as a single tear slips over her cheek. "Mommy, please don't leave me here by myself."

"Oh, sweetie, everything will be alright, I promise." I pull her in and hold her close. Her forehead is warm and sticky against my cheek. She's running a fever again.

When Doctor Yates comes in, she takes Poppy's vitals and makes notes on her chart. When she's done, she motions for me to follow her outside.

"What's wrong?" I ask immediately. "Why is her fever back?"

"We need a donor," Dr Yates tells me bluntly. "Where's the sister?"

"There's been a complication."

"Sophie," Doctor Yates begins, her brow pulled tight, "whatever the complication is I suggest you uncomplicate it as soon as possible. Until we find a donor match there is only so much we can do for your daughter. Am I making myself clear?"

She doesn't wait for an answer and instead turns and strides down the corridor leaving me burning with a fever all my own. Does she think I don't understand the gravity of the situation? Does she think that by complication I mean something easily rectified like a family spat or delayed flight? *Am I making myself clear?* How dare she imply that I need any clarification on the severity of the situation? Poppy is my daughter. She is my heart and soul. I would die for her if I thought it would help. Anger quickly consumes me, and I channel it all toward Doctor Yates mostly because I need to.

In a better state of mind, I would acknowledge that it's myself I'm angry at. It's my fault I didn't push the local GP harder when I knew something was wrong. It's my fault I didn't take her for a second opinion. It's my fault I'm not a match for my own child.

Until the day Poppy fell, I was enamored with my body and the miracle it had performed. At the age of thirty-five, I was considered geriatric in terms of naturally carrying a child to term. But I believed my body had nurtured, carried, and protected her. I thought my body had taken Bastian and I's love and manifested that beautiful emotion into new life. I had even fallen for the lie that my body had given me a second chance, a miracle in the form of Poppy. But the truth is, my body failed her on every count. When Poppy was in my womb my body hadn't protected her. It had betrayed her. My aging relic of a body failed to create her the way she deserved. Now, when she needs me most, I'm not a match.

Around me, the corridor swims and I clutch at my forehead. The day Josh died I was asleep. My body was tired, so I took a nap. I am a gross failure as a mother. I should never have been able to have children. As the room tips sideways, I feel an arm come up beneath me.

"Sophie, what's wrong? I'll get a doctor."

"No, just leave me Bastian. Go and find Harlow. Save Poppy."

His face is a blur as he leans over and looks into my eyes. "I'm getting the doctor."

"It's my fault she's sick," I mumble. "I never should have been a mother."

"You listen to me, Sophie," he says. "In my eyes, you are the true mother of all my children and if I had a choice, I'd choose you all over again. Every time. Do you hear me? Every. Single. Time."

Despite my objections and embarrassment, one of the emergency GP tells me to lie down on one of the spare gurneys. He looks me over and quickly comes to the conclusion I'm having a panic attack and need to rest.

When he eventually leaves us alone in the room, I pull myself up and look at Bastian. "What are you planning to do?"

"I've tried Harlow's cell a hundred times," he tells me. "It's turned off. The police have got roadblocks in place and are contacting everyone she knows from school."

I rest my hand against his arm and try to look encouraging. "She'll be alright."

"I have to find her before the police do. If they arrest her and she's found guilty…"

"We will," I tell him. "We'll find her."

"We? You mean, you're coming with me?"

"Bastian, you came to the US to take her back to Madelyn-May against her will. She won't trust you right now."

"Sophie, I…"

"We have to find her, Bastian. Part of me hates myself for leaving my daughter and God knows I have my issues with being a bad mother, but if I don't, Harlow will be out there with no one to help her and we may lose the only chance we have to save Poppy's life."

He nods and rests his hand on my shoulder. "Thank you, Soph, this means a lot to me."

"We have no choice, Bastian," I tell him. "We have to find Harlow. Both our daughter's lives depend on it."

Chapter Twenty-Five

HARLOW

Darcy agreed to meet me in Valley Green Road parking lot at the entrance to Wissahickon Valley Park. He said the local news stations were reporting roadblocks in every direction so getting away from Chestnut Hill by road right now would be out of the question. My only hope is to hike the Wissahickon Valley Park trails and get as close to Fairmount Park on the edge of Center City as I can. Then try to board a Greyhound Bus out of town. It will mean navigating my way through ten or so city blocks, but what choice do I have?

When I see a single headlight cut through the dark, I push up from the small wooden fence and shove my hands deep into the pockets of my black hoodie. My stomach flip-flops at the thought of facing him, but whatever Darcy feels about Kempsey's death and my involvement in it, he's here and that has to count for something.

I keep my eyes trained on the ground as he kills the engine of his trail bike. Around us, the air is alive with the chirp of frogs. The night air feels heavy, damp, and smells of moss.

"Thank you for coming," I whisper, as he approaches. "I didn't know if you'd show."

Finally, I look up and take him in. The accidental fringe that covers his forehead like the sweep of a bird's wing, perfect cream skin, and even in the dark I can see the brightness of his eyes, emerald against the backdrop of night.

He stops a few steps away and mumbles, "I can't believe she's dead. Doesn't seem real."

It's too dark to tell if he's been crying, but there's no doubt in my mind that Kempsey's death has rocked him. "Darcy, are you alright?"

He shrugs and immediately looks away, unable or unwilling to talk about how he feels.

"I don't understand any of this," I continue, not wanting to push him. "It's crazy. I mean, seriously. How does this even happen?"

This time he nods but still doesn't meet my eye.

"Even with everything, I never wished anything bad to happen to her. She was my best friend." I kick at an invisible rock and shake my head in silent disbelief. "Even though I didn't do it, what happened is still my fault. I'm so sorry, Darcy."

"You can't think like that, Harlow," he says quietly. "You didn't do this. If anything…"

"…if anything what?"

He shifts his weight from one foot to the other and finally meets my eye. "Kempsey put something in your drink that night. That's what started all of this. I shouldn't have let her convince me you're someone you're not. She didn't deserve what happened, no way. I'm just saying that's where it started is all."

I nod and shove my hands deeper into my pockets. "You really believe me then, that I didn't do it?"

To my surprise, he steps in and wraps his arms around me. "I believe you, Harlow. I wouldn't be here otherwise."

Something inside me breaks and I start to cry. "I'm sorry. I should've said something. I should've let you in. I knew… I knew you liked me, but I was too afraid. Now, look what's happened."

I bury my face into his shoulder, and he pulls me closer. "Hey, it's not your fault, alright? None of this is your fault."

He holds me while I sob, my entire body trembling. His kindness is something I didn't expect and compared to the emptiness I've been feeling it's a stark and welcome reminder that I'm not completely alone.

"Here," he says, letting me go and stepping back, "I have what you asked for."

He reaches into his back pocket and takes out an envelope.

"I can't thank you enough for this, Darcy. I don't know what else I'd do."

He smiles quickly and takes out a fake ID card. "This should work. It has the selfie you texted me with your new hair color and a new name."

I take the card and look at it closely. According to the ID card, my new name is Alexandra Smythe. "You think I look like an Alexandra?"

"Alexandra Smythe was the first girl I ever had a crush on back in grade school," he says with a sheepish look. "Felt right to give you that name."

Despite the situation, I feel a warm rush flood through me. "That's sweet, Darcy. Thank you."

"Here, I thought you might also need this."

He hands me the envelope and inside is what I guess to be at least five hundred dollars. "No, I can't take this."

"You'll need it. Take it, Harlow, please."

I nod and reluctantly tuck the envelope into my rucksack. It feels wrong to take money from Darcy but he's right. I need all the help I can get.

"So, what's your plan?" he asks, but then immediately adds, "Actually, don't tell me. If anyone asks, I'd rather not know. That way I can't be forced to say anything that might get you caught."

"I couldn't tell you even if I wanted to," I say. "All I know is that I need to get away from here. I don't even know where I'll go."

His eyes take me in, and I wonder what he's thinking.

"Are you scared?'" he asks eventually.

The truth is, I'm terrified but if I say the words out loud, I'm not sure I'll ever be able to push my fear back down. "I'll be alright," I say instead. "I have to be."

"You will be alright, Harlow. They'll catch who really killed Kempsey."

Of all my regrets, the fact I didn't have the courage to let him in when I had the chance, when life was still normal, is something I will take with me wherever I go. "Thank you, Darcy," I smile. "But they won't catch who really killed Kempsey. Not while I'm their only suspect."

Chapter Twenty-Six

VALENTINE

The waiting is driving me crazy. How hard can it be to find a seventeen-year-old girl?

I flick the television to a different channel in the hope of finding a news update. The police must be morons. She has no transport and if she's not using her cell, she has no means of communication. From what I read on those social media comments everyone she knew at school turned against her and her only friend is dead. That means no one is harboring her and without her parents to help I can't understand why they haven't picked her up.

I sigh and place my empty wine glass down on the bedside table. Next to it, the alarm clock reads eleven o'clock. If they haven't found her by morning I'll take matters into my own hands. I should have just killed her when I had the chance and to hell with the neighbor. Lesson learned.

Knowing I won't sleep, I walk over and look out the window. My hotel room is on floor one hundred and one, and down below, Center City is spread out like thousands of illuminated veins and arteries, all connected, all irrevocably linking one thing to another.

Family is just the same, I think to myself as I look down. Like it or not, blood is blood. Madelyn-May thought she could sever that bond by murdering her father and setting the trailer alight with Lacy still inside, but all she did was make herself more like them. Every time he forced himself on her he took away the life she might have had. I know because he did the same thing to my mother. He was my father too and might have done the same thing to me if he was still alive, but he never got the chance. For that, I guess I should be grateful to Madelyn-May. Maybe what she did saved me from becoming another of his victims, but I can't see it that way. I hate them both. He for the disgusting, heinous acts he carried out on my mother, and Madelyn-May for killing him.

Down below the tiny shapes of people move this way and that. It's late, but in a city like Philadelphia that matters little. Most of the shapes move in twos, some in groups of three or four and I catch myself wondering what it might feel like to have someone walk beside me. The footfall of their steps in time with mine, the moment shared between us.

At the trailer park, Lacy had been an absent grandmother at best. But as we stood staring at my mother's body that day, I saw her begin to disappear. Her shoulders narrowed and her head dipped lower. Her chest sunk as though her heart was shriveling, the aching space causing her ribs to buckle and bend. Despite the loss of her leg, she had been an imposing woman. But after seeing my mother dead on the floor of the filthy trailer Lacy had acquired from a resident drug dealer, she reminded me of a bird, its dirty wings broken and torn. I was only nine years old the day my mother died but I learned quickly the only person you can ever depend on in life is yourself. So, if the police can't find Harlow, then I'm damned sure I can.

Chapter Twenty-Seven

HARLOW

Tangled root systems push their way up from below, breaking the surface and continually catching the toe of my runners. The skin on the palms of my hands is grazed and bleeding. The track is dark and undulating making it almost impossible to see.

I've fallen twice, once worse than the other. The thick fleshy mound of my right palm is dripping blood and the other is scraped and sore. I can feel the sting of a scratch on my cheek and the toes on my left foot ache from smashing against rocks I can't see in the dark.

A sign back at the start of the trail told me I'm on the orange track. Unlike myself, who prefers to be indoors tucked up with a book, Darcy is an avid mountain bike rider and said he rides these trails most weekends. He assured me I can follow the orange trail along Wissahickon Creek, past Devil's Pool, and along to Kitchen's Bridge where it forks to the right and runs beneath Walnut Lane. Eventually, I will switch to the Wissahickon Bike Trail. That will take me as far as Ridge Avenue near Kelly Drive at Fairmount. From there I will follow the Schuylkill River along to Market Street, which if I'm lucky enough not to get caught, will take me across ten city blocks to the Greyhound Bus Terminal.

All up the trip is nine miles and should take about seven hours to complete. If I can make it to Market Street by five am, I have a shot at getting through the city before sunrise. But if I keep falling, I might not make it at all.

I hitch the rucksack higher up over my shoulders and remind myself that I need to keep going. It's only been an hour. I still have six hours of ground to cover before the sun rises and people start using the track for their morning walk. My once shoulder-length chestnut hair is now inky black and cut into a bob that doesn't fall past my chin but that doesn't mean someone won't recognize me. My face is all over the news. I'm wanted for murder. I have to make it to the bus station before sunrise.

As I walk, the night-time sounds of the forest follow me. The whistle and hoot of great horned owls. The chirp of frogs down by the creek. On each side of the track, I hear the rustling of creatures that remain unseen, and above me the screech of bats hustling for position in the trees.

My body feels warm from walking, but winter has only just turned to spring and the air is frigid against my bare cheeks. I have gloves, a beanie, and hoodie, but my face and throat are exposed. To my right, from somewhere in the brush an animal shrieks its protest at my presence and I leap in fright.

"Shit," I swear under my breath. "This is so much bullshit."

Part of me wants to cry, to lay down right here on the track and give up. The odds against me are overwhelming. I have limited money and no plan. Even if I make it to the bus terminal, where will I go? Lancaster County comes to mind. It's in Pennsylvania and the Amish settlements don't have television. No one would have seen the news or know that I'm on the run. My arrival would certainly lead to questions though, ones I couldn't answer, so I quickly scratch that idea off the list.

I keep walking, my mind racing as I try to figure out where I will go. New York is too close. Los Angeles feels too scary. Vancouver requires crossing an international border. I consider Boston, Portland, or maybe even Austin, but every city I think of feels overwhelming, empty, and unknown.

And then it hits me. Denver. I went there for a month as part of a student exchange experience back in junior high. It's somewhere I've been before and there was something about the Rocky Mountain backdrop that made me feel safe like the whole city was nestled in, the soaring ranges watching over everyone. The proximity to the mountains also means a lot of skiers, tourists, and transient people. I remember a lot of college students and artsy types flooding cafes and walking through the city streets. But most of all, I have been there before. I've lived there for a whole month, and right now I need something that feels familiar because I've never been in a world that feels so unknown.

Chapter Twenty-Eight
SOPHIE

J ust before midnight we finally get a lead on where Harlow might be. Rhonda, the woman she was staying with, called Bastian with the name of a boy from school who might still be in contact with her. I study his face as he cradles the phone between his ear and shoulder, waiting for the boy to answer.

Completely unaware of our anguish and the stakes at play, around us hospital orderlies go about their business, pushing patients on gurneys and answering phones. Back in her ward, Poppy is fast asleep, her fever finally relenting, still blissfully unaware of the danger she is in.

If this boy knows where Harlow is, it means leaving Poppy to go with Bastian. The very idea tears at my heart and conscience. When Josh died, I wasn't there. I wasn't by his side the way a mother should be. He died alone and afraid on the side of the road, wondering why his mommy wasn't there to make everything better. The thought has haunted me every day, every moment, and every second since. Now I'm faced with the decision of whether to leave my daughter lying alone in a hospital bed surrounded by strangers. If something were to happen, a complication or unexpected turn, I won't be there. She too could die alone without her mommy by her side. With Josh, it was an accident. There was nothing I could have done. But this time I have a choice to make.

"Hello, is that Darcy?" Bastian leans forward. His back stiffens and the sudden rise of his chest tells me that despite the circumstances the sound of the boy's voice has provided the hope he needs to keep going. "This is Bastian Marozzi, Harlow's father. I'm looking for my daughter and I need your help. You're not in any trouble but if you know where she is or how I can contact her you need to tell me. Right now."

I take in the rise and fall of his brow, the way his jaw clenches in and out like a heartbeat. I would do anything to hear what the boy is saying, to know if we have any hope of finding her.

"If you care about her at all you need to talk to me," Bastian tells him. "Please, I know she isn't capable of hurting anyone. This whole thing is a mistake. I have to find her before the police do, it's the only way I can help her. If you know anything…"

He nods silently and suddenly his eyes shine a little brighter. With frantic gestures, he motions at me to get him a pen and paper. Panicked at the idea I may not have anything to write on, I desperately rummage through my bag but come up empty. He glares at me, his eyes burning with frustration, and I leap out of my seat, rushing over to the nurse's station.

When I hand him the paper and pen, he scribbles a phone number, thanks the boy, and puts the phone down.

"I have a number for her," he tells me. "He said it's a burner, but hopefully she still has it with her."

I nod quickly and watch as he dials, praying she picks up.

"It's ringing," he whispers, and grabs my hand, his fingers linking through mine. "Harlow, is that you? It's Dad. Where are you?"

My heart is racing as I stare at him, trying to get a gauge of what she's saying.

"Harlow, that's ridiculous of course you can trust me. Now tell me where you are," he tells her, sterner this time. "I know you didn't, sweetheart. I know who you are. Let me help you, please."

Bastian's palm grows hotter against mine as he shifts in his seat.

"No, I won't call the police." A pause. "Because I wouldn't do that, you're my daughter." An even longer pause. "I know, but I thought with everything that was going on perhaps going back to Australia was best for you."

I hold my breath as he tries to convince her to let him help.

"Of course I'm on your side, sweetheart." Another pause. "Because you just have to trust me, Harlow. I'm your father." He gestures for me to hand him the pen and paper. "Where?"

I move closer, trying to hear her voice on the other end of the phone.

"Orange trail? How do I - ?" Clearly frustrated, he pushes air out through his teeth and clutches at the back of his neck. "Well, how long have you been walking?"

After glancing at his watch, he thinks a moment and then says, "Keep following the trail then get off and meet me at the end of Nanna and Pa's street at Blue Bird Hill. It should take you about twenty-five minutes. I'll be there, Harlow, I promise."

A look of relief washes over his face and he squeezes my hand. We have a location. All we have to do is go and pick her up. I rise to leave but suddenly Bastian tenses and clutches the phone even closer to his ear.

"Harlow, wait, what? Calm down, I can't understand you." He pulls his hand from mine and gets to his feet. "Sweetheart, listen to me very carefully. Slowly get down on the ground and do not move."

His brow is knotted and his jaw is clenched. I lean in and study his face, trying to figure out what's going on.

"Are you on the ground?" Another pause. "Harlow, can you hear me?"

Suddenly she screams so loud even I can hear the sound of her fear reverberating out of the phone.

"Harlow! What's happening? Harlow?" Bastian pulls the phone even closer to his ear and paces back and forth. "Harlow? Are you there?"

He waits a moment then lets the phone drop to his side. The color has drained from his face and his hands are trembling.

"Bastian, what happened?"

But instead of answering, he stares at me, his eyes glassy and his mouth ajar.

"Bastian, please," I try again. "What happened? Was it the police? Did they find her?"

"We have to go," he says, suddenly snapping back. "Right now."

"Go where? Bastian, what's happening?"

Without answering, he begins to run pulling me along behind him as we dodge nurses and patients on our way toward the exit.

"Just tell me what happened," I shout, as we run. "Is she alright? Did the police find her?"

"No," he shouts back over his shoulder, "and we don't have much time."

"But, Poppy..." I stop running and he lets go of my hand. "I don't know if I can leave her, Bastian. Not after... If something happens and I'm not here..."

"I thought you said - "

"I know what I said, but she's my daughter. What if..."

Bastian steps in and takes both my hands in his. He looks deep into my eyes. "I know where Harlow is, Soph, and she's hurt. Right now, except for this boy Darcy, she doesn't trust anyone, especially me. If we don't convince her to tell us what really happened, we have no chance of saving Poppy. They'll arrest her and if she's found guilty, she'll face the death penalty. Then they could both die." He lets go of my hands and steps back. "I don't know about you, but that's not something I can live with."

Chapter Twenty-Nine
HARLOW

There were so many things to be afraid of on this track. Rapists, snakes, a random night hiker seeing me and calling the police. But the thought of crossing paths with a black bear never even occurred to me.

I had been about to hang up from my dad when the giant bear ambled out of the forest and onto the track in front of me. It had to weigh at least three hundred pounds. When it turned and saw me it immediately reared up onto its back legs and then charged. It didn't make a sound. No roar, no snarl. Nothing. I didn't even have time to tell my dad goodbye.

Acting on pure adrenaline, I kick and strike out. It rears again and hovers in the air above me for what feels like forever, then slams its body weight down on top of me. My right arm instantly shatters beneath its weight and I scream out. For a moment everything goes black and I wonder if I'm dying. Around me, the forest is silent. There are no frogs chirping, no owls, and no rustling of animals in the brush. When I open my eyes again, further down the trail I see two cubs somersaulting over each other like two tiny circus clowns. They are completely unaware that their mother's attempts to keep them safe might end my life.

Before I can pull myself off the trail, the bear comes at me again. It sinks its teeth deep into my shoulder, slicing through muscle, sinew, and skin, then flicks its head tossing me over to the side of the track. I land hard in a pile of brittle leaves. Sticks and rocks push into my back. Winded, I clutch at my side and gasp for air. But it's not over. It comes at me again, but this time I manage to find a broken branch on the ground and pick it up with my left hand.

"No!" I shout, as loud as I can. "Get away! No!"

Desperate to scare the bear off before it launches another attack, I struggle to my feet and swing the branch again. "Go! Get away!"

My right arm hangs limp by my side and my left leg is dragging as I sway back and forth like a tree branch caught in the wind. The bear's eyes lock with mine and its nostrils flair, sizing me up.

"Get out of here!" I shout, with another swing of the stick. "Get away!"

Hot breath hangs in the air as the bear bellows at me. The sound reverberates through the forest and above me I hear the beating wings of bats as they take to the sky. Just trying to move creates a dazzling swirl of spots in front of my arms like all the stars are falling.

Further down the track, one of the cubs cries out in a voice almost identical to a human baby's wail. The bear glances back at the cub and then looks me over. It rears up, and bellows again, its hot sour breath clinging to the skin on my face. She is a mother. It is my last warning.

Finally, the bear turns and ambles back down the track, eventually disappearing into the brush with its cubs. I drop the stick and clutch my right arm. Just below my shoulder one of the bones has punctured the skin. The jagged tip, fragile and exposed, is jutting out at a sickening angle. I gasp at the grotesque state of my arm and feel my legs buckle beneath me. Suddenly the forest begins to spin and the ground rushes up to meet me. Then everything fades to black.

Chapter Thirty

SOPHIE

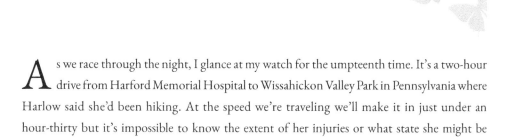

As we race through the night, I glance at my watch for the umpteenth time. It's a two-hour drive from Harford Memorial Hospital to Wissahickon Valley Park in Pennsylvania where Harlow said she'd been hiking. At the speed we're traveling we'll make it in just under an hour-thirty but it's impossible to know the extent of her injuries or what state she might be in.

Before we left, Bastian called Darcy using an encrypted app the teenager had told him to download just to be safe. He said we could use it to call him without the police or FBI being able to track or listen in to the call. Our hope is that Darcy can find her and let us know how badly she's hurt.

I glance down at the still vacant screen of Bastian's phone. It's been forty minutes since we left and still no word from Darcy. I silently will Bastian to go faster and reading my mind, he steps on the gas and the car accelerates. He knows as much as I do that we're running out of time.

"How much longer do you think?" I ask, not able to help myself.

"I'm going as fast as I can." His tone is short, frustrated.

"I know that Bastian. I was just asking."

The entire time we've been in the car, he hasn't said a word. After so many years of being apart he is finally so close to me and yet he feels further away than ever before. "This whole thing might be easier if we talk about it," I tell him. "I'm just as scared as you are."

"Harlow is out there in God-knows-what state, Sophie," he snaps. "The police think she murdered someone. I have no idea what I'm doing or how to help her. What is it exactly you think we can talk about that will make this easier?"

"I'm not trying to make you angry, I just hate this silence." He ignores me and keeps his eyes trained on the road. "We'll find her, Bastian. I know we will." He nods but doesn't say anything back. "Bastian, please. Just say something, anything."

"Christ, Sophie, can you just leave it? Don't you think you've done enough?"

I turn in my seat and stare at him. "What's that supposed to mean?"

"Nothing. Forget it."

A voice in my head screams to take his advice, that this is not the time, there's too much at stake. But despite my better judgment, the words push their way out. "Well, you obviously meant something by it."

We pass under a streetlight and I see his jaw tighten.

"It means I can't believe you kept Poppy a secret from me, Sophie. She's my daughter. What the hell were you thinking?"

"That you were trying to work things out with your *wife*." A venomous tone attaches itself to the word wife and I immediately hate myself. We were never one of those cliché couples to argue and become resentful. We were always better than that. Or so I thought.

"So, to you that justifies lying about having a child with me?" he asks.

"I didn't lie, Bastian, Jesus…"

Suddenly he pounds the steering wheel and glares at me through the dark. "You didn't tell me. You kept my child a secret. That's a lie, Sophie, any way you look at it."

"Well, she's my child too!"

"What does that even mean?"

"I don't know. I…"

Here in the dark, in my Mini that Bastian is pushing way beyond its limits, we are having our first real fight. Anything I say next will be an excuse. What I did was wrong. Even if it was done with the best of intentions. To protect Bastian. To save Poppy the confusion. And I hate to admit it, but maybe to keep her all to myself.

"What Sophie? What did you think? That I'd try and take her away from you?"

"Of course not!"

Hearing the words out loud, I realize how ridiculous it all sounds but there is truth to his accusation. There was a part of me that up until this moment, worried he would take her from me, that my history of anxiety and mental breakdowns after losing Josh would make him think it was *the right thing to do* – for *his* daughter.

"Then what? Why wouldn't you tell me about her?"

I shake my head silently as tears burn in my eyes. I was scared to tell him about her, so scared of what he would do or say, that I was willing to deprive Poppy of her father - a caring, intelligent, and wonderful man.

"Bastian, I…" I want to explain but the right words fail me. Once again, I have proven that I am not capable of being a good mother. I am selfish and useless. Maybe she would have been better off if he did take her from me. "There's nothing else to say, Bastian, other than I'm sorry."

"You're sorry?"

"Yes."

"You have a five-year-old child, Sophie, *my daughter*, and you're sorry?"

"I told you. I don't know what else to say."

The shadows in the car are all that save me. In the light of day, my broken pieces would catch in the light blinding Bastian to the love he once felt for me. He would never be able to see me the same way again.

"I can't pretend to understand what you did," he says, letting out a long breath. "And this is not the end of our conversation. But right now, we need to focus on what they need. Harlow and Poppy. Not *us*."

I nod, relieved that at least for now the fight is over. But it doesn't stop me from wondering if there will be an *us* ever again.

Finally, Bastian's phone buzzes with a message from Darcy. He found her, but she's badly hurt and too far from the entry point for him to get her back by himself.

When we arrive, following Darcy's instructions, Bastian turns onto a gravel road called Kitchen's Lane and follows it around to the back of what looks to be a horse property. It's almost one o'clock in the morning. Around us, pockets of fog hover over the grass like ghosts.

"Now what?" I ask as we get out of the car.

The musty scent of hay and horses hangs over empty paddocks that stretch back to meet the forest. There are no paths or signs that lead to the trail Harlow said she was hiking.

"Mr Marozzi?"

A chill runs the length of my arms as a figure steps out from the darkness of the tree line.

"Darcy?" Bastian asks.

The boy nods and steps in closer.

"Where is she? How do we get to her?"

Even with his face half hidden by shadow, I can see that Darcy is a good-looking boy and I wonder about his relationship with Harlow. Is he her boyfriend? Does he love her?

"Other than hiking the entire trail this is the closest access point," he tells Bastian. "We have to go through the forest. Once we navigate the slope it's not far, but sir, she's in bad shape."

"How bad?"

"I dressed the wounds as best I could and stopped the bleeding, but it's her shoulder. You'll see. Carrying her up myself would have been unbearable for her. We'll need to work together to get her out. She really needs to be in a hospital, like, now." He points toward the dense forest cloaked in darkness. "We have to get going."

The idea of us traipsing after a teenage boy through the dense, dark forest, Bastian in loafers, and me in canvas sneakers, seems like a very bad idea. But despite my fear, I turn and follow them, praying one of us doesn't end up needing to be rescued as well.

The terrain is steep. Our feet slip and slide in loose earth and more than once my foot catches on tree roots and plants, causing me to trip and fall into Bastian's back.

"Harlow?" Bastian calls out. "Harlow, can you hear me?"

"She won't answer you, sir," Darcy tells Bastian. "She can't."

Bastian stops and turns to me, his wide eyes bright in the dark. "Oh Jesus, Sophie, what if…"

He trails off and I squeeze his arm. "Don't think like that. You can't think like that."

"How much further?" he barks at Darcy.

"Almost there, sir, but you should prepare yourself. Like I said, she's in pretty bad shape."

Chapter Thirty-One
HARLOW

S omeone lifts me up and at first, I think I'm dreaming. But then the pain consumes me. I don't scream out. I don't make a sound. It's as though we have become one and I no longer know anything else. No reality, no lucidity. Just pain.

"Harlow, I'm taking you to the hospital," someone whispers. "You'll be fine, sweetheart. I've got you."

A part of my mind wants to respond but I can't find the words. My mouth is cotton and my mind is clouded. The voice is familiar and soothing, but I can't place it.

The air is frigid on my cheek as we move through the forest. I hear the chirp of a frog again and for some reason, it calms me.

"She'll be alright," a woman says. "We'll get her there in time."

"And then what?" the man replies. "How long do you think it will take before the police show up."

"What choice do we have, Bastian? She needs urgent medical care."

The world suddenly jolts up and down and I wonder if I'm falling. A vague memory of a forest appears in my mind and I wonder if I'm still there.

"Have you got her?" the woman asks. "Be careful."

"We're nearly there."

Someone gently touches my forehead and my eyes flutter half open.

"She's burning up."

"Who's there?" I manage. "Where am I?"

"It's Dad, sweetheart," the man tells me. "I'm taking you to get help."

Chapter Thirty-Two

SOPHIE

Bastian carefully rests Harlow across the back seat. She has grown so much since I saw her last. The little girl I met in Fairmount has become a teenager, more resemblant of a woman really. Her hair is tangled with blood. One eye is swollen shut but there's no denying the similarities of her features. She has the same pillowy top lip as me and the angle of her jaw is resilient and determined, just like mine. I want to smile, but instead, force sharp-tasting bile back down my throat when I see the shattered bone protruding from her right arm.

"Bastian, her arm..."

"I know," he says, tucking his sweater under her neck for support. "Come on, get in. We have to go."

As I drop her backpack onto the floor of the car, the outside flap falls open and a few items scatter across the carpet. With no time to spare, I don't bother picking them up until a card with her picture on it catches my attention. I reach in and see that it's an ID card. It has an image of Harlow with her current short dark hair and the name Alexandra Smythe.

"Wait," I say to Bastian as he puts one leg into the car. "I don't think you should be the one to take her to the hospital."

He stops and peers at me as though I have lost my mind. "What are you talking about?"

"Look..." I walk around to the other side of the car and show him the ID card. "Is this what her hair was like before the murder?"

He takes the card and looks at it closely. "Alexandra Smythe?"

Beside us, Darcy kicks at the dirt and looks uncomfortable. "Yeah, umm, I made that for her. It's a thing I do, kinda like a side hustle. My brother showed me. Not that I do it all the time or anything, just that she said she needed it to get away from here. She changed her hair tonight before she started on the track. Sorry... I, just... sorry."

I look at Bastian and try to figure out if he's going to launch at Darcy or hug him for trying to help Harlow.

"You're her father," I say before he has the chance to decide. "If you take her to the hospital, they'll know who she is. But if I take her, Alexandra Smythe, with her different hair and face all bruised and swollen, it might buy us some time. She looks so different and technically I have no connection to Harlow Marozzi."

Saying it out loud is painful, but it's true. Despite the subtle similarities of our faces, without a DNA test, no one can link me to Harlow.

Bastian thinks it over, then opens his mouth to speak but is interrupted by a call on his cell phone.

"It's a number I don't recognize," he tells me. "Should I answer it?"

My shoulders stiffen and I quickly shake my head. Call it women's intuition but I have an overwhelming feeling it's the police.

"No sir," Darcy adds quickly, "it's the feds for sure. They'll know you're in the US by now." He quickly pulls out his phone and turns it off. "Turn your phones off, now, they'll trace them."

"Christ," Bastian swears, as he switches off his phone. "This can't be happening."

"We have to focus," I tell him. "We need to get her help without alerting the authorities until we know what really happened back at that house."

He walks in a wide circle and kicks at the loose gravel. When he stops, he pushes the heels of his hands against his eyes and lets out a frustrated shout.

"Bastian, she needs a doctor. Now."

"She's right," Darcy says. "Harlow can't wait any longer. Get her to the hospital and get burner phones. Use the app I told you about and don't communicate any other way, it's too risky. Kempsey's mom already told the police I was close with Harlow."

"Okay, alright," Bastian says with a nod, clearly pulling himself back together. "You take her, Sophie."

"What about you?"

"Don't worry about me. I can walk to my parent's place from here." He takes in my face and then glances toward the back of the car. "Get her there safely, Soph, please."

I nod and slide into the driver's seat. "I can do this, Bastian. You have my word."

Chapter Thirty-Three

VALENTINE

The hunt for Harlow is the lead story on every morning news show - and so is FBI Special Agent Jasper Monroe. He's younger than I would have expected, and not bad looking with close-cropped black hair and sharp green eyes. When the shot pans back I see he isn't wearing a wedding ring and there's something about the intensity of his plea for Harlow to turn herself in that tells me he genuinely believes he can make a difference. Sad really.

Going straight to the source and finding out what they know will be the easiest way to figure out where this little brat is hiding. And I have no doubt that Special Agent Monroe is ripe for the picking.

After calling the FBI from a public phone and reporting a sighting of Harlow at a coffee shop called The Grind near Reading Terminal Market, I hang up and make my way over there.

It's time to find Harlow.

It takes about twenty minutes for Special Agent Monroe and his partner to arrive. At a table in the back, I sit and sip my latte, waiting for the right moment. As he speaks to the manager, a sandy-haired boy in glasses who can't be more than twenty-one, the agent's face looks strained. He is frustrated and who could blame him? He came to the café on the promise of a lead on his murder suspect Harlow Marozzi and got nothing for his trouble. Or so he thinks.

"Poor Special Agent Monroe," I whisper under my breath as I watch him move toward the door of the café, "but don't worry. You won't be disappointed for long."

I get up from my seat and follow him and his partner toward the door. As he steps out onto the sidewalk I make my move.

"Excuse me," I call out. "Sir, I think you dropped this."

When he turns around, I hold out a man's leather wallet. "I saw this on the ground near the counter. Did you lose it?"

He stops and inspects the wallet in my hand. "No Ma'am, that's not mine."

He has a southern drawl that to my surprise instantly wraps around me, pulling me in.

"It's not?" I pout and glance back into the café.

"No but thank you."

I let my gaze linger over the features of his face. First his eyes, then a little longer on his lips. "Well, that's too bad."

I decided to keep it natural today. No wig, no disguise, just my own black hair that falls exactly in line with my breasts, pink lip gloss, and a little mascara. Coupled with tight jeans and a soft cream sweater it would be easier to think I was a magazine model than Kempsey Karrigan's killer.

He grins and looks uncomfortable.

"You know, I think I saw you on television this morning," I continue. "You're the agent in charge of finding that missing teenager, right?"

"Yes Ma'am," he nods and stretches out his hand. "I'm FBI Special Agent Jasper Monroe."

Clearly bored by our conversation, his partner announces he'll wait in the car and leaves us standing alone on the sidewalk.

"You don't sound like you're from around here, Special Agent Monroe. And please, stop calling me Ma'am," I gush, tapping him gently on the arm. "You're making me feel a hundred years old."

"I apologize for that Ma'... I'm sorry, I didn't get your name?"

"Claire Jamieson," I smile. "But everyone calls me CJ."

"Well you're right CJ, I'm not from around here. I flew in for the case." He looks out toward where his partner is getting into a black sedan. "It's been a pleasure meeting you, but I must be going. Important work and all."

"Of course, off you go then." I give him my warmest smile and let my eyes slowly fall over the rest of his body. He nods and turns to leave but before he gets too far, I call him back. "Special Agent Monroe?"

He stops and I take a few steps forward, close enough for him to smell my perfume. "I'm sorry, I just wanted to say thank you for all you do. Keeping us safe and holding all the criminals out there accountable." Then, I lean in and kiss him softly on the cheek. What he doesn't feel is my expertly trained hand reaching in and lifting his wallet from the inside of that cheap, poorly-made suit.

"That's awful nice of you Ma'... CJ. Much appreciated. You have a good day now."

After my mother died, I had to find a way to support Lacy and me. She was the only family I had left, and we needed a way to pay rent on the trailer. When I approached my mother's dealer, a tall skinny man three trailers over with no front teeth, asking to help sell heroin he bent over laughing. But when I grinned and produced the wallet he thought was still in his pocket he looked me over and quickly said he had an idea. That was the day I started my education on how to become a professional pickpocket. By the time I was seventeen, I had successfully lifted the wallets and watches of more than a thousand unsuspecting men. I never sold drugs, never touched drugs, and swore to never let anyone get close enough to hurt me. Men were marks, nothing more. They would never break me. I was too strong.

Back in my hotel room, I rifle through Special Agent Monroe's wallet and find exactly what I'm looking for - his room key. He is staying at the Windsor Hotel on Walnut Street. I give the card a victorious slap against my palm and smile. It's time to change hotels.

Chapter Thirty-Four

HARLOW

When I wake, the first thing I see is a strange woman folded into a plastic chair by the bed. Her limbs are bent at such a strange angle that she reminds me of a crumpled-up origami swan. Her clothes are creased, her shirt is bloodstained and the soft hum of her breath filters through the hospital room.

"Hello?" I try, feeling half guilty for waking her. "Are you awake?"

She shifts in the chair, her arms and legs heavy with sleep. Then suddenly as if someone has flicked a switch, she sits bolt upright and stares at me. "Harl... Alexandra. You're awake."

A rush of panic floods through me as she says the name, Alexandra. Only Darcy and I know that's the name he gave me. Whoever this woman is, she already knows too much. "Who are you?" I demand, glancing nervously at the door. "How do you know that's my name?"

"You don't recognize me," she says, in a tone that strikes me as almost sad.

"Am I supposed to?"

"Not really, but it was too risky for your dad to come so I'm here to help you."

"Are you with the..." I lower my tone to a whisper, "...police?"

"No, I'm with your dad," she says, unfolding herself from the seat. "My name is -"

"Sophie," I finish, the memory of her suddenly flooding my mind. "I met you once when I was little."

"That's right."

She smiles like she wants to hug me, but instead I move further back in the bed. "You're my..."

"...friend who's here to help, that's all." She takes a beat. "Are you alright? How's your shoulder feeling?"

I gaze down at my bandaged arm and instinctively reach out for it. "Did I have surgery?"

"They had to reset the bone," she says. "It was a terrible break, but they said you'll make a full recovery."

I try to nod but moving my head feels like boulders crashing against the back of my eyes. I wince and move my hand from my arm to my forehead.

"You also have a slight concussion," she adds.

"No shit," I say with a sigh. "Every part of me hurts."

She leans in but doesn't seem to know what to do with her hands. Awkwardly, she pulls away and folds them into her lap.

This is the woman I have long believed to have been my egg donor. The woman who secretly provided her eggs so that I could be born. Now, at the lowest point in my life, she is sitting across from my bed making sure I'm alright. In the moment it took for me to recognize her, she instantly became more of a mother to me than Madelyn-May has ever been.

"Harlow, we need to know what really happened at the house with your friend Kempsey," she says, lowering her voice. "The only way your dad and I can help you is if we know who really killed her."

I fall back into the pillows and close my eyes. My entire body is throbbing, and my mind feels packed in cotton wool. "I was locked in a bedroom upstairs," I begin. "I heard someone in the house. They came up to the door and unlocked it, but..."

"...but what?"

"Kempsey came home. Whoever it was, went back downstairs. They killed her and left. I never saw them. I have no idea who it was." I hear her sigh out loud and carefully open my eyes. "Darcy thinks..."

"...Darcy thinks what?"

"No, it's stupid."

"Nothing is stupid... Alexandra." She leans in, this time resting her fingers on my wrist. "If there's anything you think might be related to what happened, then you have to tell me."

I roll my head to the side and look at her. Our eyes are the same. Her hair has the same chestnut highlights as mine did before I dyed it. "You're my real mother, aren't you?"

She instantly lets go of my wrist and looks away.

"Just tell me, Sophie. Are you my real mom?"

"Madelyn-May is your mom," she says, without meeting my eye. "And no matter what you think, she loves you. That day you were taken... she would have done anything to protect you."

"You were with her?"

"I was."

Memories of the car rolling over and the sound of twisting metal scrape at my insides. "But it was her fault it even happened. All she ever cared about was being famous. If she hadn't been all over the internet Lacy would never have found us."

"She loves you. You have to try and believe that."

"I can't believe you're sticking up for her," I say, frustrated. "I thought you loved my dad?"

"You know about that?"

I can tell from the shocked look on her face that her relationship with my dad was supposed to be a secret. "I know all of it Sophie and I wish you were my mother. At least you'd take care of me."

But to my surprise, she scoffs and looks away.

"What?"

"Nothing."

Her eyes are wet and I can see she's trying not to cry. "Sophie, what?"

"I'm not a good mother," she says. "Believe me, you're much better off with Madelyn-May."

"How would you even know what kind of mother you'd be? You never tried to be a mom to Harry and me. Unless…" she reluctantly meets my eye and it occurs to me that Sophie might have other children of her own "… you have other kids?"

"I have a daughter," she admits. "Her name is Poppy. And I had a son, Josh, before I met your dad. But he died in a car accident."

I take a moment and let it all sink in. If she had a son before she met my dad and a daughter after, did that mean… "You have a child with my dad? Like, a real child?"

"*You* are a real child," she reminds me, "but yes. Poppy, and she's very sick."

"Sick how?" I push myself up against the pillows and peer at her.

"She has a rare form of leukemia. If she doesn't receive a bone marrow transplant soon she could die."

I nod slowly and no matter how hard I try to push them back, tears sting my eyes. "So that's why you're here?"

"I'm here because I want to help both of you."

"It's okay, I get it," I say, my tone frosty. "I might be a donor match for her, right? Because we're siblings."

"Yes, but that's not the only reason I came."

I suddenly feel so stupid. When I saw Sophie in the chair for a moment, I actually thought I had a mother who cared for me. But then, I thought Rhonda cared as well, and look where that got me. *Stupid.*

"Please, just listen -" she tries again, but I cut her off.

"Get out."

"Harlow…"

"Don't call me that," I hiss. "Just… please leave."

"But your dad needs to know - "

"Oh, like he cares," I say, my voice wavering. "He has a new daughter, right? Poppy, is that what you said her name was?"

"That's not true. He loves you. Both your parents love you."

"But not you, huh? To you, I'm just a spare parts department for your *real* daughter."

"Harlow... no."

"I said don't call me that. Now leave, Sophie. I don't ever want to see you again."

I train my eyes on a tiny crack in the wall and for a moment, she just sits there. I can feel her eyes on me, desperate and confused. In my heart, I feel like the lowest person on earth. Somewhere a little girl is dying. I might be the only hope she has and yet the pain of being cast aside, yet again, is debilitating. I want to look Sophie in the eye and apologize. I want to say of course I'll help, but no matter how much I try to deny it I am so jealous of this little girl whose mother would go to such lengths to try and save her that I can't make my mouth say the words.

From the corner of my eye, I see Sophie get to her feet and I know it's my last chance. I hear her footsteps beside the bed, then see her cross in front of me. I know she's going to turn and look at me. I will myself to meet her eye, to say something, anything, but to my disgust, I remain silent. Her footsteps grow quieter as she makes her way toward the door, softer still, and then she is gone.

When the room falls silent, I think back to the question Sophie asked me; who do I think really killed Kempsey? It wasn't me. I didn't kill anyone. But now I can't help but wonder – did my jealousy just cost a little girl her life?

Chapter Thirty-Five

SOPHIE

When I messaged Bastian using the encrypted app Darcy told us about to let him know Harlow was awake and in recovery, the first thing he said was thank you. The second was that we needed to talk.

Now, as I wait for him to open the door to his hotel room my stomach flip-flops in anticipation.

"Soph, come in," he says, stepping back to make way for me.

As I brush by him, I can't help but notice his rich, familiar scent - sandalwood, musk, and cedar. Before he has a chance to see, I grab at my own sweater and smell the material. Sweat, blood, and dank earth. *Great.*

He follows me into the room, which despite its generous space instantly feels cramped like we're on top of each other.

"You want a drink?" he asks, bending to look in the room's mini fridge. "There's water, soft drink, juice? I could make you a coffee?"

"I'm okay," I tell him. "But thanks."

They are pleasantries. Formalities. And they make me uncomfortable. "So, Harlow is doing well," I tell him, eager to move on to something real. "They re-set her arm. The rest looks bad but there's nothing that won't heal."

"I'm so glad." His smile is warm and creases the edges of his eyes. "What you did, Soph... that was really something."

I shrug and let my eyes fall. "She needed help."

Silence falls between us and I swallow hard. "Bastian, at the hospital Harlow got upset."

"About?" He takes a seat at a small round table by the window.

I follow suit and sit across from him. "She asked if I was the one who donated the egg to Madelyn May."

"I see." He takes a sip of water and crosses one leg over the other.

"Bastian, did you tell her about us?" I ask. "She seemed to know a lot about what happened."

"Not intentionally. After the accident when she was a kid the doctors were talking to us about the potential need for a blood donor. They were asking a bunch of questions about our medical history and just to be safe Madelyn-May told them about the egg donation. We thought Harlow was too out of it at the time to take anything in."

"And about you and I?"

"Harlow's a smart kid. A few years later she asked me about you," he explains. "It bothered her to think that the woman whose egg she came from, was *'some random'*, as she put it. So, I told her that you were a lot more to me than that."

There was never any question about what Bastian and I meant to each other, but my body still warms at his words. "And how did she take it?"

"Well, it was a lot to try and explain. She hated Madelyn-May for the lies," he says, "and then me for cheating. But I think she always saw what her mother did as the greater betrayal. It just added to Harlow's resentment about being forced into the public eye whether she and Harry wanted to be or not. She thinks the accident wouldn't have happened if Madelyn-May hadn't been so hell-bent on building an online empire with them at the center of it."

I nod and try to imagine what it would be like if Poppy hated me. If she will hate me for leaving her alone at the hospital.

As if reading my mind, Bastian reaches across the table and gently places his hand over mine. "Soph, we need to talk about Poppy."

"I know." I meet his eye and try to read his thoughts. "I never meant to hurt you."

He takes a deep breath and moves his hand away. "I just can't believe that after everything we've been through you wouldn't tell me about her. I thought... I thought we were more than that."

"I wanted to." I reach out and take his hand back into mine. "You have to believe me. There were just so many reasons that stopped me, Bastian. We were over. You were trying to put your family back together. We were oceans apart."

"Maybe in distance, Sophie, but Christ," he swears, "it's us. You and me."

I search my mind for the right words but come up empty. He's right and I can't help but wonder if Madelyn-May and I are more alike than I care to imagine. We've both kept monumental secrets from him, both betrayed him with our silence. I want to cry but feel like if I do it will be a cop-out. Bastian deserves more than tears. He deserves an explanation.

"I was scared," I begin, "scared that you'd think Poppy would be better off in Australia with you."

He gets to his feet and paces the length of the window. "Why would you think that?"

"Because," I manage over the lump in my throat, "Josh died, and I wasn't even there. The last time you were with me I was crippled by panic attacks. I would hardly be the person you want raising your child, especially when you have..."

He stops pacing and stares at me. "...especially when I have what?"

"Everything," I whisper. "You have everything to offer her."

"Not everything," he replies, his voice quiet. "I don't have you."

Chapter Thirty-Six
VALENTINE

"CJ? Is that you?"

I take another sip of my coffee and slowly turn around. "Special Agent Monroe, what a surprise."

"Are you staying here in the hotel?" he asks. "I thought you were a local."

I look him over, slowly enough to make sure he feels my eyes on him, then smile. "No, I'm here in Philly for business."

It's not a total lie. Making sure Harlow is captured and held accountable for murdering that poor girl is definitely my business.

"I see." He hovers a moment then glances over at the breakfast bar.

Taking the cue, I follow his gaze. "I was just about to eat," I tell him. "Would you like to join me?"

He hesitates and glances over his shoulder. "You know, my partner never eats breakfast. He does take his time coming down though."

"A coffee then?"

As we sit and chat, I quickly discover Special Agent Monroe comes from a small town called Brusly near Baton Rouge where he and his three brothers all grew up under the watchful eye of a single mom named Evelyn. He smiles when he mentions her name and I know immediately that she's the in I need.

"Single moms are special," I tell him, a warm smile lighting up my eyes. "My mom was... unlike any other woman I know." *Wasn't she just.*

He leans in, his eyes searching mine. "You're the daughter of a single mom as well?"

"Her name was Melody."

"You said, *was*. Has she passed?"

Images of her pale dead body flash through my mind. "Yes, when I was nine." *With a needle in her arm.*

He sits back in his seat and pushes out a long breath. "That's tough. I'm so sorry you had to go through that and so young."

Knowing he is on the hook I push my mug away and focus all my energy on letting my eyes mist over. "I still miss her every day."

"Of course you do and again, I'm so sorry for your loss CJ, really."

He reaches out and covers my hand with his. My initial impulse is to pull away. I hate being touched, especially by a man, but for the sake of the ruse, I have to let him comfort me. "Thank you, Jasper," I say, purposely using his first name, "that means a lot."

He holds my gaze, then removes his hand and clears his throat. "So," he begins, "what kind of business brings you to Philly?"

The murdering kind.

"I'm an art curator back in California," I tell him without the slightest flinch. "I'm here for a meeting at the PMA."

"PMA?"

"Philadelphia Museum of Art."

"Oh, sorry." His cheeks color and I take it as a good sign. He cares what I think of him. "Law enforcement and art don't quite go together."

I catch his eye and smile. "I wouldn't say that."

He folds his napkin, and I take it as a sign he is about to wrap things up. "CJ listen, I think you're lovely -"

"Then ask me out," I interrupt before he can finish. "Nothing serious. Just for the company. Unless... it wouldn't be right for you to be seen out to dinner when you're on a case?"

"That would definitely be a bad look on my part."

"Then room service it is," I say with a smile. "We'll order in, have a glass of wine, a chat, then I'll say goodnight." He hesitates and I make my final move. "Jasper, it's just for the company. My meeting in the morning is a job interview and I'm super nervous. It would be a great distraction and I have to be in bed early anyway."

"Well, I can't say a beautiful woman has ever asked me to be her distraction before."

I give a coy laugh and feign embarrassment. "I probably shouldn't have put it quite like that."

"I guess you put it just fine because the answer is yes," he says. "Seven o'clock work?"

"Seven o'clock is perfect," I tell him. "I'm looking forward to it."

Poor Jasper, I think as I watch him drain the rest of his coffee and get to his feet. He looks so content. If only he knew, the thing I'm looking forward to most is being in his room so I can access his case files.

Chapter Thirty-Seven
SOPHIE

When I found out I was pregnant with Poppy, my first thought had been to call Bastian. I loved him and he was her father. More than that, he was a good man and one who would never make her feel second best or allow her to want for anything. So why didn't I tell him?

My fears seemed so rational at the time. He had seen me at my worst. I allowed that, encouraged it even. At the time, I believed it brought us closer, made the connection between us stronger. He wasn't my husband, but we weren't dating. He and I lived in a kind of limbo, a place between truth and fiction where we could make our own rules, where the light of day shone only through tiny cracks, never harsh enough to cast a shadow. There were no expectations or broken promises. There was just he and I, holding hands while the world fell in around us. In that private place, I could show myself to him. All my shortcomings and flaws, my fears and insecurities, because he would never consider them baggage he might one day have to carry. He already had a wife. He was free to walk away from me at any time; the thing was, he never did. But when that tiny red plus sign emerged on the pregnancy test, everything changed.

He was an ocean away trying to stitch his family back together and I had started a new life, one where I was trying to untangle him from my heart.

So many times, before I found out I was pregnant I picked up the phone to text him. Nothing monumental, just the truth. *I miss you*. But I never hit send. What would be the point? Our time was over, or so I thought.

And then suddenly there was Poppy. Technically nothing more than a tiny cluster of cells and a cross on a test, but instantly she was everything. She was him and she was me. She was our child, the manifestation of a love that had saved my life. And that was the thing. To Bastian, I had been a life that needed saving. What would he think of me raising his child?

As she grew inside me, every day, and week, and month my fear of losing her became more and more irrational. I lost Josh, what if I lost Poppy as well? What if my anxiety resurfaced and

I couldn't care for her? What if she was in an accident? What if I told Bastian and he knew I couldn't be the mother she needed?

The first two were things I could try to prevent, but the last, once I told him, was out of my hands. And so, by the time my pregnancy was at thirty-two weeks, I had made the decision not to tell him about her. I couldn't. More truthfully, I wouldn't.

But now, standing in front of him, as he tucks my hair back behind my ear the way he always has, I wonder what the hell I was thinking. Bastian would never take Poppy from me. He would have told Madelyn-May and together we could have worked something out. My daughter could have had a father - a great one. Now, because of my fear, it may be too late.

"Bastian," I begin, "I should never have kept Poppy from you. I don't know what I was thinking."

He gazes into my eyes, his finger softly tracing the length of my cheek. "You hurt me, Sophie."

My eyes drop. "I know."

"I understand your reasons, but you have to know I would never try and take her from you."

"I know that too."

"Look at me..."

I gather the strength to look up, to be held accountable by the man I love.

"Sophie, I think you are one of the strongest women I have ever met. You lost your child and your husband. What you felt after that, the way your mind and body reacted, was natural. You were a mother without a child and yet you pulled through. More than that, you saved Miss Molly and gave her a home. You found love in your heart for me, and you saved our son when he was trapped in a car wreck."

"Bastian..."

"No, I mean it, Sophie. You need to hear this. I would never try to take Poppy from you. I love you. I mean it."

I nod as quiet tears roll down my cheeks. "I love you too and I'm so sorry."

He pulls me close and my head nestles perfectly into the warm nook beneath his shoulder. I feel the soft rise and fall of his breath. In this moment Poppy is not sick and Harlow is not in the hospital. Madelyn-May doesn't wear his ring and we are not in a hotel room. We are home. I pull back just far enough to take in his face. "I've missed you."

"I've missed you too."

He leans in and I close my eyes, anticipating the soft touch of his lips. And then my phone rings.

"Don't answer," he whispers.

But it could be the hospital and as much as I want his lips on mine if I missed a call about our daughter, I would never forgive myself. I glance at the screen and my stomach twists when I see the hospital's number.

"Sophie, it's Doctor Yates. You need to get back here as soon as you can."

"What's wrong? What's happened?"

"Poppy's fever is spiking again. We're having trouble bringing it down. If we can't..."

She trails off and I'm already grabbing for my purse. "I'm coming. Just, please do everything possible. I'll be there as soon as I can."

I shove the phone into my purse and quickly shrug on my jacket, tears burning in my eyes. "This can't happen," I sob. "It can't..."

Bastian grabs both my shoulders. "Hey, just breathe," he says. "I'm coming with you."

"No, you have to stay here. Harlow needs you close by."

"You can't drive in this state, Sophie, it's not safe."

"Find a way to speak to Harlow. She hates me, Bastian," I tell him. "She thinks the only reason I brought her to the hospital was so she could be spare parts, *her words*, for Poppy. Somehow you need to explain that's not the case."

He pushes out a long breath, then reaches into his pocket and pulls out a scrap of paper with a number scribbled on it. "I got a burner like Darcy said. Call me the minute you know what's going on and use the encrypted app. I'll figure out a way to help Harlow. The sooner we do that, the sooner they'll both be safe."

Chapter Thirty-Eight
VALENTINE

Jasper's one-bedroom suite has the same layout as mine but it's so tidy it's hard to believe anyone has been staying in it. I'd like to think he tidied it up to impress me, but I get the feeling he is one of those people who likes everything in his world to be organized and in its place.

"How long have you been staying here?" I ask as I glance around the suite.

"Just a couple of days. Since the case started."

"You're very tidy."

He looks around the room and shrugs. "Probably because of my time at Quantico. We learned early on that everything requires order. My mom never cared much for mess either matter of fact. With four boys in the house that was a tough ask mind you."

"I'm sure you all did your best." I smile and take a seat at one of two small loungers at the end of the living room.

"So, what are you in the mood for?" he asks.

I know he's referring to dinner, but all I can think about is getting into his computer and finding out what the FBI knows about Harlow and her whereabouts.

"Something spicy," I tell him, my brow raised. "If you're game."

We order two Thai curries and he pours us both a glass of wine. Over dinner, he surprises me with warm humor and perfect manners. He tells me about growing up on the west side of the Mississippi, about the trouble he and his brothers caused growing up, and how last year he had to travel home when his mother was diagnosed with breast cancer.

As he speaks, I watch him closely looking for tells. Fortunately for me, he is open, honest, and surprisingly willing to share himself with a stranger. Midway through a tale about he and his teenage brothers bringing a stray horse into their backyard, it strikes me that our life experiences could not be any further apart. Growing up he knew love and laughter and because of it, Jasper has clearly become a man who is responsible and walks with his head held high. He doesn't creep in shadows or shut people out. I tell myself that I feel sorry for him, that he is naive and weak, but the truth is, as I watch him laugh and sip his wine, I'm jealous of this man who seems to have had a perfect life.

"I just need to check my email to make sure nothing has changed for my interview in the morning," I tell him as I take my phone out. "Don't think I'm being rude."

"Course not," he says. "Go for it."

After fiddling with my phone for a couple of seconds I let out a long sigh. "Shit, my internet isn't working."

"Really? You want me to take a look?"

"And see all my private photos?" I say with a grin. "Not just yet."

He laughs and points to a side table in by the bed. "You can use my laptop if you like."

"You sure?"

"You're not a spy are you?"

I throw my head back and laugh. "Yeah right, gallery curator by day, secret agent by night."

"Go on in, take your time," he tells me, getting to his feet. "You want another glass?"

"Sure," I call back, knowing it will distract him. "Thank you."

When he is busy in the small kitchenette, I log onto a fake email account just in case he checks the search history, then click off and scan my eyes over his file list. He has worked on a number of missing persons cases and one high-profile murder in New York that I saw on the news last year.

"You get in okay?" he calls from the kitchen.

"Yep, and lucky I checked. They brought my interview forward an hour. Just give me a sec to write a response."

When I find the case file marked Marozzi, I push a USB stick into the laptop and hit copy. As the files transfer, I pretend to write an email and pray it doesn't take too long.

"You want your wine in there?" Suddenly he is hovering in the doorway and I gently move my knee over the USB.

"No, I want it out there with you, silly. I'm almost done."

A green tick appears on the screen and when he turns and heads back to the living area, I pull out the USB and quickly shove it into my jeans pocket.

"All done," I sing out. "And... oh my God, is it that late already?"

He glances at his watch. "Shit, where did the night go?"

It's just past eleven. I have actually stayed later than I intended. "I'd love to stay and drink that glass of wine, but I better get going," I tell him. "Especially now my interview is at eight-thirty in the morning."

He nods and I can see by the way his shoulders fall he's disappointed that I'm leaving.

"I had such a great night," I tell him, as I scoop my bag up over my shoulder. "Thank you. It was exactly what I needed."

He walks me to the door and leans one shoulder against the wall. "I had a good time."

I give him a coy smile, then touch his arm. "I did too."

"Can I see you again? You know, just to see how the interview went considering I was such a good distraction."

I surprise myself by laughing because it's genuine. "I guess that would be alright."

"Great. I'll call you when I'm done tomorrow evening."

And then the biggest surprise of all comes when I hear myself say, "I'm looking forward to it."

Chapter Thirty-Nine
HARLOW

I use the remote control to switch on the hospital room's television and try to distract myself from the relentless throbbing in my shoulder. After flicking through a trashy reality show, the cooking channel, and a game of football, I land on the news where the top story is me.

I use the remote control to switch on the hospital room's television and try to distract myself from the relentless throbbing in my shoulder. After flicking through a trashy reality show, the cooking channel, and a game of football, I land on the news where the top story is me.

"The manhunt continues for missing teen Harlow Marozzi, the main suspect in the murder of seventeen-year-old Kempsey Karrigan at her family home two days ago. Marozzi was staying at the home at the time of the murder and is believed to have fled the scene."

My face flashes up on the screen and I swallow and glance over at the door. I've done all I can to alter my appearance but once the swelling in my face goes down it won't take long for hospital staff to figure out who I am.

Up on the screen, a handsome detective speaks to the camera, his name coming up along the bottom as FBI Special Agent Jasper Monroe.

"Ms Marozzi if you are watching this, know that we will find you. It is in your best interest to make contact and come forward as soon as possible."

I turn off the television and slump back against the pillows. I have twenty-four hours tops before being here will become dangerous, but where will I go? Even though my dad is here in the US, the minute I call him they'll be onto me and I can't trust Sophie. All she cares about is her own daughter and using me as a spare parts department. I have to figure this out on my own. And the first thing I need to do is tell the FBI the truth; that I didn't kill Kempsey.

Making my way along the hospital corridor is a struggle. An IV tube runs from my arm to a dolly that I need to wheel along beside me. Every step sends a hot pain shooting up my arm and into my shoulder. When I finally make it outside, I squint in the sunlight and shuffle toward a seat by the bustling taxi rank.

Once I ease myself down, I take out the burner phone and dial the number that flashed up at the end of the news story. It rings and I hold my breath. This will have to be quick.

"Crime Stoppers."

"I'm calling with information about Harlow Marozzi that teen the FBI is looking for."

"What's your name please?"

"I'd like to talk to the agent in charge."

"Name please."

"Not until I speak to Special Agent Monroe."

I hear a long sigh on the other end of the line. "I can't transfer the call until you tell me your name."

"Fine, this is Harlow Marozzi. Now put me through. I won't be calling back."

A part of me expected her to shriek in surprise that the target of a nationwide FBI manhunt is on the line but instead she says, "Please hold," and the line goes quiet.

When he picks up the call, I notice he has more of a southern drawl than I heard on the television. "This is Special Agent Monroe. Who am I speaking with?"

This is it. I have one shot at telling the truth. "It's Harlow. I didn't kill Kempsey. I need you to know that."

"Harlow, if it's really you, you need to come in. Where are you?"

"Listen to me, please," I try again. "I didn't kill her. I was upstairs. There was an intruder. I think it was a woman. I saw her run across the front yard after she... killed Kempsey."

"Can you identify this woman?"

"No, because like I said, she was in the dark. Kempsey was already dead by the time I got downstairs. It wasn't me."

"Then let us pick you up and we can work this all out."

"No," I tell him. "Not until you find the real killer."

"Harlow, you need to come in."

"Lacy Myers. Speak to her. She's in prison for trying to kidnap me."

"We know about Lacy."

"Then ask her. She did this after she found out where I was."

"Harlow-"

"Don't you get it? I was the target, not Kempsey. She just came home at the wrong time."

"Then all the more reason you should let us pick you up."

"Speak to Lacy."

I hang up and use my left arm to push up from the seat. Even though it's a burner, it won't take long for them to track the location of the phone. In front of me, a man who looks to be in his thirties with a plaster cast on his leg is being helped into a taxi by one of the hospital staff.

"Excuse me," I say to the orderly, "I'm sorry but I think I need some help getting back to my room. I'm not feeling so good."

They both look at me and the young male orderly nods. "Of course, if you can wait just a moment, I'll be right with you."

When he turns to help the man with the cast into the car, I take a deep breath and throw myself down onto the ground as though I have fainted.

"Oh, my goodness" the orderly shrieks, dropping the man's bag onto the ground. "I'll get help."

"Shit, are you alright?" The plaster cast patient leans out from the taxi and looks me over.

I pretend to come around and clutch onto his sports bag to help drag myself up. "Yeah, I... I think I fainted."

When the bag is under my chest, I slip the phone inside. Hospital staff come running out with a gurney, while beside me a nurse quickly puts his bag into the taxi. The door closes and it pulls away as they wheel me back inside the hospital.

Chapter Forty

SOPHIE

I cradle Poppy's burning forehead against my chest and rock her back and forth. I feel so helpless and wonder if I did the wrong thing walking out of Harlow's hospital room. Maybe I shouldn't have even taken her there. Maybe I should have been brave enough and selfish enough to instead make the trip back here where at least the girls would be under the same roof. That way they could do the test and if there was a match before the FBI tracked Harlow down. But then I remind myself, that in many ways Harlow is my child too. The injury to her shoulder was severe and if we hadn't made it in time…

I let the thought trail off and immediately feel guilty for having even considered it. But I carried Poppy for nine months. I felt every twitch, tear, and trauma of giving birth to her. I am her mother in every possible way.

I pull my tiny daughter closer and feel her face hot and sticky against my cheek. Harlow came from my egg, but the truth is, I don't feel like a mother to her. Maybe if Poppy wasn't in the world the connection would be stronger, but right now, as my daughter lies dying in my arms, I regret leaving Harlow back in that hospital room. She was right there in front of me, the answer to saving Poppy's life residing inside her, and I walked away. Now Poppy might die.

"Sophie," Dr Yates appears by the bed, as usual, with a clipboard in her hand.

"Is Poppy alright? Will she be okay?" I ask brushing the hair from my daughter's forehead and hoping desperately that somewhere on that clipboard is the solution to keeping her alive.

"Unfortunately, until we find a donor Poppy will be at risk, Sophie," she tells me, her voice low and stern. "Did you have any luck securing her sibling?"

I shake my head and find that I can't bring myself to meet her eye. This doctor is an expert in her field. She is a surgeon and can save lives. I can't even find a way to bring Harlow to the hospital.

For all the times I have felt like a failure as a mother, this moment exceeds all of them. All I need to do is get Harlow here and this doctor can potentially save my child. But instead, I'm just sitting here watching her fade away.

"Is there anything you can try in the meantime?" I ask. "A way to buy us some more time?"

"We could try a blood transfusion. That may provide enough red blood cells to keep her stable. We could also consider starting her on chemotherapy, but it's a risk. If your donor doesn't come through and we don't locate a match on the register in time, it means her immune system will be compromised from the treatment."

"And if we don't?"

"It means when you do have a donor, she'll still have to wait at least ten days before we can begin the transplant process."

My head is spinning. There are so many variables but when you break it all down, there's only one question I need to answer. Do I believe I can get Harlow to this hospital in less than ten days?

"Can I have a minute?" I ask. "I need to call her father before I make any decisions."

The words sound foreign as they hang in the air between us. Having to consider Bastian's opinion is new. I have attached so much fear and apprehension to him having a say in her life, but having someone to share the burden, if I'm honest, is a relief.

He picks up on the third ring, and right away I know something is wrong. "Bastian? What's happening? You sound different."

"Soph, there's been a development."

I take a deep breath and as quickly as it came, the reassurance I felt about being able to safely call him instead turns to anxiety. "What kind of development?"

I listen as he explains what happened at the hospital and that he's waiting to be questioned by the FBI about his role in Harlow's escape. He tells me there's a high chance he will be charged with aiding and abetting and expects to have his phone confiscated at any time.

"So, what are you saying Bastian? That I'm on my own?"

"I'll work this out, Sophie. I'm sorry. I didn't mean for it to go like this."

"What were you thinking going to the hospital like that?"

"I had a plan. I still do but I don't want to get your hopes up."

"Get my hopes up?"

"Special Agent Monroe said Harlow called him this morning. She told him she thinks Lacy was involved in killing that girl."

"Lacy?" I quickly think back to what Harlow had started to say in the hospital. *Darcy thinks...*

"I think she tried to tell me the same thing," I tell him. "Before I mentioned Poppy."

"How is Poppy?" he asks. "Is she alright?"

I swallow down the lump in my throat. "Not really. She needs Harlow, Bastian. I don't know what to do."

But even as I say the words, I know there is only one thing I can do. If Harlow is right and Lacy is involved, then I need to pay a visit to the prison.

Chapter Forty-One
VALENTINE

I know more about Harlow than the FBI. After reading through all Jasper's notes and background information the only thing I've discovered, to my disgust, is that the FBI has no idea where she is.

I am down to his last entry and beginning to wonder why I wasted my time on him when suddenly I find what I've been looking for in his call logs. Harlow called him. Yesterday, just after ten o'clock in the morning.

I read over the transcript of their call and catch my breath when I come to the part where she begs him to speak to Lacy. So, she knows it wasn't a break-in. I'm surprised, and a little impressed. She's smarter than I gave her credit for. But did he take her seriously?

There are pages of notes in his file about Lacy and the accident. How she groomed and then tried to kidnap Harlow. How Harlow tried to strangle her while she was driving, the resulting crash flipping the car, all three of them in a critical condition and Harlow suffering the worst of it after being thrown through the windscreen.

I click to close the file and wonder if Harlow would have the balls to go to Lacy herself. With so much heat on her, she couldn't possibly get into a prison without being caught. No, she wouldn't dare. Would she?

While I try to pre-empt Harlow's next move, I type her name into the internet search bar to see if there's been any news updates on the case. The first thing I find is a link uploaded forty minutes ago. When I click on it, it takes me to a shaky cell phone video of Jasper and a hoard of FBI agents running across what looks like the grounds of a hospital, then crash-tackling none other than Madelyn-May's husband to the ground.

"What the hell?" I lean in closer and read that after being surgically treated for a shoulder injury, Harlow escaped from a hospital located just an hour outside Philadelphia.

"Brat," I sigh, unwilling to admit to myself this girl and her tenacity are starting to grow on me. "Where have you gone?"

The story goes on to say agents found dirt bike tracks on the trail where she disappeared but could not be sure there was an accomplice as the area is a renowned hotspot for trail bike riders.

"Well of course she had an accomplice," I say out loud to the empty room. "How else do you think she disappeared?" *Idiots.*

I slap the laptop closed. A seventeen-year-old girl is outsmarting the FBI; she and whoever is helping her. By now Bastian in all his wisdom will be in custody for aiding and abetting a fugitive, so he's off limits. And he wasn't the one who helped her escape. So, who does that leave I wonder as I pace back and forth across the room. Who would be willing to help a suspected murderer escape the FBI?

I flip the laptop back open and type into the search bar looking for the infamous video of Harlow at the bar. She doesn't have any adult friends who have spoken out on her behalf so whoever is helping her has to be another teenager. And I'm willing to put money on the fact they are in that video with her. All I have to do is figure out who it is.

Chapter Forty-Two
HARLOW

I wake up to realize the nurse who wheeled me back to my room must have added an extra painkiller to my IV drip. Outside my window, the sun is setting and although my intention had been to immediately get my things and make an escape, almost eight hours later, I'm still here.

"Shit," I swear out loud, unable to believe the FBI hasn't tracked me here already.

Being asleep all day has left no time to plan, and I still have no idea where I'm going to go. But I can't let that stop me. I clench my teeth, squeeze my eyes closed, and carefully slide the IV drip out of my hand. When it's detached, I pull out my old clothes only to realize they are torn and covered in dried blood.

"Shit, shit," I swear again.

With no other choice, I shuffle down the hospital corridor hoping no one notices that I'm no longer attached to the drip dolly.

"Are you alright?" a nurse calls from the station, just outside my room.

"Oh, um, yep, just going to the bathroom."

"Do you need help?"

"Nope," I call back. "I can manage."

When she doesn't insist, I move along the corridor until I find a girl about my age asleep in one of the rooms. As quietly as I can, I slip inside and find her overnight bag on a shelf near the door.

"Jackpot," I whisper, as I slowly and carefully thread the bag over my good arm.

In the bathroom, I change into her jeans and struggle to pull a navy-blue sweater over my head. The pain in my shoulder cuts to the core. The runners are a size too small and immediately begin to rub as I head down the corridor, past an empty staff room, and away from the nurse's station.

As I wait for the elevator, movement back down the corridor catches my eye and I turn to see the man from the television, Special Agent Jasper Monroe standing flanked by six other men at the nurse's station.

"Oh no," I breathe, as the nurse points toward the lady's bathroom. "Shit."

With as little fanfare as possible, I turn and try to find an exit before they find me. I turn corner after corner, mindful not to run no matter how much my brain screams at me to do just that. It has to be here. There has to be a way out. But when even more agents appear up ahead, I know I'm not going to make it.

"There!" a man dressed in dark pants and an FBI windbreaker calls. "That's her."

They move toward me in a pack and I have no choice but to turn and run back toward Special Agent Monroe. I'm on the first floor. One of the rooms will have windows that open. I quickly remember seeing an empty staff room. If I go in one of two things will happen. I can jump out the window before the agents catch up to me or the window will be sealed, and I'll be trapped.

I dart into the staff room and to my relief find that it's still empty. I lock the door behind me and head over to the window. Lifting the old wooden frame with my injury is going to be excruciating. I curl my fingers around the handles, count one, two, three, then brace myself and lift. The old window groans and I cry out in a mix of pain and joy as it opens. Without looking back, I crawl onto the ledge and drop over the side onto the grass below.

"Stop right there!" I freeze at the sound of a man's voice behind me. "Don't you move young lady."

His voice is wavering. It sounds like it belongs to an older man. "I'm turning around," I tell him in a calm tone. "Don't do anything crazy."

"Slowly."

I turn with my hands up to find a hospital security guard who looks to be in his sixties, his legs spread wide and a rubber baton in his hand.

"Let's not get crazy," I tell him. "I didn't do anything to anyone. You need to know that. This is all a mistake."

"Do not move." He pulls a two-way radio from his belt with one hand and keeps the baton trained on me with the other.

"Harlow!"

I turn and am shocked to see my dad coming toward me from the other side of the lawn.

The security guard's face reddens at the sight of my dad, and his weight shifts from one foot to the other. "Stop where you are," he shouts. "Both of you. No one moves."

"Harlow, come on, we have to get out of here," my dad calls, ignoring him. "There's no time!"

I glance at the security guard and then up at the window where the agents are now staring down at me.

"Harlow, now!"

Praying for a miracle, I turn and run toward my dad. It's been so long since I've seen him. I want to stop and throw my arms around him, but know I can't. "Now what do we do?" I call, as I close the gap between us.

"Keep running we're almost there."

"Almost where?"

As I approach, he turns and I run behind him to the edge of the carpark where the hospital grounds meet woodland. When we reach the edge, he stops and turns to me.

"Alright," he says, his hands coming to rest on my shoulder. "I love you. Your mom loves you. We know you didn't do it. I'll work this out, you have my word."

"Dad, wait, what?"

Deep shadows press into the skin beneath his eyes. He looks tired. Scared. "Run, Harlow. If I stay with you it will only make things harder. Run down that trail and don't stop for anything."

I stare down the empty trail that leads into dense woodland. "What? To where?"

"Just trust me, sweetheart. Run as fast as you can."

"What about you?"

"I'll be fine. Now go."

I hesitate and try to take a mental picture of him in my mind. Whatever he's feeling, whatever he's going through, I know it's my fault.

"Go, sweetheart. I'll fix this, but you have to go."

Tears sting my eyes as I turn and run as fast as I can along the winding track. Behind me, he shouts out and I hear the muffled reply of FBI agents. I want to stop and turn back, but instead I keep running, not knowing where I'm going or why my dad chose this track. But as I turn the next corner, almost out of breath, suddenly it all makes sense. Sitting on his dirt bike waiting for me is Darcy.

Chapter Forty-Three
SOPHIE

Poppy is stable. The blood transfusion worked, for now, but we're not out of the woods. If we start the chemo, I have ten days to find Harlow, prove she didn't kill her friend and convince her to help save my daughter's life. If I don't, Poppy could slip back into a critical condition at any time.

I lean against the door and watch my daughter sleeping. I'm facing the biggest challenge of my life and with Bastian at the FBI, I'm in this all on my own. I take a sip of coffee from a paper cup and let it warm me. There was a time, not so long ago, when I could barely leave the house without being heavily medicated. Without the support of my lovely Miss Molly and a handful of anti-anxiety meds, panic would almost always get the better of me. Our walks were short, and my recovery was long. There are times even now that I still struggle with the creeping sensation that something inside me isn't quite right. When my stomach clutches and my vision blurs. When a quiet voice whispers that something terrible is about to happen, something out of my control that will pick me up and carry me away in its devilish embrace. But I'm stronger now. I've learned to control the physicality of my condition. My mind, on the other hand, remains huddled in the dark, forever shackled to my failures.

The drive, if I choose to make it, to the prison will take about three hours each way. That's another day I will need to be away from Poppy.

As I think about making the trip to see Lacy, my mind travels back to the day she tried to kidnap the children. I had been so desperate to meet Harlow and Harry just to know if they bore any resemblance to Josh, or if they carried Bastian and my features. I had been a mother without a child, longing for the simple act of seeing them, just to know that somewhere out there they existed. By bringing them to my house that afternoon, even though she knew the truth about Bastian and me, Madelyn-May offered the kindest gesture I have ever been privileged to receive. When they drove away and I saw Lacy following in the car behind, I had no choice. They were in danger and despite my shortcomings and panic attacks, the right thing to do was try and help.

That afternoon, Harlow, just like Harry, was Madelyn-May's child, not mine, but it didn't stop me from trying to save her.

As I stand here now, gazing at my sick child, I realize nothing has changed. Madelyn-May for all her faults and failures gave me something I didn't deserve that day. As a mother, she understood my pain and did what she could to take it away. Right now, my child is in trouble, but so is hers. We are both mothers and our daughters are in dire need of saving.

I take my phone out of my pocket and Google the number for Muncy State Correctional Institution. Now the only question is - will Lacy agree to see me?

Chapter Forty-Four
HARLOW

I wrap my arms tighter around Darcy's waist as he accelerates the bike faster and harder along the heavily wooded track. There was no time to talk when I jumped onto the back, but my dad must have organized all of this. I have no idea where he is now or what happened back at the hospital, but the heavy feeling in my stomach tells me the FBI has him in custody.

When Darcy eventually stops the bike in an old underground rail tunnel, I climb off and remove my helmet. "I can't believe you did that!" I tell him, my voice echoing through the cavernous space. "Are you crazy? You could get arrested."

"Your dad said you needed my help. This isn't your fault, Harlow. We all know that."

"Do you know where he is now? My dad, I mean. Was there a plan? Is he meeting us?"

Darcy glances up to the road that runs along the edge of the woods. "He was getting a different car. You were supposed to meet him on the road. He said something about taking you to a different hospital."

"Poppy," I whisper. "He was taking me to Poppy."

"Whose Poppy?"

I look at Darcy. With dirt smeared across his cheek and a slick of sweat that holds his fringe to his forehead, he has risked so much for me. I quickly make a silent promise that if I ever get out of this, I'm going to do everything I can to make sure he stays in my life.

"She's my sister," I tell him in a ginger tone. "I only just found out about her. She's sick."

"Sick how?"

"Cancer... leukemia... something like that. She needs a bone marrow transplant and they're pretty sure I'll be a match."

He nods and thrusts one hip up onto the bike seat. "And you were going there to help her?"

I wish I could tell him yes, that despite everything going on in my life I was willing to risk it all to try and save little Poppy. But it would be a lie and Darcy deserves better than that.

"No, I wasn't," I admit, sick to my stomach at the thought. "It felt like they were only trying to help me out of all this so I could save her. It was like, they didn't really believe me or care what was happening so long as Poppy was going to be okay."

"Like they had already given up and were replacing you?"

I nod and silently scream at myself not to cry.

"But do you really think that, Harlow?"

"I don't know," I mumble, ashamed of myself because the truth is that I don't.

"Do you want to go and help her?"

"I do… I mean, of course I do, but I also have to figure out who really killed Kempsey or there's no way I'm not going to jail." I run my hand through my hair and sigh. "I can't stay on the run and I can't keep putting you and my family at risk like this. My dad's probably already in custody because of me. The last thing I want is…" Despite my attempts to stay calm, I start to cry, and Darcy immediately hops off the bike and puts his arms around me. "The last thing I want is to ruin your life too," I finish. "It's not fair."

He holds me close until I stop crying, then pulls back and slowly searches my face. His eyes come to rest on my lips. I've never had a boyfriend or any kind of meaningful relationship with a boy. The only emotion being intimate ever ignited in me was the need to escape. But not this time.

I tilt my head toward him, and his lips find mine. They feel soft and warm. The sensation travels through my body, causing a shiver of warmth to flutter along my arms. It's a feeling I have never experienced before and yet every part of me knows it's right, that this is how it's supposed to be.

When we break apart, I feel warmth in my cheeks and hope that I'm not blushing.

"I've wanted to do that for so long," he says with a grin. "Was definitely worth waiting for."

Despite the circumstances and everything that's going on, I find myself giggling and realize that even I, as closed off and guarded as I am, can turn to mush in the company of the right boy.

"Me too," I tell him, "but I meant what I said, Darcy. I don't want you getting caught up in this any more than you already are."

"The truth will come out, Harlow," he tells me in a tone more mature than I ever expected. "It always does. But until then you have a decision to make. Do you want to go to the hospital and help your sister, or head to the prison and confront Lacy about who really killed Kempsey?"

Chapter Forty-Five

VALENTINE

When Jasper called to say he would be working late, three things happened. First, I was furious. Who was he to stand me up? Second, I was frustrated because I needed to know what happened at the hospital when Harlow escaped. Third, and worst of all, I was livid at myself because there was no denying the disappointment I felt that we wouldn't be seeing each other.

Now every time I think of him, I chastise myself. He is a mark, nothing more. I don't do men. I don't compromise or allow myself to go all stupid and powerless. I'm stronger and smarter than that. Always have been. And yet...

I glance at the empty phone screen. It's unusual for a man to prioritize anything over me, even work. It's always to their detriment of course because let's face it, I'm never in their company just for the enjoyment of it. There's always a motive.

"This is ridiculous," I tell myself. "Get a grip. He's a mark. That's all."

Knowing there is only one thing to do, I pull on a pair of black jeans and a leather jacket, then head out. I need to remind myself that I am in control. That men serve me, not the other way around.

Two blocks from the hotel I find a grotty-looking sports bar and go inside. Up on the wall, various matches blast out from screen after screen. Basketball, football, tennis, and soccer. Attractive young women in tiny shorts serve drinks, laughing out loud at things I am certain aren't funny, and turning the other cheek as male patrons slap them on the bottom.

I take a seat in one of the empty booths and order a vodka straight up from a waitress with blonde hair, fake eyelashes, and a name tag that reads *Kandy* with a K. As she takes my order, I consider asking whether she remembers the exact moment her self-esteem plummeted low enough to think working here was acceptable. But instead, I keep my mouth shut and stare vacantly at a basketball game showing up on the screen.

"Now why would a woman of your caliber be sitting in this bullshit sports bar all on her own?"

Bingo.

The line is even worse than his too-tight T-shirt and over-tanned arms. Clearly a gym junkie or bodybuilder, the guy looks to be in his mid-thirties with bleached hair and a silver eyebrow ring.

I look him up and down and take a long mouthful of my drink, purposely making him wait. When I'm done, I put the glass down and smile. "I didn't realize there were any eyebrow rings left after 1999."

"Sassy," he replies, clearly amused by what he must consider a flirtatious challenge. "I like it."

"Do you just?"

Without being asked he slides into the seat across from me. "I'm Marcus."

"I'm sure you are."

"And you are?"

Already bored with you. I let out a long breath as though he's twisted my arm. "Samantha. Sammy to my friends."

"Sammy, huh?"

"To my friends," I reiterate. "You and I are definitely not friends."

He grins and nods to himself like he gets it. Like he's down with the hunt. "Okay, alright. I'll play along."

I drain my drink and fix him with a look. "So, you like games then?"

"Depends what kinds of games," he tells me. "But I should warn you, losing is not in my vocabulary."

Not rolling my eyes at this point is almost impossible, but I stay the course. "Sounds like you're in the right bar then."

He glances over at the sports screens and chuckles. "Looks that way."

His eyes run over me and when they settle on my lips I almost gag. Blowing off steam on this guy is going to be exactly what I need. "Marcus, how about we take this outside?"

"I like a woman who knows what she wants." He grins, flashing me with ultra-white veneers. "My car is in the parking lot out back, but I hope you know what you're in for if you know what I mean." He reaches down and grabs hold of his crotch to let me know that at least in his opinion he's well endowed.

"Oh, I know exactly what I'm in for," I assure him. "Let me go freshen up. Meet you out there in five."

When I make my way out to the rear parking lot, he's standing against a souped-up metallic blue muscle car with fat tires and gleaming mag wheels.

"Well, that's a little obvious isn't it?"

"The chicks dig it."

He has a heavy-set jaw and the minute he says the word *chicks* I imagine the sweet sound of it shattering under my boot heel. "I can only imagine."

"So, you want to take this someplace else or you good with fucking right here?"

The fact that he actually believes I'm going to let him penetrate me in the back of that monstrosity of a car is truly mind-boggling. Out of habit, I look around and check for cameras. Deeming the coast to be clear, I turn back to him. "I think right here will be fine."

"Sick." He presses a button on his keys and the car clicks open. "Get in."

"You know what, Marcus," I begin. "That's a little boring."

His brow arches in surprise. "Babe, I'm anything but boring. You'll see. Now get in."

"But backseat sex is so cliché," I say with a pout, "and besides, there's no chance of anyone seeing us in there. Don't you just love the idea that out here maybe someone could be watching?"

"Fuck yeah," he replies, grabbing for me. "That's hot. Come here."

He pulls me in and thrusts his lips onto mine. The moment they touch I feel bile rising up in my throat and immediately think of Jasper. *It would feel different with him.*

As we kiss, I fight the urge to reach for the pocket knife in the back of my jeans. That would be too easy and I want to enjoy hurting him.

Suddenly he pulls back and flips me around and my breasts push hard up against the side of his car. He gathers my hair in his fist and lifts it up exposing the bare nape of my neck. The rough stubble on his chin scrapes against my skin and I wince.

"That's too rough," I manage. "Slow down."

"Fuck that," he breathes. "You know what you came out here for."

His hands slide against my waist and then up to my breasts. He squeezes so hard that I gasp and try to pull away. "I said slow down."

"And I said, *fuck that.*"

His breath quickens and he pushes himself against me. I can feel his excitement growing as he shoves his groin into my buttocks. Any opportunity to catch him off guard has been lost now and up against the car I'm in a very vulnerable position. With limited options, I steady myself, then stamp my heel down onto his foot as hard as I can.

"You fuckin' bitch," he swears, jumping back. "What the fuck?"

"I told you to *slow down.*" I turn and step forward creating some space between my back and the car.

"And I told you, *fuck that.*"

He holds my gaze and his eyes harden. I came here tonight to blow off steam, to beat up some arrogant shmuck who thinks women exist for their own entertainment. I thought it would calm me, interrupt my thoughts of Jasper. But the situation is quickly getting out of hand. If I show weakness, he'll try to overpower me.

"So that's how it's going to be?" I ask.

"That's how it's going to be." He reaches into the back of his jeans and to my surprise, pulls out a black handgun. "Let me tell you what's going to happen. First. you're going to get on your knees and swallow my dick. When you're done I'll tell you what's next. You got it?"

I quickly consider my options. Having him in a vulnerable position would be ideal, but if he thinks his dick is coming anywhere near my mouth he's got another think coming. "Okay, alright." I hold my hands up in surrender and get down onto my knees. "You win. Just take it easy."

When I'm down on the ground he steps forward and places the gun on the roof of the car. "Fuckin' bitches. You're all talk 'till someone like me comes along. Now you're going to get what you deserve."

He unzips his jeans and pulls out his penis. "And don't go getting any ideas. One hand will be on your head, the other right up here." He taps the gun and spreads his legs for balance.

Loose rocks dig into my knees and the musty scent of his skin wafts across my nostrils. I know that biting his genitals will get me shot, but there is no way I am putting that thing in my mouth.

"Hurry the fuck up," he threatens. "I'm waiting."

Slowly I reach around to my back pocket and take out the blade. I have to get this right the first time.

"Suck it you fuckin' bitch or I swear I'll put a bullet in your head. It wouldn't be the first time I - "

His words stop mid-sentence as I plunge the blade deep into his right testicle. Blood immediately spurts out, splattering across my hand and face. At first, he doesn't scream or make any sound at all. He stares down in shocked silence, then releases a guttural roar that reverberates through the empty car park. Knowing his first instinct will be to reach for the gun, I leap to my feet and stab him again, this time in the shoulder.

"You fuckin' whore," he wails, as the gun clatters to the ground. "What the fuck have you done?"

"You were going to rape me you piece of shit," I tell him. "You're a fucking rapist."

As he clutches wildly at his injuries, I bend to pick up the gun but before my fingers close around it, he knees me hard in the ribs and I go down. From behind he gathers my hair in his fist and smashes my face into the asphalt. Once, twice, three times, four times until the entire world is spinning. I can feel the warm trickle of his blood dripping onto my cheek as he stands over me. On the ground, I see the outline of the gun but I can't move.

"Now you're going to get what you deserve," he tells me, as the gun is lifted into the air and out of view.

"Hey, what's going on over there?" someone calls out from the street. "Jesus, I think that guy has a gun!"

I hold my breath and wonder if I could possibly get this lucky. I came out here for all the wrong reasons and have paid the price. If I get away with this, it will be a miracle.

"Someone call the police!" the voice calls out. "There's a guy over there with a gun!"

I lift my head as Marcus' feet crunch in the loose dirt. The car door opens and closes, then the engine roars. Whoever called out has just saved my life.

The sound of footsteps comes toward me. Heavy. Running. I try to lift my head but the world spins.

"Hey, there's an ambulance on the way," a man's voice tells me. I can't focus on his face, but I can tell he's crouched over me. "You'll be alright."

"No, no ambulance," I manage.

"You're hurt. You need help."

A light shining across the carpark catches my blade and I crawl my figures toward it. "I said, no ambulance."

"But - " The man's words catch as I pull the knife around and hold it toward him as best I can.

"Jesus Christ," he exclaims. "Everyone in this city has gone batshit crazy. Alright, sweetheart, you're on your own. Fuck this."

Knowing I have limited time before the ambulance arrives, I pull myself up to my feet and grab onto a parked car for balance. I can't get a taxi or call an Uber. Blood is trickling down both sides of my head and I can already feel my right eye has swollen shut.

I stumble across the carpark toward a back lane that runs behind the sports bar. It's too far to walk back to the hotel looking like this. Too many people will see me. With no other options, I take out my phone and dial. When he picks up, I have no choice but to be honest. "Jasper," I whisper. "I need your help."

Chapter Forty-Six
HARLOW

I hate the smell of hospitals. The sterile ammonia-laced corridors punctuated here and there by the fragrance of vomit and fear. Ever since the accident when I was a kid I've avoided them, and yet in the past week I've found myself inside two. Suffice it to say, I don't plan on visiting a third any time soon. When Darcy asked me to choose between confronting Lacy and trying to save little Poppy, I'd like to say the choice was easy but it wasn't. Coming here before I have cleared my name is likely to land me in prison where I won't be able to help anyone. But I also realized there isn't much point re-instating my life if it's riddled with the guilt of letting a little girl die.

I keep my head down, and my hands shoved deep inside the pockets of a gray hoodie Darcy gave me. Beneath the hood, my hair is now platinum blonde thanks to a packet dye Darcy rubbed all over my head in the dirty bathroom of a gas station three miles out from the hospital. My eyes are rimmed with heavy black pencil. My lips are stained a shade of violet that reminds me of pansies that grew in the garden of our home in Chestnut Hill. I thought life was so difficult back then. Mom making us pose for all her stupid online content and not letting me have any social media of my own. Our world was about making her look like the perfect mother and I hated her for it. But now, if I was honest, I would do anything to be back in my room whining to the girls from school about how shitty it was to be the daughter of Madelyn-May Marozzi. My life had been so removed from reality. I had no idea what it was like to make hard choices or sacrifice anything. Perhaps that's why it's been so hard for me to come to the hospital. The only person I've ever had to think of is myself. Maybe for someone else, deciding to help Poppy would have been a no-brainer but for me, it's been the hardest decision I've ever had to make. Putting a stranger, and one who my father may end up loving more than me first isn't an easy choice. Not for me at least. Maybe not for anyone.

I take the elevator up to the pediatric wing and hope that I can find her on my own. The last thing I need is to draw additional attention to myself. Once I take the test to see if I'm a match it will be impossible to stay under the radar. I only hope that my brand-new ID from Darcy, the one that now says I'm Chloe Miller, coupled with yet another look, will buy me the time I need to get this over with before the police realize there's a connection between Sophie and me.

Keeping my eyes down, I walk quickly along the corridor toward a sign that says oncology. The word sends a shiver through me. It feels so final, so end of the road. To be at the very start of your life and already facing the end seems so unfair. I wonder how much a five-year-old might understand about what is at stake. Does she know what death is? Does she have her own thoughts on what happens to us when we die? Is she scared?

I shove my hands deeper into my pockets and try to push the thoughts from my mind. I have done all I can by coming here. At any moment Special Agent Monroe and his team could come around the corner, but I'm trying. I'm doing the right thing.

As I approach the first room, I look up and try to find a name on the door. Before I can read anything a woman carrying a hot cup of coffee hurries out and crashes right into me, the scalding liquid burning through my hoodie and onto my chest.

"Shit!" I gasp. "What the -"

"Harlow?" she gushes in a hushed tone. "Is that you?"

"If you have to ask then that's a good thing," I manage, still wincing from the burn. "I don't know how long we have before they catch onto the fact that I'm here, Sophie, so let's get this done."

She grabs me by the crook of my elbow and pulls me inside the hospital room where I cannot help but look at the little girl asleep in the bed. She's so tiny. Her skin is pale, almost translucent. There are so many cords coming out of her that it reminds me of a scene from a sci-fi movie.

"She's... she's so small," I manage, unable to take my eyes off her. "Is she in pain?"

"Harlow, listen to me," Sophie says, stepping between my line of sight and Poppy. "If we do this, they will arrest you. You'll have to give blood and go through a million tests. There's no possible way we can do this without you getting caught."

I nod and sidestep her to look at Poppy one more time. "I know. I'm just glad I got here when I did."

She stares at me until I meet her eye, then grabs my hand. "I don't know how to thank you for this, Harlow."

I swallow hard, knowing there is only one thing I could ever want in return. "Just, when this is all said and done don't forget about me, alright?"

"Oh, Harlow..."

Tears sting at my eyes and I quickly blink them away. "That's all I want."

"Of course, sweetheart. Never."

Sophie forces a smile and it dawns on me how tired she looks, like the life has been drained away and only her skin is holding her together. It's so unfair that this woman, who would clearly do anything for her child, should be faced with watching her daughter slip away before her eyes. Whatever I was thinking that held me back from coming here suddenly feels petty and stupid. Even the fear of going to prison fades in comparison to the horror of watching a little girl die before my eyes.

"Let's do this," I tell her. "How do I take the test?"

To my surprise, the test is nothing more invasive than a cheek swab. It's the technician's questions that make me uncomfortable. What is my relationship to Poppy? Who are my birth parents? All the questions that could at any moment trigger a call to the FBI. When we're done, she tells me that in usual circumstances it can take weeks, even months, to find out if I'm a match but due to the severity of Poppy's condition, we should know within hours.

"I don't think I should stay here while we wait," I tell Sophie after the technician leaves the room. "If someone recognizes me it could be all over."

"No, I don't want you coming and going in front of everyone," she says. "Stay put in Poppy's room. No one will see you there."

Reluctantly I agree, knowing I will be a sitting duck if anyone does call the police. But I've come this far. I have to see it through. "Alright, but we should figure out a plan B. Just in case."

Chapter Forty-Seven
SOPHIE

The prison had called to say Lacy agreed to see me. I was running out to call Bastian and tell him the good news when I crashed right into Harlow. My plan had been to drive out there right away. I hoped that maybe Lacy's time behind bars had changed her, that she would no longer be the psychotic, heartless monster who tried to kidnap Harry and Harlow. I hoped that maybe, under the circumstances, she would help me. But all that went out the window the moment I saw Harlow.

Now, as we wait for the results of her test, I cannot help but feel elated. I know what's at stake for Harlow and what she's risked by coming here. I know that at any moment the FBI could burst in and arrest her. But I also know that at any moment we could find out she's a match for Poppy. At any moment, my daughter's life could be spared.

"Do you have any questions?" I ask, trying to put myself in her place. "There must be so many things running through your mind right now." She's slumped in a plastic chair, staring at Poppy. Her face is hard to read and with so much going on it's difficult to tell what she might be thinking. "If there's anything you want to ask me, I'd be happy to try and answer."

I expect her to ask me about Poppy's condition or if I think she's guilty of killing her friend, but the question she asks catches me off guard.

"Do you think my mom deserved what happened?"

I pause and wonder if I heard her correctly. "You mean about your dad and me?"

She finally tears her eyes off Poppy and looks at me. "Yeah, I mean, I get it. She's... a lot."

"I didn't know much about your mom back at the start," I tell her honestly, "so, I can't say it happened because she wasn't a good person or wife. It was never about that for me, and to be honest, I don't think it was really about that for your dad either."

"Then what was it about?"

I think back to when Bastian and I's relationship began and feel a chill creep into my bones. I was in so much pain. The world was so dark, like the sun would never rise again. "My husband

and son were killed," I begin. "On the day they died it was like I died too except my body was still alive. It's hard to explain but it was like all the air around me was gone. I was suffocating."

"But my dad changed that?"

I have no idea how to explain why Bastian was different or how he found a way in. All I know is that he did. "He never pushed me," I try. "Back then there was nothing romantic between us. Some days, despite my objections he would come to the house and just sit next to me. He didn't say anything. He would just sit there. I thought because he was my boss it was a welfare check, that eventually he would tell me I had to get therapy or resign, but he didn't. He just kept showing up on my doorstep."

"And that helped?"

Despite the circumstances a smile tugs at the corner of my lip. "It did actually. Some days I would cry, others I would just stare at the wall. Then eventually one day I spoke. I said, '*I feel like everything I ever loved is gone*'. And you know what he told me?"

"No, what?"

"He said, *then find something you just like a lot*."

Harlow gives me a quizzical look. "That's weird."

"Not really," I tell her. "I told him that I liked having him sit there beside me. Then one day to my surprise, it occurred to me that I really liked him sitting beside me. That day was the first time I held his hand. As the weeks and months went by, I came to love having him sit by me. And eventually, I just loved him. He became the light in a dark world and over time I found myself moving toward it. Just by being there, he brought me back to life."

As I wait for her response, I wonder if I have answered her question. No one deserves to be hurt or betrayed. Not Madelyn-May or any woman who marries a man expecting him to be faithful. No one deserves to lose a child. No one deserves to feel unloved or to be accused of something they didn't do. None of us deserve the scars we carry and yet they make us who we are. The truth is, what Bastian and I did to Madelyn-May was wrong and it was hurtful, but we were each other's oxygen; without the other, we would have suffocated.

"I get it," she replies eventually. "My mom does too. That's why she brought us to meet you that day."

"You remember that?"

She nods and gives a half-hearted smile. "I remember thinking your hair was just like mine."

"What your mom did for me that day was undeserved."

"She and my dad were miserable back then. All they did was fight." She pauses and looks down at her feet. "I don't know why they even stayed together."

"It's hard to let go of the only life you know," I tell her. "Believe me."

"I get that too," Harlow says, looking back at me. "That's why I stayed in Philly. But I kinda wish now that I'd gone to Australia with them. At least I wouldn't be in this mess."

My heart breaks for Harlow. She is clearly confused and so afraid. "How are you holding up? You've been through so much."

But she just shrugs and scrunches up her nose. "I'm getting through it. What else can I do?"

"You experienced a trauma that most people wouldn't know how to cope with, Harlow. You saw your friend dead. Not to mention being the one accused of her murder."

She re-crosses her legs and gives me an intent look. "The funny thing is, I was so closed off before all this. I hated everyone and to be honest, the night I heard someone downstairs I..." she looks away and I see the first tremble of her jaw, "...was cutting my wrist."

"Harlow, what?" I immediately reach out to her.

"I was just in a really dark place," she continues. "I know I didn't lose what you did, your husband and son, but I get what you said before about there being no air. I just couldn't deal with everyone hating on me and all the online trolling. I felt worthless. I couldn't breathe. I just wanted it over."

"And now?"

"I found a light too," she smiles. "Darcy. He's done so much to help me. I mean, he's put himself in danger to make sure I'm safe. I've never had that before."

I smile and am genuinely happy that Harlow has a person in her corner who she trusts. With everything she has to deal with, she needs someone to lean on.

"It's like, just knowing he's there makes it all bearable, you know? Like what you said before about Dad."

I squeeze her hand and nod. "I'm glad you have Darcy, I really am. But Harlow, he's not the only person who has put themselves in harm's way to try and keep you safe. Your dad has, and your mom did too. I know your relationship with her is strained but try to remember that for all her faults, she loves you."

"I know," she says with a sigh. "I just wish things had been different between us. Like, I wish it would have felt like having a real mom."

She looks away and I know our heart-to-heart is over. But I'm glad we had time to talk. Really talk.

As if on cue, Dr Yates appears in the doorway, and for the first time since Poppy was admitted she looks at me and smiles. "Congratulations," she says. "We have a match."

Chapter Forty-Eight

VALENTINE

"**S**o, let me get this straight," Jasper tries again, as he presses an ice pack against my throbbing eye. "You were walking to the Wawa and someone tried to snatch your bag. You tried fighting him off, but he pushed you and you hit your head on the sidewalk?"

"That's what I said," I tell him, wishing he would just let me go back to my own suite already.

"But, CJ, you have multiple lacerations on your forehead."

I push his hand away. "Multiple lacerations? What is this, *Law and Order*?"

"I'm just saying it's obvious that you hit your head more than once. What aren't you telling me?"

"Nothing, Jasper, Jesus." I get to my feet and pad over to the kitchenette. "I was dizzy. I fell a couple of times trying to get up."

"And this man," he continues, following me, "was he tall, short, old, young?"

"I didn't get a good look at him. Middle-aged, I think. He had a beanie and dark glasses on."

"At night?"

"He's a bag snatcher."

Jasper lets out a long sigh. "You're just not giving me much to go on."

"Well, that doesn't matter because I don't want you to do anything," I tell him, my tone frustrated. "I was being stupid and not paying attention to my surroundings. We don't need to conduct a nationwide manhunt. Don't you already have your hands full with one of those? How's that going by the way? Any leads?"

I turn around and in the confined space of the kitchenette, Jasper is right in my face. "CJ, you don't look so good."

"Thanks," I huff. "Actually, I really just want to go to bed. I'm going to head back to my suite."

He peers into my eyes and rests his palm across my forehead. "No really, you look pale. Do you have a headache?"

I want to object to all his fussing but suddenly can't find the words. Everything in my head is jumbled. "I... what..."

"CJ!" The last thing I hear is him call out my name as my legs buckle and the floor rushes up to meet me.

When my eyes eventually flutter open, the first thing I see is Jasper looking down at me.

"You're awake," he says softly.

The room is swimming. Everything is soft focus. "What happened?"

"You fainted," he tells me. "I carried you in here and put you in my bed. An ambulance is on the way."

"What? No, no ambulance."

"Just as a precaution," he says.

"No!" I pull myself up and the room spins even faster. "Cancel it."

"What? I don't -"

"Cancel it. Now."

"Alright, Jesus." He walks out of the room and I hear the muffled sounds of his voice talking to someone on the phone.

When he comes back, I feel the weight of his questions before he even opens his mouth. "Look, Jasper," I begin, "you don't know everything about me."

He sits down on the edge of the bed and to my surprise, takes my hand in his. "Okay, so tell me."

A glass of water has been placed on the bedside table. My mouth feels so dry, and I can't be sure if it's because I fainted or because I'm about to lie right to Jasper's face. I take a long drink and begin. "The job interview wasn't the only reason I came here. Back in California, my husband... he was abusive. I ran but I know he's looking for me."

"CJ, that's horrible and I'm so sorry you had to go through that," he says in a gentle tone. "But you're safe with me. It's safe to call an ambulance when you're hurt."

"No, my medical insurance. They'll contact him. He'll find me."

"CJ, I'm an FBI agent. We can sort all of that out."

"No," I snap. "Look, I appreciate everything you're trying to do but I don't want to take any chances. Please respect that."

He nods then lets out a long sigh. "Well in that case there's only one thing to do."

"And what's that?"

"Looks like I'm going to have to take care of you myself." A grin pulls at the corner of his lip and quickly turns into a smile. "I do have some medical training you know."

"Jasper, that's ridiculous. You have more important things to do, like finding that missing girl."

"Well, how about I look after you for the rest of the night and we'll see how you feel in the morning. Deal?"

I think back to all the men I have crossed paths with in my life. Those who wanted me to sell drugs and those who wanted me to steal. Those who wanted to fuck me and those who wanted to fuck with me just for their own amusement. There were those I stole from, and those I used for whatever I needed. But no matter who was running the play, every relationship I ever experienced was transactional. This was supposed to be no different. I needed Jasper's intel to find Harlow. I thought the FBI would have no trouble figuring out where she was, and I could beat them to the punch. But he has no idea where she is and while I have no doubt he's thought about sleeping with me, Jasper has made no move to make it happen. That leaves two people, alone in a hotel suite, asking nothing of each other but to share the space. It's a foreign concept and one I have no idea how to navigate. Every instinct I have says to run, to get out of here, and yet I hear myself say, "Alright, Jasper. You have a deal."

While I lie in bed, he orders us a pizza and tosses me the remote control. "You want to choose a pay-per-view?"

"Pizza and a movie in bed? Are we married?" I say with a nervous laugh. "What's next? Strolling around the weekend markets?"

"Would that be so bad?"

He's handsome in a way that's fresh and wholesome. He smells like soap even after a full day at work and hasn't the slightest hint of an agenda. Jasper is the marrying kind. When he meets the right girl, he will spoil her, marry her, and be a father to their children. Until then he is committed to his career and catching the bad guys. The only trouble is that right now, the bad guy is me.

"Like I said, I've been through -"

"Hey," he cuts me off, "all you have to worry about right now is what we're going to watch when the pizza comes. Let me take care of the rest."

I choose a comedy to avoid any sex scenes or awkward emotional drama. When we finish the pizza, he lies on top of the quilt and pulls me in under his arm.

"You feeling alright?" he asks.

"I am. I think I just need a good night's sleep."

"When the movie is done, I'll take the couch," he says. "You need to rest."

"Oh, no I can go back to my room."

"Nonsense. I'm here to take care of you."

I pull back and take him in. He really is handsome.

"What?" he asks.

"Nothing, I just... I don't think I've ever met anyone like you before," I tell him, and this time it's the truth.

He holds my gaze and without thinking I lean in and kiss him. Softly, gently. He kisses me back but doesn't move in closer. He doesn't force himself on me or try to take anything that isn't ready to be given. I kiss him again, deeper and longer.

He pulls back and gently traces his finger across the flutter of blue butterflies tattooed along my arm.

"CJ, I don't want to push..."

"I want you, Jasper, " I whisper.

"Are you sure?" he asks. "I mean -"

"Jasper?" He pulls back to meet my eye. "Shut up."

As we make love, I push the past away and allow myself to be present with him. He moves slowly inside me and I am no longer a hustler who grew up in a trailer park. I am not the girl whose family was the victim of incest. I am not the child who found her mother dead or a woman who has killed. I am no longer filled with rage or the need for revenge. My body arches against his and in this moment, I am none of those things. Instead, I am free.

Chapter Forty-Nine
HARLOW

Now that I'm a match for Poppy the chances of the FBI being alerted to my whereabouts have gone up tenfold. Fortunately for little Poppy, my human leukocyte antigen, or HLA, as the doctor keeps calling it, was a close match. That means the chance my donation will save her life, at least for now, is high. Unfortunately for me, it also means a series of blood tests, evaluations, discussions, and endless possibilities that my real identity will be revealed.

The other problem is that I'm still a minor which means we need parental consent for me to donate. Sophie needs to be my real mom.

The television screen in Poppy's room is showing the news and the top story is still the FBI's search for me. I look different in the pictures they are showing, but I can't change my face completely. Sooner or later, someone in this hospital is going to figure out that donor Chloe Miller with her short blonde hair and gothic make-up is actually Harlow Marozzi, murder suspect and fugitive.

"Sophie, they're going to find me," I tell her, not taking my eyes off the screen. "It's only a matter of time now. There'll be a DNA match in the system."

Footage of the house I lived in with Kempsey and her parents flashes across the screen. Flashbacks of her vacant staring eyes fill my mind and I shiver. It is a sight I will see for the rest of my life.

"Mommy?" Beside us, Poppy stirs and opens her eyes.

"Hi, sweetheart," Sophie coos, gently brushing her daughter's hair back from her forehead. "How are you feeling?"

Poppy shrugs and trains her eyes on me. I can see she is part inquisitive, part nervous about this strange girl with weird make-up who is suddenly in her room.

"Hi, Poppy," I say with a smile. "I'm Chloe."

Saying the fake name out loud makes me uncomfortable and the idea of lying about my identity to a terminally ill five-year-old does not sit well at all.

"Poppy, this lovely young lady is going to help you get better," Sophie explains.

I watch as she looks at Sophie with huge eyes, and although she doesn't say the words, I know she is asking, *Mommy am I safe?*

"You see, Poppy," I tell her, as I sit down on the edge of the bed, "you and I have something in common."

"We do?"

"Sure, we do," I tell her with a reassuring smile. I can feel Sophie's eyes on me. She must be terrified I'm going to tell this little girl that I'm her sister but now is not the time. "We have the same kind of magic beans inside us. But right now, your beans have lost their power, so you know what?"

"What?" she asks, clearly intrigued by the idea of magic beans.

"I'm going to loan you some of mine till yours get better."

She holds my gaze and then glances at her mom. "Am I allowed, Mommy?"

Sophie clearly fights her tears and I pray to God that we are able to make this donation before Special Agent Monroe and his team drags me out of here in handcuffs.

"Of course, you're allowed, sweetheart," Sophie tells her daughter. "And once you have Chloe's magic beans we can go home. How great is that?"

Poppy smiles and although I have heard the expression about someone's smile lighting up a room, I have never seen it happen until this moment.

"And we can see Miss Molly?" she asks.

"And we can see Miss Molly," Sophie says with a smile.

"Miss Molly is our dog," Poppy tells me. "She's yellow like the sun."

Memories of stroking Miss Molly when I was just a girl flood my mind and I smile. "She sounds like a great dog and I bet she misses you a lot."

Poppy smiles again and then closes her eyes, leaving us to watch her fall back to sleep.

"Sophie," I whisper once I'm sure Poppy won't hear me, "we can't let the FBI mess this up."

"I know. The surname on your fake ID means so far they think you're my daughter but once we start the process they'll need all your details."

I try to hide the stab of hearing Sophie say the doctors *think* I'm her daughter, but it must show on my face.

"Well, you know..." she adds quickly, "my daughter as in officially on my medical files."

"Sure, yeah, I know. So, what do we do?"

"Ladies," Dr Yates announces as she suddenly appears in the doorway, "are we ready for the next round of tests?"

Sophie and I exchange a glance. There is no time to figure this out. We have to keep pushing forward with the donation process. But the further we go the sooner my true identity will be revealed.

Chapter Fifty
SOPHIE

While Harlow has her bloods done, I wrack my mind trying to think of a way out of this mess. The hospital will ask for *Chloe's* medical insurance before they start the harvesting process and once that happens we're screwed.

I try Bastian but don't expect him to pick up. By now the FBI will have taken his phone and probably have him locked away in an interrogation room. But to my surprise, he answers.

"Bastian, oh my God, you picked up."

"I'm still at the FBI," he tells me, "but I don't think I'm being charged."

"Really?"

"Technically I was just coming to see if Harlow was really at the hospital. When she ran, I was chasing her, trying to bring her in."

"And they bought it?"

"Well, I'm not in handcuffs."

"Okay, well..." I pause and lower my voice to a whisper, "she's here."

"Who?"

"Do I need to spell it out? We're at the hospital in Maryland and Bastian... she's a match for Poppy."

"You're serious?"

"Yes, they're doing the final blood work now. Poppy's been undergoing chemo treatment so they should be good to do the transfusion any day now."

"So long as the FBI doesn't find Harlow first."

"Exactly," I agree. "There is one problem though."

I explain about the insurance and wait for his reply. I had been hoping for a miracle, that he would have the answer, but just like me, he is stumped. Until...

"What if we just pay for the procedure?" he suggests.

"Pay for it? Bastian, it would be hundreds of thousands of dollars. I don't have that kind of money."

For a moment the line is silent and then he says, "I know, Soph, but I do."

"You're serious?"

"They're our children," he tells me. "Of course, I'm serious."

"And Madelyn-May? It's her money too."

"Let me talk to Madelyn-May. In fact…"

"What?" My stomach tightens with the feeling that Bastian is about to drop a bombshell.

"She's on her way here. When I was taken into custody she got on a plane."

For a moment, I can't find my voice. "Sure, that makes sense," I say eventually. "She's your wife and Harlow's mother."

Throughout this ordeal, I have convinced myself that I am not Harlow's mother. I have sung Madelyn-May's praises and done all I can to remind Harlow that she can repair their relationship but that was when Madelyn-May was on the other side of the world. Now that Harlow is here with me and helping to save Poppy's life, things feel different. Not to mention the fact that Bastian and I are a team again. He and I against the world. But now she is coming. His real wife. Harlow's real mother. And once again, I will be relegated to the sidelines.

"Sophie, are you there?"

I snap back and quickly remind myself that all we have to do is make sure Poppy's transplant goes ahead. After that Bastian and Madelyn-May can help Harlow and do whatever they need to do. My priority has to be Poppy.

"I'm here," I tell him.

"Are you alright?"

"'Course I am," I tell him in a tone that sounds a lot brighter than I feel. "Everything is working out. All we have to do is keep the FBI from finding out Harlow is here and we're all set."

"Sophie…"

"No really, it's fine."

"It *will* be fine Sophie," he reassures me. "I promise."

I want to believe him but there's so much at stake and too much residual pain that lingers. "Don't do that, Bastian."

"Don't do what?"

"Make promises you can't keep. That's not what we do, you and I."

Chapter Fifty-One

VALENTINE

Despite the throbbing lump on my forehead, I feel a lot better than I did last night. Before he left for work this morning Jasper brought me a coffee and kissed me gently on the lips. He said he'd see me tonight and it suddenly occurred to me that I have royally fucked up. I let him in. I opened myself up. Worst of all, I think I *care*.

I can't be in a relationship, especially with an FBI agent. And yet, when I think about last night a warmth washes over me, unlike anything I have ever felt before. For the first time in my life, I don't feel like I'm pushing back the tide of the entire world all by myself. I don't feel like everyone is against me or that I have to kill or be killed. Instead, I feel inclined to sit and let the sun warm my face. And maybe once this Harlow business is sorted out, things could be different. Once she is dead everything goes back to even. If I can just fix what needs to be fixed, maybe I could finally let go.

I push open the door to my own suite and lock it behind me. Up on the wall are all the news clippings from Harlow's murder case and a myriad of sticky notes I used to write down my thoughts on who could be helping her, along with pictures I found on social media of other kids who were at the club that night.

I flop down onto the couch and stare up at the wall. Almost everyone in the pictures from the night Harlow rose to notoriety has written scathing comments about their so-called friend online. After cross-referencing their social media profiles and comments on the *Kaleidoscope* article, only one person who was at the bar that night chose not to comment. A boy named Darcy Jones. I didn't consider him at first because Kempsey, that girl who got in my way in the kitchen, was his girlfriend. So why would he be helping the one person everyone thinks is her killer? I stare up at his picture and try to figure it out. Was he cheating on Kempsey with Harlow? Doesn't seem likely. After all, Kempsey was a prom-queen kind of girl and from what I can tell, after the car accident Harlow grew up to become a bookish nerd with no real friends.

"Well, there's only one way to find out,'" I say out loud, "and if the FBI can't find Harlow maybe I can make Harlow find me."

I quickly set up a fake social media profile pretending to be Madelyn-May's private account. Darcy doesn't have to see the contents of the page. All I need to do is use it to private message him. After all, someone as famous as Madelyn-May would never accept a random teenage boy onto her private page. But she would try to reach out to someone her daughter trusts, especially now her husband is in custody.

Madelyn-May: *Darcy this is Harlow's mom. I have just arrived in the US and need to find my daughter. I know the two of you are close and that maybe you've been helping her. Please meet me by the pond at Pastorious Park, Chestnut Hill. Nine o'clock tonight. I need your help.*

I hit send and wait. If I'm right, Darcy will take the bait. If I'm wrong, he'll either tell me to get lost or just ignore the message completely. It only takes a few seconds for the message to come up as *seen* and a speech bubble to appear. He's answering.

Darcy: *I don't know where she is*

It's a start.

Madelyn-May: *Her dad was arrested. I need to find her. Please, I really need your help. Will you meet me?*

Once again, the message reads *seen* and I wait as he types.

Darcy: *He was?*

Now to reel him in.

Madelyn-May: *I flew all the way here from Australia to try and help her. I'm not asking you to bring her to the park, just come and talk to me. Tell me how I can get her to trust me again. I'm the only one who can keep her out of prison. Please, if you care about her come and meet me. I just want to talk.*

I hold my breath and wait as he types back.

Darcy: *OK*

When Jasper calls just after six-thirty to let me know he's leaving work, I tell him my headache has come back and that I just need to sleep. The sooner I can get this resolved the sooner I can put it all behind me. But I know he will come by to check on me, so at seven o'clock I pull on a pair of satin pajamas and get ready. Sure enough, when I hear a knock at the door, I open it a crack and peek out.

"Just wanted to check in on you," he tells me with a warm smile.

He looks so handsome with his navy FBI windbreaker and concerned look. I curse myself as my heart melts, just a little more. "That's sweet,'" I tell him, "but I'm fine. Just tired."

He peers in at the lump on my head and frowns. "I really wish you'd see a doctor."

"Why do I need a doctor when I have you?"

He chuckles and nods. "You sure you don't want some company? I can get dinner."

"I'm sure. I just need to sleep. Tomorrow night?"

"Count on it," he says with a smile. "And call me if you need anything, I'm just down the hall."

"I will," I tell him. A pause and then, "Any luck finding that girl?"

"Not yet, but her mother flew in from Australia today. We'll put her on every news station pleading for her daughter to turn herself in. Hopefully, that resonates."

I can't show it, but it's hard to contain my excitement. Madelyn-May is in the US. Not only does it fit perfectly with what I just told Darcy, but it provides an unexpected opportunity. Hearing your daughter is dead is one thing but being forced to watch her die is even better.

Chapter Fifty-Two

HARLOW

"So, I have good news and bad news," Sophie announces as she comes back into the hospital room. "Actually, two lots of good news. One bad."

"Great, we need some good news," I reply. "What is it?"

"Your dad is going to organize the money for me to pay for the procedure. There's a risk they might trace it but right hopefully by then it will be already done."

"And the other good news?"

"He's still at the FBI but he thinks they're going to let him go soon."

Sophie is right. They are two pieces of good news. All I have to do now is avoid the FBI until the procedure is complete. But she also said there was bad news. "So, what's the downer?" She looks uncomfortable and doesn't answer right away. "Sophie, just tell me. What's the bad news?"

Eventually, she meets my eye and visibly swallows before she speaks. "It's your mom. She's on her way here."

I fall back into the plastic seat and clutch at my forehead. "No, no, no. This can't be happening."

"She left Sydney yesterday so there's every chance she's already landed."

I take it in and try to steady myself. At least I won't have to see her. I can't see her. In fact, the minute the media finds out she's here it's going to be a shit storm. Which gives me an idea. "The media are going to be all over her," I say, thinking out loud. "Which is actually kinda perfect."

"How do you mean?"

I pull myself out of the chair and pace back and forth along the length of Poppy's bed. "What if we created a diversion? Made the media and FBI think I contacted her from somewhere far from here. It might just buy us the time we need to get this done."

Sophie nods as she mulls it over. "How do we do that?"

"Well, if they thought I had contacted her from say Ohio or West Virginia they'd have to follow any lead associated with that tip."

"Alright, but how would we create leads like that?"

I take a moment and I continue pacing. I already know the answer but hate myself for even thinking about it.

"Harlow, how do we do it?" she asks again.

I finally stop pacing and look at her. "We don't. Mom's fans do."

All my life I have hated my mom's online platform and the legions of fans who devoted their lives to following her every word. Even when the dirty secrets of her past came out after Lacy tried to kidnap Harry and me, her followers begged her to keep the site going. For them, her torrid past and the fact she had overcome being raised by such a terrible mother of her own only strengthened their devotion to her. Not for a moment did they think any of the perfect mom routine was a set up or make-believe. All it did was make them love her more. If she were to ask for their help in the search for her missing daughter I have absolutely no doubt that hundreds of thousands of women would suddenly start seeing me everywhere from Ohio to West Virginia, and probably all the way to Timbuktu if they thought it will help the once famous, now infamous, Madelyn-May Marozzi.

As I explain the plan to Sophie, she nods and takes it all in. When I'm done, I step back and wait for her response.

"So, you need your mom to activate her social media and ask her fans to help find you?"

"Not just ask them," I say. "Tell them she heard from me and that I'm somewhere in Ohio. Then ask them to call in any sightings to the police. She'll post that I'm on the run and could be anywhere in Ohio or maybe I could have even traveled further by now."

"And you think she'll do it?"

I let out a long breath. This is going to be the hard part. "Well, that depends..."

"On?"

"How it's explained to her."

Sophie searches my face and I can tell the moment she understands what I'm suggesting. "Oh, you want me to ask her?" she exclaims. "No, I can't do that."

I step forward and take her hands in mine. "You have to, Sophie, it's the only way to keep them off my back until we do the procedure."

"No, I can't..."

I lock eyes with her and stand firm. "You have to. Everything depends on it."

She looks past me at her daughter sleeping in the bed. "Okay, you're right. I know you're right."

"Call my dad and get him to arrange a meeting. Mom will think he's the one coming. Somewhere private. Somewhere the FBI won't see you." I think for a moment. "A hotel room, someplace big enough that you can blend in with a bunch of people in the lobby when you go in."

"Alright," she agrees. "But you stay in this room, do you hear me? Do not under any circumstances leave these four walls."

"Of course, I won't," I tell her. "Now get going. We don't have much time."

Chapter Fifty-Three
SOPHIE

Bastian set the meeting and booked a room in his name at the Hilton Garden Inn right in the middle of Center City. As I drive back to Philadelphia, my stomach is in knots at the idea of seeing Madelyn-May face-to-face.

As I drive, I remind myself that although this is the best way to help Poppy, it's also helping Harlow. Once the procedure is over and Poppy is in recovery, I will go to Muncy myself and make Lacy tell me who really killed that girl. Then we can clear Harlow's name and hopefully all move on with our lives.

Behind me, the sun is sinking and as the white lines on the road turn to a blur, I let myself wonder what that future might look like. If Poppy is healthy and Harlow is safe where will that leave Bastian and me? Harlow said she thinks he and Madelyn-May are still unhappy despite their new start. Does that mean there could be a chance for us to start over? Harry has already gone back to Australia and once this is over, so will Madelyn-May. Maybe Harlow, Bastian, Poppy, and I could stay here together and be a family.

I quickly catch myself and push the idea from my mind. How inappropriate that on my way to meet Madelyn-May I'm fantasizing about stealing her family from her. What kind of person does that? I quickly remind myself that I'm just over-tired, that I'm being ridiculous, and am in dire need of a good night's sleep. That of course, I would never try and take her family from her. *Would I?*

When I get to the hotel, I keep my head down and take the elevator to the fifth floor. Outside the door, I take a deep breath and try to steady myself. I can't mess this up. I can't let my emotions get the better of me. Whatever her reaction, I have to convince Madelyn-May to follow the plan. There is so much at stake.

When the door opens, I force myself not to look down or apologize. Instead, I gather myself, meet her eye and make sure my feet stay planted to the floor. "I know I'm not who you were expecting," I begin, "but I need to talk to you."

Madelyn-May looks me over and then steps forward and peers past me down the hallway.

"Bastian's not here if that's who you're looking for," I tell her. "He's still with the FBI."

She looks at me skeptically and then leans on the door frame, a move that is clearly not an invitation to come in.

"You've got balls coming here, I'll give you that, Sophie," she says. "Even after everything you've done to try and destroy my family, here you are again."

"I really am trying to help," I tell her. "I'm not here to cause trouble."

"Bastian asked you to come?"

Even in the most trying of times, Madelyn-May has retained her air of elegance. Her champagne-blonde hair is perfect, and barely-there makeup is just enough to accentuate her features while still allowing her to look natural and beautiful.

"No, Harlow actually," I tell her. "I know where she is Madelyn-May and she asked me to come here. We have a plan, but we need your help."

Bastian's wife looks me over. To her, I must look like a deranged lunatic with my unkempt hair and unwashed jeans.

"She needs my help, or *you* need my help?"

"We both do," I admit. "If I could just come in and explain."

Reluctantly she steps aside and after taking one last look down the hall, turns and closes the door behind me.

"So, how is my family?" she asks, her tone sarcastic. "It seems that one way or another you always know that better than I do."

There is no air in the room, and I begin to feel the onset of a panic attack but I can't let the girls down. I have to hold my own in front of Madelyn-May.

"Look, I know this is awkward for both of us, but Harlow wants to help Poppy," I begin. "She's a match for the bone marrow transplant my daughter needs. We are just a day or two away from completing the procedure. Once she's in the clear I'm going to see Lacy and force her to tell me who really killed that girl. I don't care what I have to do but I am going to make this right for Harlow, I promise."

Madelyn-May slowly crosses her legs, never taking her eyes off mine. "So, my daughter is hiding out in an oncology center in where, Annapolis?"

"Maryland," I tell her. "But she has a fake ID and extremely short blonde hair. She looks very different and there's no connection to me so for now there's no reason for the FBI to look for her there."

"No connection to you," Madelyn-May repeats and it's impossible to miss the tone of her voice. Resentful. Hurt. Disbelieving. "And what's her fake name?"

"It's Chloe."

She fixes me with a stare so intense it causes my toe to tap with nerves.

"Chloe, *what*?"

"Madelyn-May, please..."

"Chloe, *what*?"

"Miller, but just so we could do the tests without raising any questions."

She nods slowly and then gives a grin of what I think is disbelief. "So, let me get this straight. You're here with my husband and now our daughter has your last name?"

"No, it's not like that."

"Oh, who are you trying to fool, Sophie?" she asks. "Of course, it's like that. It's always like that when it comes to you and him. Do you really think I don't know?"

"I..." I want to tell her that she's wrong, that I don't want to steal her family but even on my way here it was all I could think about. "...I love them, Madelyn-May."

"Excuse me?"

I have been intimidated by her and felt second best for what feels like forever. I know they're her family, but the truth is I do love them. I love Bastian with every piece of my heart and Harlow is the most incredible young woman I have ever met. To say anything else would be untrue and Madelyn-May is an intelligent woman. She can see through my lies. If we are ever going to get anywhere with this, I have to tell her the truth.

"You got me," I tell her. "I love them, and I'm sorry that I do, but I do. I never meant to fall pregnant with Poppy and I tried to do the right thing. I cut all ties with Bastian and I stayed away but it doesn't mean that I don't love him. And Harlow, she's..."

"... headstrong, impossible, and outrageously smart?"

"Yes," I agree. "She's all those things and more."

"And your daughter? What's she like?"

I think back to that day on the park bench when a chance encounter saw Madelyn-May and I first meet. My mother was dying and Madelyn-May was terrified that her inability to have children was going to cost her the only man she had ever loved. Back then neither of us knew what it meant to be a mother or how far we would go to protect our children. We had made a pact. I would give her my eggs and she would pay for my mother's treatment. It was a partnership forged out of desperation between two women who thought they would never see each other again. If only we had known what we did that day would stay with us for the rest of our lives, that we were irreversibly tying ourselves to each other with knots so tight they would never come undone.

"Poppy's road has been tough," I tell her honestly. "I didn't know she was so sick. I mean, I took her to the local GP so many times, but they didn't find it. I didn't know she was..." I can't bring myself to say the word *terminal*.

"And now?"

"She needs a bone marrow transplant. I hoped I'd be a match, but I'm not." Despite my resolution not to let emotions overcome me, I start to cry. "I feel so helpless."

"And Harlow is a match?"

"Yes," I manage. "And she wants to help. And I want to help her too. I know she didn't kill that girl."

Madelyn-May leans forward and looks at me. "You said you planned on going to Muncy to see Lacy. Why?"

"We think Lacy had something to do with the murder."

"That's impossible," Madelyn-May replies with a shake of her head. "She's still incarcerated and over seventy years old now."

"When Harlow had that incident at the bar, there was a lot of online trolling," I explain. "Someone dropped her address in an online chat room. We think that maybe somehow Lacy got hold of it and sent someone to finish the job she couldn't."

"But why? That was all so long ago."

"You don't think she'd hold a grudge?"

"No, in fact, she wrote to me a while back. She said it was part of making amends and that she was sorry for everything. I didn't reply of course, nor do I forgive her, but the attempt felt genuine."

The news has me perplexed. If Lacy wasn't involved then who came to the house trying to hurt Harlow? Could it really have been just a break-in?

"There was something though, now that you mention it," she continues. "At the time I didn't think much of it. I thought she was just being Lacy or misusing her words, but in one of the sentences, she wrote *we shouldn't have done what we did*. She used the word *we*."

"We?"

"Yes, like maybe there was someone else involved."

"Do you have any idea who it could be?"

But Madelyn-May shakes her head and says she has no idea, that Lacy never mentioned anyone else and she always thought it had been just her behind the whole thing.

"Help me understand," I say. "Originally, Lacy wanted revenge for what you did to your dad, even though he... hurt you."

"I know, it makes no sense," Madelyn-May says. "You'd think she would be grateful to be rid of that monster but she couldn't let go. I just wanted to leave the past behind me. We both did. You'd think she would have too."

"You *both*?"

"My sister. We both ran that night. Unfortunately, she went back. Lacy said she ended up a drug addict and eventually died in the trailer park from an overdose."

"That's horrible. I'm so sorry."

Madelyn-May nods and I can see the weight of her past has stayed with her, even now.

"We were twins, Melody and I," she says, surprising me that she would go into detail. "It must run in the family, what with Harry and Harlow being twins as well."

"They do say that."

"I had an older sister too," she adds. "Her name was Mercy. She took off long before that night though."

"Do you think she could be the one doing this with Lacy?"

But again Madelyn-May shakes her head. "No, she was long gone. She hated all of us. There's no way she would do anything to help anyone, especially Lacy after what our dad did." She pauses then continues. "Lacy always knew what Daddy was doing to us. That's the thing I could never get past. She knew and didn't do a thing to stop him. How can that be?"

I wish I had the right words for Madelyn-May. Despite her perfect exterior, inside she is still broken, that much is clear and who could blame her? After what she endured as a teenager it surprises me she can function at all.

"Anyway, that's not why you came to see me," she says, snapping back. "So, tell me what scheme my daughter has put you up to. Do I need a drink to hear it?"

As she gets up and walks over to the mini-bar, I feel a smile tug at my lips. Madelyn-May's answer is going to be yes. She's going to help us. That's the thing about she and I. Somehow, no matter how far apart we are or what we do to each other, like bizarre sisters, we always seem to end up inextricably tangled in each other's mess.

Chapter Fifty-Four

VALENTINE

The night is alive with the sound of crickets chirping by the pond. At this time of night, the park is deserted and I know we won't be interrupted. I don't want to kill another kid, but Darcy will decide his own fate when he gets here. At seventeen he is almost a man and the last thing this world needs is another one of those. From what I can tell he is the only friend Harlow has. Maybe it would be worth killing him, I think to myself, just to cause her more pain.

When the sound of a dirt bike grows closer I ready myself. Not willing to take any more chances after what happened at the sports bar, I brought a handgun this time. A Glock 43 I picked up in a store down on Torresdale Avenue along with a Ruger precision rifle. On the off-chance Harlow might be stupid enough to come with Darcy, I want to be prepared.

I get down lower in the surrounding brush and wait. The sound of the bike gets louder, and I know he is in the parking lot. The engine goes quiet and I reach for the rifle, praying she is with him. If I could just get one shot off, I could finish this here and now. I could wake up tomorrow morning free of this burden and able to move on with my life.

But it is only a single shape that enters the park. He walks slowly toward the pond, stops and looks around then continues toward a seat by the water.

"Damn it, Harlow," I whisper to myself. "Why couldn't you have just come with him."

Due to Madelyn-May's celebrity status, I cannot pretend to be her. Everyone on the planet knows what she looks like. My only chance is scaring him into either making Harlow come here or telling me where she is. Either will do, but I want to finish this tonight.

I silently step out of the brush and walk toward him, my gun aimed at the back of his head. He's facing the pond which is unbelievably stupid given he's meeting someone in a park in the middle of the night.

"Don't turn around," I tell him as I approach. "I have a gun and I will use it."

His arms immediately fly up as though this is some kind of old-fashioned stickup.

"You can have my wallet," he stammers. "It's in my back pocket."

The fool thinks I'm going to rob him and it's all I can do not to laugh.

"I'm here to meet someone," he says. "She'll be here any minute. Just take my wallet. I won't turn around I swear."

I press the muzzle of the gun against the back of his neck. "I know you are Darcy. And guess what? I'm already here."

He starts to turn and then thinks better of it. "Mrs Marozzi? I don't..."

"Mrs Marozzi couldn't make it."

"Oh shit," he manages. "It's you. You're the one who killed Kempsey."

"Get Harlow on the phone and tell her to come down here and meet you."

"Why are you doing this?" he asks. "I don't get it. Why kill Kempsey? She didn't do anything."

He's visibly trembling. I want to feel bad for him, but I just don't have it in me. "You don't have to get it, kid. Just get Harlow down here."

But he shakes his head and shrugs. "I can't, she doesn't have a phone."

I cock the gun so he can hear the sound of the bullet click into the chamber. "Maybe you didn't hear me correctly."

"No, I swear!" He shifts his weight and half turns around. "She knew the FBI would trace it. There's no way for me to call her. I mean it, please. I'll help but don't kill me."

"How are you going to help me?"

He begins to turn but I use my free hand to push him back. "If you turn around, kid, I will have to kill you and strangely enough I don't want to do that."

He nods quickly and stays facing the pond.

"Well? How is it you think you can help me?"

"I know she was planning to go and see someone about Kempsey's death. Someone in prison. Her grandmother I think."

"When?"

"Huh?"

"When is she going to see Lacy?"

"I don't know," he mumbles. "I picked her up when she ran from the hospital and dropped her by the side of the road. She said she had to find out who really killed Kempsey for all this to be over."

I chuckle at the idea of Lacy helping anyone but herself. If Harlow thinks risking everything to go and see that old bag will help she's going to be bitterly disappointed, but it will give me the opportunity I need.

"Get up."

"What?"

"I said get up. And don't turn around."

The kid slowly gets to his feet and starts to cry. "Please don't kill me," he sobs. "I don't want to die."

"Walk."

As we walk toward a cluster of trees he sobs, snotty disgusting sounds that almost make me wretch.

"Get down on your knees."

"Oh my God, please, I'm begging you," he exclaims between sobs. "I won't say anything about this I swear."

"I know you won't."

"But I haven't even seen your face. I won't say anything. Please, I've told you everything, there's nothing left to tell. I…"

I don't hear the rest of his blathering because by the time he finishes, I'm already too far away.

Chapter Fifty-Five
HARLOW

I'm sound asleep in the chair beside Poppy's bed when a commotion in the hallway wakes me.

"I said you can't run in here," one of the nurses tells someone in a curt tone. "You aren't even supposed to be in here. I'm calling security."

Someone is in the hallway who shouldn't be. Instantly my pulse races and I leap to my feet. They've found me. The only question is, is it the FBI or Kempsey's killer?

When he bursts through the door, I squeeze my eyes and clutch at my chest expecting the worst.

"Harlow, we were right," he exclaims. "Someone is after you."

"Darcy?" I open my eyes and am shocked to see him standing in front of me. "No, you can't be here. You have to go."

"I had to come, Harlow, it was the killer. She tricked me. I met her at the park thinking it was your mom."

"You did what?"

"Harlow, she's after you. I told her you were going to the prison so she wouldn't know I brought you here instead, but she had a gun. She held it against the back of my head. I had to say something, but I didn't tell her where you are, I swear.

"A gun? Oh my God, are you alright?" I rush forward and wrap my arms around him. "I'm so sorry you got mixed up in all of this."

"What in the world?"

I let go of him when I hear Sophie's voice in the doorway.

"You have to be kidding, Harlow. What is Darcy doing here?" She looks past him at me as though I am the most stupid person on earth.

"The killer held a gun on him," I manage. "He came here to warn us."

Her eyes widen and she takes two steps toward us. "You saw the killer?"

"Well, not exactly," Darcy says, looking at the ground. "I was sitting in a park. It was dark. She came up behind me with a gun, but I didn't tell her where Harlow is, I swear. I just rode for hours to get here and tell you."

"What did she say?"

As Darcy fills us in on the details of his encounter we listen intently, Sophie nodding as she takes it in.

"I said a woman in prison, and she said the name Lacy," Darcy adds at the end. "They definitely know each other I could tell."

At the mention of her name, Sophie and I exchange a glance that isn't lost on Darcy.

"So, I was right," he says with a nod. "This does have something to do with your grandmother."

"Well, if there was ever any question before there isn't anymore," Sophie says, casting a worried glance at Poppy, "but still, you shouldn't have come here, Darcy. You're putting everything at risk. What if the FBI is watching you?"

"Well, if they are, they should have taken out the woman in the park with a gun to my head."

Sophie nods and seems satisfied that he's made a good point. "Alright, fine but you can't stay. You have to go."

Darcy nods and then looks at me intently. "Are you alright?"

"Me?" I exclaim. "What about you? You're the one who had a gun pointed at you."

"There," a nurse says, appearing in the doorway and pointing Darcy out to a security guard. "I told him no running and no visiting. It's one o'clock in the morning and he's in here causing a ruckus. This is the pediatric oncology wing. It isn't any place to be running around and acting stupid."

All three of us exchange glances and Darcy holds up his hands in surrender. "I'm going, I'm going. I apologize."

"Not so fast," the security guard says. "Now you have to wait for the police."

"The police?" Sophie breathes. "Why did you call the police?"

"Standard procedure."

"It's standard procedure to call the police for no reason?" I exclaim. "Are you serious?"

"He looked like a threat," the nurse says, "being all boisterous and loud at this ungodly hour. And in here of all places."

"I wasn't being loud," Darcy pleads, looking at the security guard and then toward Sophie and me. "I swear. I hurried, that's all."

"It's the middle of the night and you came in here with your hoodie up and running like you were about to do something you shouldn't," the nurse says. "I had no choice."

Darcy turns and stares at her in disbelief. "You called the police because I have a hoodie on? It's freezing out."

"Well," she quips, "these days you can't be too careful."

"Oh my God," Darcy says with a long sigh. "This is ridiculous."

"Chloe, why don't you go and get us a coffee from the machine down the hall while we wait for the police," Sophie suggests with a knowing look.

But before I can move the security guard interjects. "Sorry, Ma'am, everyone needs to stay here until the police arrive. Hospital policy. If this is nothing, then it won't take long to get sorted out."

"Sir, my daughter is sick," Sophie says gesturing toward Poppy. "My other daughter is here to provide a life-saving bone marrow transplant. This is her boyfriend. He did a stupid thing, but please, is this really necessary?"

The security guard looks at little Poppy as she stirs and begins to wake up. "She has cancer?"

"Yes," Sophie answers, "leukemia, and please, can we not do this in here? Or at all? It's really not necessary I assure you."

The security guard's face softens, and the nurse throws up her arms. "Fine, but no more running you hear me?" she scolds Darcy. "And there's to be no visiting on this floor unless you're family. Understood?"

"Yes, Ma'am," Darcy says. "I'm so sorry."

"Well get out of here," she says, shooing him away like a stray cat. "And I don't want to see you back here again. Ever. Are we clear?"

Darcy nods and my shoulders drop with relief as the nurse and security guard turn to leave. When their backs are to us Sophie looks at me and rolls her eyes in disbelief. She doesn't say a word, but I know exactly what she's thinking; that was way too close. We follow them out into the hall, and I say my goodbyes to Darcy. But as he turns to leave, my heart sinks as two police officers step out of the elevator and stare straight at me.

Chapter Fifty-Six

SOPHIE

"You need to get out of here, but do not run," I whisper to Harlow, who is frozen to the spot beside me.

She nods and turns to leave but right away the policewoman quickens her step and calls out for Harlow to stop.

"I need everyone to stay where they are," she announces, as she approaches us. "At least until we clear this up."

Harlow stops and drops her head, while Darcy huffs and shoves his hands into his pockets.

"This is just a misunderstanding," I begin. "My daughter's boyfriend came in at a stupid time and he's extremely sorry. It's just that my Chloe here is preparing to donate bone marrow to her little sister. It's been extremely emotional for all of us and I apologize for the disruption. It won't happen again."

The male officer flips open a small notepad and writes something down while the woman takes a closer look at Harlow.

"I'd really like to get back to my daughter if you don't mind," I continue. "As you can see, she's in oncology and is extremely ill."

Neither of the officers respond. Instead, the man keeps scribbling and the woman moves in on Harlow.

"You look familiar," she says. "Why would that be?"

"She did some modeling a while back," I say quickly. "Fashion magazines and such."

The female officer looks her over one last time, then meets my eye. "Nope, don't read fashion magazines."

I nod and glance quickly at Harlow who looks about to cry. "Well, then I really can't say but as I told you, my daughter -"

"- is sick, yes I know," she finishes. "We're in a hospital."

It is all I can do not to reach out and wrap my hands around Darcy's throat. I know why he came but his presence here has put everything at risk.

"I've definitely seen you somewhere," the officer continues, casting her attention back to Harlow. "I just can't put my finger on it."

"I've got all I need," her partner says. "I'm good to go if you are."

I want to breathe out but don't have the courage. We are so close now. All she has to do is walk away. But instead, she rubs her chin for a moment and then says something to Harlow that sends a chill down my back.

"Can I see some ID please?"

"ID?" Harlow replies, her voice so small I can barely hear it.

"Yes. Is there a problem?"

Harlow shakes her head and reaches into her back jeans pocket. "Here you go."

I don't dare to move as the officer takes the ID and stares at it.

"Chloe Miller. That's you?"

"Yes," Harlow whispers, catching Darcy's eye.

They don't speak but I know exactly what they're thinking. *Will the fake ID hold up?*

Eventually, the officer hands the ID card back to Harlow. She nods but there is a heaviness on her brow. Her lips are tight.

"Alright then," she announces in a curt tone, "I don't expect to be called back here. You understand?"

We all nod, and I don't think I am the only one trying to make myself seem as small as possible.

"Have a good evening then."

The male officer tips his head and turns to follow her down the hall. It's over. They're leaving.

Beside me, Harlow lets out a breath so long and deep I can actually hear it. "Oh my God, that was so close."

"Darcy, Jesus Christ," I hiss, "do you have any idea what could have happened? Are you stupid?"

"I'm sorry," he mumbles, "I wanted to warn Harlow."

"Don't say her name!" I grip him by the shoulder and pull him into Poppy's room. "My daughter's life depends on Harlow being able to go through with the donation procedure. If she doesn't Poppy will die. Do you get that?"

Beside us, Poppy stirs and opens her eyes. "Mommy, who's Harlow?"

"Hi, sweetheart," I coo, immediately changing my tone. "How are you feeling?"

"Okay," she says, rubbing at her eyes. "Who's Harlow?"

"No one, sweetheart. Go back to sleep."

"Who's that?" She points at Darcy and waits for me to answer.

"A friend of Mommy's but he was just leaving." I stare at Darcy and he gets the message.

"I'm sorry, really," he manages. "I don't want to cause trouble. I just care about Harlow."

"I know and I appreciate that, but you need to go."

He nods and makes his way out into the hall to say his goodbyes while I sit down on the side of Poppy's bed.

"Hey, Soph, we're going to go see if the cafeteria has any vending machines before Darcy goes," Harlow says from the door. "He hasn't eaten in hours and it's a long ride back to Philly."

"Okay but be quiet and walk slowly. Then I want Darcy out of here. You got it?"

She nods and they disappear leaving me to finally breathe out. I slide onto the bed and pull Poppy in under my shoulder. "Just another day or two and you'll be all better young lady."

She nuzzles into me and I breathe in the gentle scent of her hair. It's impossible to find words for how much I love her. This tiny little girl with my hair and Bastian's eyes. If I could, I would give my life for hers.

"Excuse me."

I look up and my heart lurches when I see the officers have returned. They're standing in the doorway, the man has his pad out and a pen poised and ready to write.

"I have one more question," the woman says, and my chest tightens. "Where's the girl's father?"

"I'm sorry?"

"Their father. Where is he?"

"Why does that matter?"

"Well, you said the little one has cancer. Seems odd he's not here."

Her question catches me off guard and I'm not sure if I'm obliged to answer something so personal. "He's away for work."

"Away for work," she repeats. "While both his daughters are about to undertake a significant medical procedure."

"He has an important job."

"Can I get his name?"

Shit.

My pulse is racing, and I have no idea what to say. "Okay fine, the truth is I don't have contact with him anymore. I don't like to talk about it in front of my kids." I tip my head toward Poppy. "It's upsetting for them."

She nods and for a moment I think I see a hint of compassion in her eyes. "Expensive procedure for a single mom. You have insurance?"

"Why does any of this matter?" I ask. "The boy was running when he shouldn't have been. That's all."

She looks taken aback and I curse myself. She was fishing and I just hooked myself.

"Ms Miller, is there a problem?

"No," I say with a sigh. "I just have a lot on my plate and it's late. I just want to lie here with my daughter if that's okay?"

"May I?" She indicates that she would like to step in closer to Poppy and I nod.

"Hi there," she says to Poppy in a tone so gentle I wonder if behind her badge is a mom just like me.

"Hello," my daughter whispers back.

"I understand your sister is going to help you get better."

The minute she says it, I realize what's happening. She's using my daughter to fish for more information and it's a step too far.

"Alright, that's enough," I tell her, getting back to my feet. "I think it's time for you to go."

We face off, neither of us backing down. Eventually, it is she who steps back. "I hope the procedure goes well."

I am about to show her the door when Poppy's little voice says, "I'm getting magic beans."

At that, she stops and turns back toward the bed. "You are? Well, that sounds exciting. And is your sister Chloe giving you these magic beans?"

"Poppy, ssh now, you need to rest because -"

"No, I don't have a sister," she tells the officer. "A nice girl is giving them to me. Mommy is her name Harlow?"

I catch my breath and grab onto the plastic seat beside me.

"All units, I have a location on Harlow Marozzi," the officer shouts into a walkie-talkie. "Maryland Harford Memorial Hospital. Alert the FBI now!"

She glances from the door to me, and then to her partner. "Watch her. I'm going to find the girl."

"Mommy, what's happening?"

I move back to Poppy's side to try and comfort her but inside my stomach churns and I think I'm going to be sick. It must show on my face because the officer steps forward and peers at me.

"You alright?"

"No, no, I'm not." I feel the start of a panic attack rush through me and it gives me an idea. "Oh my God, I can't breathe."

"Ma'am, you need to stay calm."

"I can't... I can't breathe!" I fall forward and grab onto Poppy's bed.

"Mommy!"

I reach up and squeeze Poppy's hand and give her a quick wink and a smile. "Mommy is just playing," I mouth to her. "It's okay."

But the minute the words leave my lips I look at the officer with wild eyes. "Get a doctor."

He is obviously torn, so I slide onto the floor and clutch at my throat.

"Shit," he swears. "Doctor! We need a doctor in here!"

As he dashes off down the corridor I get to my feet and kiss Poppy on the forehead. "Mommy is fine, alright, but I have to find Harlow."

She nods and I hurry from the room and down the corridor toward the elevator that will take me to the cafeteria. I have no idea how we are going to complete the procedure now but if I don't find Harlow before the police, we are all out of options.

Chapter Fifty-Seven
HARLOW

"I really am sorry," Darcy says, as we wander slowly across the hospital carpark toward his bike. "The last thing I wanted was to make things harder for you."

Above us, the night sky hugs the stars, and I long to feel the warmth of his embrace. "I still can't believe this is happening. Honestly, I don't know how much more I can take. I just want it to be over."

"Come here..."

He opens his arms and I nuzzle into him. The warmth of his body almost makes me feel like I'm safe, but I know that isn't true. There's an entire team of police and FBI out there just waiting to rip me away from him. "Darcy, I'm scared. What if I can't help Poppy in time? What if I can never prove I didn't kill Kempsey?"

"You will, and we will, Harlow. I promise."

I nod and press myself even further into him. "I wish I could stay here forever."

"Umm... Harlow?"

"What is it?"

"Do you hear that?"

I step back and listen. Sirens. They're in the distance but definitely getting closer. "Oh my God, Darcy, they know I'm here."

"Harlow!" Suddenly Sophie is running across the carpark waving her arms. "They know you're here. We have to go. Now!"

She quickly closes the distance between us, and I stare at her in disbelief. "Go where?"

"To see Lacy," she manages, gasping for air. "We have to get her to tell us who killed Kempsey."

"But Poppy..."

"You can't help Poppy from prison. Now, come on. We have to go."

"How?"

"On foot, at least to my friend's house. It's no more than a fifteen-minute walk from here. I'll get her car and we can drive straight there."

"I'll never get into the prison," I tell her. "I'm too hot. They'll be looking for me."

"She's right," Darcy agrees. "It's too risky for her to attempt going into a prison."

"I'll go," Sophie says. "Lacy already approved me for her visitation list."

"She did?"

"Apparently, she's looking for forgiveness. Maybe that includes me since I was involved in the car crash she caused all those years ago."

"Then why would she try to kill me? It makes no sense."

Sophie looks at me and shrugs. "I don't know, Harlow, but it's the only shot we have and I'm not letting you out of my sight until I get answers. Now come on, we have to go."

Chapter Fifty-Eight
VALENTINE

It's been six years since I've seen my grandmother, Lacy. Six years since she royally fucked up my plan to kidnap Harlow and sell her off to the highest bidder. That's my specialty, after all, fencing stolen items. Don't get me wrong, I've killed when necessary, but I never considered it as a profession - way too messy. But stealing, that's an art form and one I have been perfecting since I was a child. Harlow is too old for kidnapping now of course. She was only eleven back then. Unfortunately, no one is interested in a headstrong, rebellious seventeen-year-old.

I know it seems cold to think I could sell off a kid to God knows who, but that's how I was raised. Children were considered the property of someone else. Everyone around me saw fit to use us as commodities for whatever they needed at the time. Selling drugs, stealing, sex. I guess that's why I haven't been able to forgive Madelyn-May. Our father betrayed her but that's what life was like and we accepted it. My grandmother accepted it, and so did my mother, but not Madelyn-May. She thought she was different like she was so much better than everyone else. So much better that our father deserved to have his head smashed in with a hammer. So much better that my grandmother deserved to almost burn to death and lose a leg. So much better that my mother should have to sacrifice herself, not just to our father but to drug dealers after he was dead. How dare she think she was so much better than all of us or deserved a better life? She comes from the dirt just like us, and pretty soon I'm going to make sure she and Harlow are covered in it.

When Lacy limps out her appearance shocks me. Her face is gaunt, and her shoulders are hunched over, arthritic, and bony. As she shuffles toward me, she looks over and I meet her gaze expecting a look of surprise or hope but there's nothing.

"Lacy," I say as she sits across from me, "it's been a while."

"What do you want?"

I search her face and try to figure out how to play this. Her reaction to seeing me is not what I expected. "How are you?"

She scoffs and looks across the room. "Like you care."

"I asked, didn't I?"

Her mouth twists and she rolls her eyes. "How do I look to you?"

I take a moment and consider my answer. "You've looked better."

"Lung cancer," she says eventually. "From the smokes."

I nod and do my best to look like it matters. "I'm sorry to hear that."

"Cut the bullshit, kid," she says, her response interrupted by a ghastly cough. "We both know you're not here because you give a shit. So, what do you want?"

I lean back in the chair and smile. "Still as feisty as ever."

"I ain't got all day."

"Fine," I say leaning in across the table. "Has Harlow been to see you?"

"Harlow?"

I can tell from the surprised look on her face that she hasn't. "Yes, remember little Harlow? Although she's seventeen now and wanted for murder."

"Murder?" Finally, Lacy's eyes flicker with interest. "She killed someone?"

"Technically no, but the police don't know that."

She nods and a knowing look falls across her face. "You set her up."

I smile and shrug, knowing I look smug as hell and not caring in the slightest.

"Ah, let it go kid, for Christ's sake," Lacy tells me with a long sigh. "This really how you want to spend your days, all churned up with hate?"

"That's rich coming from you. You're in prison."

"Exactly, and I'm probably going to die in here. Take a look at your future, kid, because this is it right here in front of you if you don't let that shit go."

Thoughts of Jasper and the life we could have flicker through my mind. I hate that Lacy is already starting to get to me. "Don't play games with me old woman. I don't have the time."

"Well, that's the difference between you and me. I ain't got nothing but time in here. But I ain't playing games. Just being honest."

"Honest?"

She nods and looks around as though she is already tiring of me.

"Then tell me this, *honestly*. Are you really comfortable with forgiving Madelyn-May for what she did to all of us?"

"I'm not forgiving her, kid, I'm letting it go. Ain't the same thing."

"How do you figure?"

"Well, way I see it forgiving is something you do for the person who hurt you. Letting go is something you do for yourself and I ain't planning on dying thinking about how much she hurt me. You shouldn't either."

"She... you both... took everything from me." As I say the words, I feel my voice crack and I silently scream at myself not to cry.

"That's where you're wrong, kiddo. People make their own choices, just like you're doin' now. But take a good look at yourself. You're heading down a dangerous path."

"I'm not you.'

"No, you're stronger than that. So, don't waste your strength on wars you ain't gonna win."

"It's not a war, Lacy. I just have to make things right."

"I don't mean a war with Madelyn-May," she says. "I mean the one you're having with yourself."

I shake my head and wave my hand dismissively. "You don't know what you're talking about."

She nods slowly and purses her lips. "Maybe. Maybe not. But you get a lot of time to think in here, that's all I'm sayin'."

I sit back and look around the room at different women chatting with their visitors. Some are older like Lacy, but others are young, my age. A blonde woman in the corner leans in toward a little girl and I watch her closely. An average-looking man with brown hair and hairy arms places his hand against the little girl's back and gently pushes her forward. When the child doesn't move, he whispers something in her ear but she spins around and throws herself back into his arms, burying her head in his shoulder. The woman looks about to cry as the man shrugs and busies himself comforting the child.

"Don't ruin your life," Lacy says, as though she's reading my mind. "You're smart and have been lucky so far. But everyone's luck runs out eventually, Valentine. Even yours."

Before I can respond, Lacy raises her hand to let the guard know our visit is over.

"Wait... you still owe me," I tell her.

Her hand still up, she looks back over her shoulder. "I don't owe you shit, kid."

"You took something from me."

"I never took nothin' from you," she says as a guard approaches our table. "If memory serves me right, it was you who gave something away."

I watch as the guard helps her up. "If Harlow comes, don't tell her about me," I say. "I have to make things even."

Lacy looks back one last time, but I can't read her face. As she is led away, I know without a doubt we will never see each other again.

"You owe me Lacy…" I call after her. "You owe me."

Chapter Fifty-Nine
HARLOW

Ominous clouds gather on the horizon, suffocating the sunrise as we drive toward Muncy Correctional Facility. We've been traveling since three in the morning and it's almost six am. While the idea of facing Lacy after what she did to me as a kid is scary, I'm disappointed I won't be able to confront her in person. When she tried to kidnap me, I never really knew what she planned to do. I knew she did it to punish my mother for what happened back at the trailer park in California but if the car hadn't crashed then what? Was she going to kill me? Keep me hostage?

For years after, I had nightmares about the crash. I could never understand how she would do such terrible things to her own flesh and blood. But after learning what my mother's childhood was like, being sexually abused by her own father, I guess hurting your family wasn't uncommon for them.

"Penny for your thoughts?"

I snap back and look at Sophie. "I was just thinking about everything."

"You might need to be a little more specific," she says. "Right now, *everything* is a lot."

"About Lacy and Mom. I hate that I'm related to them. It's all so disgusting and depraved."

"You mean what happened with your grandfather?"

"All of it," I say with a sneer. "I mean, it makes me hate myself for even being a part of that family."

"Do you think that's part of the reason you don't want to see your mom anymore?"

I shrug and force myself to stare out the window so she won't see that I'm about to cry.

"Harlow, what happened to your mom when she was a little girl wasn't her fault. She knew it was wrong and that it was unacceptable. She shouldn't have killed him, but she was a kid being tortured and abused. She was trying to protect herself and her sister. What happened to them shouldn't happen to anyone."

"She killed him. Lacy tried to kill me. Now I'm being accused of murdering my best friend. It runs in the family. There's no way anyone is ever going to see past that. Since I was old enough to make my own choices I've done everything I can not to be like them. I hate being related to them. I'm a murderer and trash by association."

"Well," Sophie says with a click of her tongue, "there's millions of women out there who don't think your mom is trash despite her past."

"Brainwashed by the internet."

Sophie laughs, and I wipe at my tears. "Probably," she continues, "but it does go to show that not everyone judges people by where they come from, Harlow. Things are different now. You can be whoever you want to be. Madelyn-May is perfect proof of that. I know you feel robbed of having what felt like a real mom, but step back and look at where she came from and what she achieved. Anything is possible. And you and I, we have to hold onto that if we're ever going to get through this."

"Wait, you want my *mom* to be our role model?"

"I want us to believe that we can come out the other side of all this. Your mom did and we can too."

When it's time for Sophie to go in and see Lacy, I find myself fidgeting and pulling at my hair. "You're sure you can make her tell you the truth?" I ask one more time. "What if she's just the same bitch who hates me and wishes I was dead?"

"Harlow, everything is riding on this. I'm going to do everything I possibly can. You have my word."

"But what makes you think she's going to tell you?"

Sophie looks thoughtful then turns to face me. "Your mom said Lacy wrote to her apologizing for everything. She's in her seventies now, and she's had a lot of time to think. If she's sick or feeling remorseful then she'll want to help just to clear her own conscious."

"I hope you're right."

"Have faith," Sophie tells me as she gets out of the car. "This will work."

"It better," I call after her, "or we're all finished."

Chapter Sixty
SOPHIE

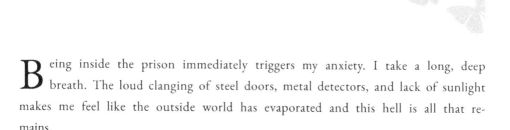

Being inside the prison immediately triggers my anxiety. I take a long, deep breath. The loud clanging of steel doors, metal detectors, and lack of sunlight makes me feel like the outside world has evaporated and this hell is all that remains.

As I wait for Lacy to be brought out, I imagine Harlow locked away in a place like this for something she didn't do. If I can't get Lacy to tell me the truth it won't just be Poppy who loses her life. For Harlow, life as she knows it will be over. There will be things that happen to her in prison, things she doesn't deserve, and things she will never recover from. There will be things that push and pull at her, remolding the girl she is now into someone new. Someone we won't recognize.

When Lacy comes out I can see she is confused. She doesn't recognize me, nor does she know why I'm here. She sits down and coughs, a raspy hollow noise that rattles down her throat and disappears somewhere inside her chest. Right away I understand why she wrote to Madelyn-May. It's a cough I've heard before. The same one my mother had when the cancer spread to her lungs.

"Lacy, I'm Sophie," I tell her. "Thank you for approving my request to visit."

"Must be my lucky week," she tells me in a sarcastic tone. "You're the second person who's come in as many days. I ain't had no one come in four, maybe five years, now there's been two of yous."

"Really," I reply. "That must be nice for you."

"Nice for me? There ain't nothin' nice about that girl."

"Madelyn-May came to see you?"

"Madelyn-May?' Lacy coughs again, this time hacking flehm and blood up into a tissue.

"Someone else then?"

"Who are you anyway?" she asks, tucking the tissue somewhere under her leg.

"I'm here because of Harlow," I tell her. "I'm trying to help her. The FBI, they're trying to arrest her for murder but -"

"- she didn't do it?"

"No, I don't believe she did."

"And you think I know who did?"

I take a moment and try to think of the best thing to say. Eventually, I settle for, "I'm hoping you do."

Lacy closes her eyes and I wonder for a moment if she's fallen asleep. "Lacy?"

"I'm thinking," she snaps. "Just give me a minute."

I wait while Lacy ponders her next move, praying she'll tell me something I can use.

"Alright," she announces, eventually opening her eyes, "I might know somethin' about it."

"You do?"

"Yep," she nods her head and holds my gaze. "But ain't nothing free in this world, sweetheart. Ya gotta give to receive."

"Was it you?" I ask, ignoring the last part of her remark. "Did you send someone to kill her?"

"Me?" Lacy looks genuinely taken aback. "I ain't got no issues with all that no more."

"Okay, then what do you want?"

"I got another two years left on my sentence and I can tell from the way you looked at me before that you know I ain't got that much left in the tank."

"You have lung cancer."

"Damned straight, and I need a real doctor, proper meds, enough to see out my time and get out of here. Can you make that happen?"

"Lacy, I…"

"That's my final offer. Take it or leave it."

"Getting a specialist like that in here to see you will take time. Time Harlow doesn't have. We can't wait."

"We?" she asks, looking at me closer. "Whose *we*?"

If I lay out all my cards Lacy will take advantage. If she knows Poppy's life is on the line the stakes will get even higher. I can't let her see how much I need this. I have to get something out of her, right here and right now.

"Harlow and Madelyn-May. She's here in the US. Bastian too. They came to try and help."

"Then why aren't they the ones here asking me for help?"

"They weren't sure you'd be agreeable to seeing them," I explain. "But Madelyn-May said you wrote to her. If you could help save Harlow, I'm sure she'd be grateful, maybe even agreeable to making amends. They have a beautiful home in Australia right on Sydney Harbor. Once you're out of here you could live out your days sitting by the ocean, the salt air on your face, surrounded by family. Doesn't that sound nice?"

The truth is I have no idea where Bastian and Madelyn-May live, but looking around here, I can't think of anywhere I would long for more than the ocean.

"You really think so?"

"Anything is possible, Lacy, but we need your help."

"And you'll get me a doctor?"

"I will, but there's going to be red tape. You're in prison. It will take time that Harlow doesn't have. If we don't help her, very soon she's going to be a seventeen-year-old girl locked in a place like this for something you *know* she didn't do."

"Probably be the best place for her," Lacy mumbles.

"Excuse me?"

Lacy leans in and glances around the room to make sure no one is listening. "You have to get her away from here, you hearin' me? The FBI ain't the only ones on her tail."

"Yes, we know. Whoever killed her friend is looking for her."

"Not *looking* for her," Lacy whispers. "*Hunting* her."

The way she says it sends a cold shiver down my back and the hair on my neck stands on end.

"And when she finds her, little Harlow won't stand a chance."

"Who is this person? Why is she doing this?"

Lacy sits back and folds her arms across her chest. "You ever come across a dog that ain't no one ever loved?"

I think back to the day I found Miss Molly cowering in the corner of the pound in Philadelphia. "I got my golden retriever from the shelter," I begin, "she -"

"I ain't talking about no doe-eyed golden retriever," Lacy snaps. "I'm talking about a dog bred from fighters and mongrels. A dog that spent its life starving, out in the weather chained to a pole, getting kicked, tormented, and fucked by all the other dogs."

I swallow and try to push the thought from my mind.

"Now imagine one day that dog gets loose and the only thing on its mind is getting payback for being tied to that pole all them years. It's savage, desperate, completely without remorse." Lacy leans forward and stares at me. "That's what's after your little Harlow."

She holds my gaze as I move back in my seat. "Who is she?"

Lacy looks away and a cloud forms over her eyes. "She's the worst parts of us all."

I think back to what the news said when Madelyn-May's past was revealed after the accident, that in the trailer park she and her sister both fell pregnant when they were young. Madelyn-May had a botched abortion but what if... "The woman after Harlow is your granddaughter?"

"Listen to me," Lacy says, snapping back and staring at me with a look so intense my breath catches in my throat. "She's here. If Harlow is here too, then you need to move her as far away as possible. You hearin' me?"

"I can't do that. I..."

"When she finds her, and she will, Harlow's going to wish the FBI locked her in prison and threw away the key. You need to move her. Have them take her back to Australia."

"She'd never make it through airport security." I think of Poppy and know that immigration officers are not the only reason Harlow can't go to Australia right now.

"Then you got to get her to the other side of the country. I know someone. They'll give her a safe place to stay."

"What? Who?"

"The less anyone knows the better. Get Harlow on a bus to California. Have her get off in San Diego. I'll make sure there's someone there to meet her."

"San Diego?"

"Organize a doctor and I'll tell the FBI what I know. I'll lead them right to my granddaughter. Then maybe Harlow can come back to Philly or go to Australia or whatever the hell she wants to do, but she'll be safe."

"No, that's not going to work," I tell her. "You need to tell the FBI now."

"And then what? I rot in here? Not gonna happen. I want my medicine."

"You have to tell me how to find your granddaughter."

Lacy laughs and signals to the guard that she wants to go back to her cell. "You won't find her," she says, as the guard walks over. "But don't worry. I have a feeling pretty soon she's going to find you."

Chapter Sixty-One
VALENTINE

It's been a long time since I shot a rifle. It felt heavy in my hands yesterday as I crouched to set up the rig in woodland about half a mile from the prison car park. Harlow will try to see Lacy, I can feel it. I know it may take a day, maybe even a week, but with the FBI closing in my guess is that it won't be too long before she shows her face.

Imagine my joy when less than twenty-four hours after arriving, I see that little arsehole climb out of a silver sedan and take a few steps toward a chestnut-haired woman I've never seen before coming out of the prison.

On the ground, the rifle is set up on a large flat rock in front of me. It was cold out last night but I couldn't risk leaving. I shivered my way through the night, my back flat against the icy-cold ground, a tangle of shrubbery hiding my weapon. By now Jasper will be wondering where I am. I could call and lie but I don't want to do that. Once I take the shot and get out of here it's over. I can go back to him with a clean slate. After that, the future will be mine, maybe ours, to create.

I peer through the scope and slow my breathing, just like I was taught. The dealers back in the trailer park thought it would be hilarious to teach a ten-year-old girl how to shoot a rifle. As it turned out, I was a natural and I enjoyed it. Whenever I closed one eye, steadied my breathing, and peered through the scope it was just me against myself. I could take my time, still my body, and when the bullet released it was like letting go. With every bullet I shot a part of my pain went with it, hurtling out into the world to strike something down. It was therapeutic and calmed me in a way nothing else seemed to.

In the carpark, Harlow is moving away from the car toward the woman coming out of the prison. I've seen Madelyn-May in the thousands of photos of her online, so I know it isn't her and it's clearly not the boy. So, who is this woman helping Harlow?

I push the thought away and focus. Her identity doesn't matter. What matters is that I need to make a choice. Do I attempt to take them both out or just Harlow? I fix my sights on Harlow first. If I have time, I'll kill the woman as well just for getting in my way. Out in front, the woman gives a thumbs up to Harlow as I slowly squeeze the trigger. The bullet leaves the chamber as Harlow throws up her arms in what appears to be joy then dashes toward the woman.

"Shit!"

The bullet misses and smashes into a car windshield next to the sedan. As the glass explodes, Harlow and the woman throw themselves down onto the ground and I know I've blown my chance. Within minutes the police will be crawling all over this place.

"Goddamn it!" I curse again, as I quickly pack up my gear. "This kid has got to be blessed."

I pack up as quickly as I can, making sure to pick up the bullet casing and any evidence I was ever here. With my rifle and gear slung over my shoulder, I hurry down the woodland track toward the road where I parked. Is it possible Lacy was right, I wonder as I make my way along the track. There's something about this whole thing that's starting to feel off balance and there's a nagging feeling in my gut that something terrible is about to happen.

I glance over my shoulder and then throw my bag into the trunk of the car. No, I can't let this go. Not yet. Not until it's over.

Chapter Sixty-Two

HARLOW

"Oh my God!" I shout at Sophie. "Did someone just shoot at us?"

"Get in the trunk!" she yells, ignoring the question. "Now Harlow, I'm not kidding."

"What? Sophie, no."

"Get in the trunk, Harlow. We have to get out of here."

I glance at the trunk of the car and imagine being locked inside that dark, confined space.

"Get in!" Her voice is frantic. She already has the lid open and is ushering me toward the cavernous space inside. "The police are going to be swarming all over here any second. They can't see you. We have to go."

Reluctantly, I climb into the trunk and pull my legs up against my chest. I glance up and Sophie meets my eye. She tries her best to give me a reassuring look. I nod and then everything goes dark.

The engine starts and I feel the vibration of the car running. I'm immediately nauseous as the car moves forward and I focus on trying not to scream. As we pull out onto the highway, I try to think about anything to distract myself. I think about Darcy and how it felt to have his arms around me. I think about the day this will all be over. There'll be television cameras and reporters. In a bid to forget that I am a fugitive locked in the trunk of a car, I practice what I'll say to the media when the real killer is found.

'I didn't want to stay on the run but a little girl's life depended on me. I knew that eventually the real killer would be found. I always had faith in the FBI and that justice would prevail. Now I'm just looking forward to moving on with my life.'

Moving on with my life. What will that look like, I suddenly wonder. I've been so focused on not getting caught and trying to help Poppy that what might happen next never crossed my mind. When Sophie came out of the prison, she gave me the thumbs up. That must mean Lacy told her who the real killer is. But once we go to the FBI and tell them the truth then what? Where will I go? Sophie will be busy helping Poppy recover and Mom and Dad will go back to Australia. My only friend is dead, and Darcy... I know I want him in my life but we're only seventeen. Maybe one day we can start to build a life together, but it's way too soon for that. So, where does that leave me?

When the car eventually slows to a stop, I hear the door open and close. We must be at the FBI or a police station, I think. They'll probably arrest me. I need to be prepared for that, but it will only be temporary. Now that Sophie knows the identity of the real killer it will just be a matter of time before the FBI arrests them, and I'll be set free. I just hope it's not too late for little Poppy.

But as I wait for Sophie to open the trunk, the minutes tick by and I start to panic. Where is she? Why isn't she letting me out? My heart races and my stomach clutches. It feels as though there's no air and I want to scream out, but I don't know where we are or who might hear me. I clutch at the neck of my sweater and try to calm myself. She wouldn't leave me in here. I'm too important to Poppy. There has to be a reason she's not letting me out.

When the trunk finally opens, I squint against the brightness of the day and shield my eyes. "What the hell? Where were you?"

Sophie leans in and helps me out, but when my feet hit the sidewalk I'm surprised to see we are parked in a back alley.

"What's going on?" I ask, looking around. "Why aren't we at the FBI or the police station? She told you, right? When you came out you gave me the thumbs up. Lacy told you who killed Kempsey."

Sophie places her hands on my shoulders and looks me deep in the eye. "Listen to me, Harlow, you need to leave Pennsylvania."

"What are you talking about? No, we need to go to the FBI and tell them who really killed Kempsey."

"You're not safe here, Harlow. That shot was fired to try and kill you."

I shake my head and wonder why she isn't listening to me. "Did Lacy tell you who killed Kempsey or not?"

Sophie drops her eyes and takes a deep breath. "Yes, but it's not as simple as that."

"Why not?"

"All I know is that she's Lacy's granddaughter, the daughter of Madelyn-May's sister."

"Mom's sister?"

"Your grandfather, he got both girls pregnant. Your mom had a termination, the one that stopped her from having any other children of her own, but her sister..."

"... had the baby."

"For all we know she was born in secret in that trailer park and who knows what happened after that? She may not even have a birth certificate or any record that she even exists. It could take them months to find her. In that time she could kill you, Harlow." Sophie pauses and looks away. "Lacy told me things about her, things that scared me. She's not like you and me Harlow, she's..."

"But Poppy..."

"Poppy might find another donor through the register. It's a long shot, but it's possible."

"And what about you?" I ask. "The police know you helped me."

"I honestly don't know, but what I do know is that you have to get out of here before she finds you again."

She hands me a greyhound bus ticket that reads destination San Diego. "What am I supposed to do with this?"

"Get somewhere safe," she says. "I know this is going to sound crazy but Lacy will have someone meet you when you arrive."

"Lacy?" I can't believe what Sophie is suggesting. "You just said they were trying to kill me."

"Not Lacy. She's dying, Harlow," Sophie says. "She wants to make this right and I believe her. She wants to make amends."

I stare down at the ticket as my mind spins. "What about Dad? Where is he?"

"I don't know. I tried his cell but he's not answering."

"And Mom?"

Sophie looks back at me and I know from the pull of her brow that we are out of options.

"Your Mom agreed to your idea about the social media posts, but Darcy coming to the hospital threw a spanner in the works. Harlow, the FBI knows you're here in Pennsylvania. This woman is trying to kill you. I can't get your dad and have no direct contact for your mom. You can't stay here it's too dangerous."

"Are you going to tell the FBI what Lacy said?"

"Of course I am. But right now, I need to get you out of danger. It's only a matter of time until she finds you again."

I stare at the ticket again and try to steady myself. "I want my dad."

"I know, sweetheart, but I don't know where he is. The FBI may have taken his phone. He thought he was being released but who knows what happened." She pulls me in and gently smooths my hair. "I don't know what else to do."

"You really think it's safe?" I look down at the ticket and find it hard to believe Lacy would ever want to help me.

She pulls back and nods. "Lacy has cancer. My guess is she only has months left. This is her one chance to make things right."

"I don't know, Sophie…" The thought of trusting the woman who kidnapped me is hard to swallow. And going to a strange place on the other side of the country all alone is terrifying.

"It's just till the FBI finds this woman, Harlow, then it will all be over. It's temporary. You just need to focus on that one thing. That it's temporary."

I feel the first tear fall and the ticket trembles in my hand. "Do you promise?"

"I promise, sweetheart," she says. "As soon as this is over your mom and dad will come and get you."

One tear turns to many as I begin to sob. "But what if I want you to come and get me?"

Once again, Sophie pulls me into an embrace. "Everything will work out, you'll see. But right now, you have a bus to catch. Alright?"

I nod but cannot find my voice to agree out loud.

"Here, take these." Sophie hands me a hoodie and a wad of rolled-up bills.

"What? No, I can't take money from you."

"Take it, Harlow. It's a thousand dollars. It's all I could withdraw from the ATM, but it will help you get some new clothes and whatever else you need until this is sorted out."

I throw my arms around her and wish I never had to let go. "I love you, Sophie, I know you want Madelyn-May to be my mom, but I love you."

"I love you too," she whispers into my hair. "Keep that hoodie over your face as much as you can and try to make the money last. Now go on. You can't miss that bus."

Chapter Sixty-Three

SOPHIE

When Harlow is out of sight, I climb back into the car and let my head fall against the steering wheel. Watching the only donor match I have for Poppy walk away feels like someone reaching in and removing my heart with their bare hands.

There is no way to save my daughter now. Unless a miracle match from a stranger turns up on the register Poppy is going to die.

It took everything I had not to drag Harlow by the arm back into the hospital and force them to do the procedure. In my mind, I see it play out. Me as the crazed mother holding the hospital staff and doctor at gunpoint while they save my daughter's life. I see myself single-handedly fighting back the FBI like some kind of movie heroine as they storm the building. One by one I take them out until none remain and I am left crouched in the corridor, one knee bent, one arm up, in a superhero stance. Poppy runs toward me, her face glowing. She's laughing, her hair fanned out behind her. She throws herself into my arms and I hold her taking in her beautiful scent, the one that became uniquely hers the moment she was born. I tell her everything is going to be okay, that Mommy saved her.

But slowly I open my eyes and am confronted by the truth - that I am not a superhero and I cannot save her. Instead, I am a middle-aged woman in a borrowed car, parked in a dirty alleyway, unsure if I am wanted by the FBI and helpless to save my child.

Reluctantly I turn on the engine and move the car forward. If I'm wanted by the FBI, they will find me soon enough because there is only one place I want to go - to see Poppy. I have been away from her long enough, and there is no place I would rather be than by her side. My only hope is that my trip back isn't to say goodbye.

Chapter Sixty-Four

VALENTINE

I stir and glance at the clock on my bedside table. It's just after two in the morning and the hair on the back of my neck immediately bristles. Someone is in the living room.

When I got back yesterday, I slung all of my gear onto the kitchen counter and spent the afternoon trying to come up with some way to finish this. The kid could be anywhere by now and with someone helping her there's no telling where she's gone.

I slip quietly out of bed and tiptoe along the wall until I reach the doorway. All I have is the element of surprise. If I wait for them to step into the room I can take them from behind. But first I need to get a look at who and what I'm dealing with.

Slowly and carefully, I creep my head around just far enough to see who is out there. In the living room, a lamp is on and I gasp when in the warm glow I see Jasper standing in the middle of the room. He's staring up at the pictures of Harlow on the wall.

"What the hell?" he breathes to himself, reaching one hand up to rub the back of his neck.

He's still in uniform. I saw on the news he traveled up to the prison this afternoon. Did he speak to Lacy, I wonder? Did she give me up? Is that why he's suddenly standing in my suite?

Sensing my presence, he glances toward the bedroom door and I quickly pull back out of sight. This is a disaster. There's no way I can explain those images up on the wall. If he looks inside the bags on the counter he'll find my rifle and handgun.

"CJ," he calls out. "I need you to come out here."

My mind is racing, everything I imagined for us quickly disintegrating. Since I was nine years old, I have managed to outsmart everyone around me. Now there's an FBI agent standing in my room. What the hell was I thinking letting him into my life?

"Jasper, I can explain." I slowly make my way out into the living room and gesture toward the wall. "I wanted to help. After I was hurt, I had a lot of free time on my hands. I thought maybe I could figure out where she was for you. You know, like those web detectives who solve crimes on the internet."

He studies my face, then looks back to the wall. "There was a shooting today at the prison where Harlow's grandmother is serving out her sentence."

"Yes, I saw it on the news." I want to go and throw my arms around him but I don't dare take another step.

"A sniper," he continues. "They missed the shot but it was close."

"Any leads?"

He looks back at me but doesn't answer my question. "Where have you been? I haven't heard from you. I was worried."

"I know and I'm sorry. I should have called."

His brow is strained, his face hard. "I got your key from reception. I thought I'd come up here and make sure you were alright." Once again, he stares up at the wall. "I never expected to find... this."

"Like I said, I just thought I could help."

He nods slowly and rests his hands on his hips, the tips of his fingers just touching the holster of his sidearm.

"Jasper, I -"

"Where were you today?"

I take a step back as my heart races so hard I can feel it smashing against my ribs. *He knows.*

As he meets my eye, an entire life that could have been flashes through my mind. Our first home together. Waking up in the middle of the night and finding each other in the dark. His fingers intertwined with mine on a sunny summer afternoon. Laughing, kissing, trust, love, forever... gone, just like that.

"Jasper, listen to me please," I begin. "I can explain."

Slowly he unclips the holster, never taking his eyes from mine. "CJ, where were you?"

"I never meant for this to happen."

He removes the gun and hesitates a moment before raising it toward me. "Who are you?"

I drop my eyes. The pain of knowing any future we might have had is now lost hits me like a bullet to the chest. Until this moment, avenging my past has felt right - necessary. But now as Jasper looks at me, his eyes a mix of pain and outrage, I realize with devastating clarity that I was wrong. Madelyn-May and I are no different. She felt betrayed by what happened to her and her sisters in that trailer. They were abused by their father, but even worse, they were forced to feel the heartbreak of having a mother who was unwilling to stop it. A mother who was unwilling to love her child enough to save her.

"I'm a person who has made mistakes, Jasper, but I can fix them. If you'll just let me explain."

"It was you," he says in a voice so quiet I wonder if even he doesn't want to hear the words out loud. "Why?"

"Harlow's mother," I manage. "She destroyed my family."

"So, what... you try and kill her daughter? Murder an innocent young girl in the process?"

Hearing it from his lips sounds ludicrous like I'm a deranged person. "You don't understand."

"No," he says, his tone adamant, "I don't."

"Can you please put the gun down?"

"I have to take you in, CJ," he tells me. "You've left me no choice."

"My name isn't CJ," I whisper. "It's Valentine."

"Jesus Christ," he breathes.

"I'm sorry. I never meant for any of this to happen."

"For any of what to happen? Falling in love with you?"

The words catch me unaware and pull the air from my lungs. "You love me?"

All my life I have wondered what it would feel like to be loved. I wondered if it really was like in the movies where people can't breathe without each other or if it would feel more like the comfort of a favorite sweater, reassuring and cozy. For me, life has always been about survival, about stopping people taking things from me. To be loved is something I never considered - until now.

"I thought I did, but clearly that was a mistake," he says. "I don't even know who you are."

Just a few steps would close the space between us. "Jasper, I'm so sorry. If I could take it all back I would. You have to believe me."

"You're sorry?"

"I didn't mean for this to happen."

"You know, you keep saying that CJ... Valentine... whatever your name really is, but it did happen. You played me."

"No, that's not true."

He shakes his head in clear disbelief and then seems to re-center himself. "CJ Sinclaire you're under arrest for the murder of Kempsey Karrigan and the attempted murder of Harlow Marozzi and Sophie Miller," he announces in a voice that is cold and unrecognizable.

"Jasper, no. Don't do this."

"Stay where you are and do not move." With his free hand, he reaches for his handcuffs never taking the gun off me.

"Don't, please. Let's talk. If you let me explain you'll understand. I know you will."

He steps closer and survival mode kicks in. I am a fighter. I always have been and to defend myself is natural instinct. Before he realizes what's happening, I launch a swift side blow to his forearm. It surprises him and the gun comes free. It clatters to the floor and our eyes meet.

"I don't want this," I try one last time. "I never wanted this." He glances at the gun on the floor and I know he's going to go for it. "Don't, Jasper, please."

Ignoring my pleas, he dives for it but my foot gets there first. I kick it further out of reach. He grabs at my leg, pulling me off balance. I fall to the floor and he rolls over attempting to pin me with his weight.

"Jasper, stop," I shout, but he doesn't listen.

We wrestle until my knee finds his groin and he rolls off, groaning in pain. I have to get the gun and unload it. I have to take it out of play before one of us gets hurt. As he gathers himself behind me, I crawl toward the gun and grab it by the muzzle.

"Stop!" he shouts and I hear the click of a bullet entering the chamber. "Just stop where you are. Don't make me shoot you, please."

Ankle holster. I know before I even turn around. "Okay," I tell him. "Alright. I'm stopping."

"Lay down on the ground and don't move. I mean it."

I do as he says, but slowly pull the gun in under my stomach. Within seconds he is standing over me, ordering me to put my hands behind my back. If I let him arrest me, my life is over.

In the moments I allowed myself to imagine a different life something changed in me. I know I want more. I want love. I want a life. I want a second chance - with him.

"Jasper, listen to me," I try. "I messed up. I know that. When I was a kid, I was left to fend for myself. I'm not proud of what I've done in my life, but it was the only way I could survive. You gave me hope. You made me imagine something different, that I could be different."

"Save it," he tells me. "I'm not stupid enough to fall for it again."

"I'm telling you the truth," I plead. "It's not too late for us. If you can just try to understand. Just give me a chance." I long to see his face but don't dare move.

"Even if that's true, do you really think I'd want to be with someone like you?" he asks. "You murdered an innocent teenager and tried to kill another. You're a sociopath. God knows what else you've done that I don't know about."

"No, you don't mean that."

"It makes me sick that I ever touched you," he tells me. "How could I have been so blind not to see it."

"Jasper please, don't say those things. You love me, remember?"

"Love you?" To my surprise, he laughs out loud. "I would never love someone like you and neither would anyone else."

The words strike me and I gasp as though I've been physically hit. Every muscle in my body tightens. Clenching and straining until my arms and legs ache. Every memory of feeling unloved, of being used, abused, and cast aside floods my mind. Heat sears through me and my entire body burns. My skin is alight. Blood rushes. A wild tide of agonizing pain. I squeeze my eyes closed. Try desperately to calm my heart but it's too late. My thoughts crash and collide in an uncontrollable rage. My mind explodes and I flip over to see the shock in his eyes. He glances at the gun in my hand and only hesitates for a second, but it's long enough for me to pull the trigger. Blood splatters across my face, sticky and hot as he falls back, his eyes still wide with surprise. His body hits the floor with a heavy thud and I close my eyes. I was so close, I think to myself. So close. But who was I kidding? Love stories and happy endings were never meant for people like me. Jasper was right. I was raised in the dirt with blood on my hands. I was never made to be loved.

I get to my feet and for the second time in my life, stare down at the body of someone I was stupid enough to open my heart to.

"I didn't want this," I whisper. "But you were right, a man like you would never love a woman like me."

I dress quickly, grab my belongings, and swing the weapons bag over my shoulder. At the door, I glance back at Jasper's body, and a single tear slips over my cheek. In his chest, is lodged the last of my pain, shot from a gun that I will take with me on my road to inevitable and absolute ruin.

Chapter Sixty-Five
HARLOW

I lean my head against the window. Outside the scenery transitions from a blur of concrete to a blur of green pastures. I want to cry but it would draw the attention of other passengers and that's the last thing I need. I have no idea where my parents are or what has happened to them, but what I do know is that I let Sophie down. If Poppy dies, it will be my fault just like it was with Kempsey.

The bus speeds along and passengers chat and laugh oblivious to the fact the world is falling in around me. I have never been to California and it feels like an entire world away. How do I know for sure that Lacy isn't setting me up? Out there no one can help me. I'll be all alone. I quickly remind myself that Sophie wouldn't have sacrificed her only chance to save Poppy unless she was sure it would be safe. It has to be.

As the hours slip by and day turns to night, I find myself thinking about my mother. There was a time many years ago, when she was close to my age, that she took a bus trip very similar to this one. After killing her father and setting the trailer alight, she ran from California and took a bus to Philadelphia where a stranger was to meet her and provide safe haven.

For so many years she kept her life a secret, but when Lacy was arrested for trying to kidnap my brother and me, the world found out about her past. When the story broke, my mom sat down with all of us and tried to explain. She cried when she spoke of what her father had done to her and why she couldn't have children of her own. She wouldn't look at me when she explained how she met Sophie and together they had conspired to keep a secret so big it could tear us all apart.

I was eleven then and didn't understand. All I heard was that she lied and used us to try and become someone she wasn't. I hated her and refused to find any compassion or sympathy for what she had been through. Looking back, I couldn't see how fortunate I was to have been spared a life so full of pain and struggle. All I could see was that she neglected us and put me and my brother in danger.

Outside an inky sky pushes against the horizon. Soon the other passengers will try to fall asleep. The seats are cramped and uncomfortable and I know that for me, sleep will not come. My mind is racing, trying to imagine my mom all those years ago on a bus just like this one, desperate to get away from the only home she had ever known. I always thought we were so different, that I had made myself into someone who would never be like her. But here I am on the same bus, making the same trip, in fear for my life for something that was never my fault to begin with.

For so long I have hated her and yet suddenly I long for her. My chest aches and I fidget in my seat as I realize that for the first time since I was eleven years old, I want my mom and she's nowhere to be found.

Chapter Sixty-Six
SOPHIE

After being grilled for more than seven hours by two FBI agents, I was finally allowed to go free. They asked question after question about why I allowed Harlow to pose as my daughter and if I knew the penalty for harboring a fugitive could be up to a year in prison. They wanted to know where Harlow might go next and if I expected her to make contact. In the end, I told them I didn't know where she would go but if it was my life in danger I would do everything I could to get out of the country, especially when my parents had a home on the other side of the world. I also took the opportunity to tell them everything I knew about Lacy, her granddaughter, and Madelyn-May's past. The agent and his partner took pages of notes, nodding and making grunting noises that I think meant they were listening. When we were finally done, I asked if the new information meant they would pivot their investigation and start searching for Lacy's granddaughter instead of Harlow. But all I got was a stiff reply that as always, they *would be following all available leads.*

Now that I'm finally back by Poppy's side, I let out a long breath and try to call Bastian again. I need to tell him where Harlow is but I don't dare do it over the phone even with the encrypted app. I need to see him in person. When the phone finally picks up my heart swells but my relief is short-lived.

"Hello, this is Madelyn-May."

"Oh..." I stammer, "I... it's Sophie."

"Sophie, where is my daughter?"

"That's why I'm calling," I tell her. "She's fine but we need to talk."

"Well, I assume you wanted Bastian but the FBI kept him for almost two days without sleep. I had no contact for you, and I have been out of my mind. I tried calling the hospital several times, but you were never there."

The words sting and I immediately feel guilty for not having been here by Poppy's side.

"I need to see one of you," I say, hating that I know it's going to be her. "We need to talk."

"Are you at the hospital?"

"Yes, I'm back and I won't be leaving again."

"Fine, I'm on my way. Bastian wanted to call you right away but his phone was dead. By the time it charged he passed out and I didn't have the password to get your number."

We're both making excuses for our failures, hoping we don't appear to each other as bad parents making terrible choices in what has to be the worst of situations.

"We're in the pediatric oncology ward. It's a long drive but you'll want to hear what I have to say."

When Madelyn-May arrives almost three hours later, she hovers in the doorway staring at Poppy.

"Would you like to meet her?" I ask quietly.

I follow her gaze to my sleeping child and wonder what she must be thinking. Poppy is not only the result of her husband's affair but everything she was unable to provide him - a naturally conceived child. It would be understandable if she bore ill will toward my daughter, but Poppy is also a terminally ill little girl. The clash of emotions for Madelyn-May must be enormous and I find myself lost for the right thing to say.

"No, I can't," she replies. "Maybe someday but not right now.'

Her tone is gentle and genuine and I understand why it's too hard for her. "Should we go to the café and talk?"

She nods and tears her eyes away from Poppy. "If it's not too much trouble would you mind if I charge my phone? The car charger wasn't working. I was on the road for hours. It's almost dead and Bastian will be calling wanting to know where Harlow is the minute he wakes up."

I plug Madelyn May's phone into my charger then give Poppy a gentle kiss on the forehead and we head down toward the café.

Inside, we take a seat as far away from other people as we can, and both lean in close. "I put Harlow on a bus to San Diego."

"You did what?" Madelyn-May immediately pulls back in surprise. "Why on earth would you send my daughter to California?"

"Lacy told me who is trying to kill Harlow."

"And?"

"It's her granddaughter. Do you know her?"

Immediately Madelyn-May shakes her head. "No, that can't be right. Harlow and Harry are Lacy's only grandchildren."

My stomach flip-flops and for the first time, I wonder if I have made a huge mistake trusting Lacy. "But I read the stories they wrote about you and your family back when Lacy was arrested. It said both you and your sister had been pregnant."

"Melody never had that baby."

"Are you certain?"

Madelyn-May falls silent and I wait for her to answer. "She couldn't have. That would be an abomination. He was our father. She was fifteen." I search her face and wonder again how she ever found the strength to survive what was done to her as a child. "No, she couldn't have," she says again. "It's impossible."

"But what if she did?"

Madelyn-May meets my eye and she openly shudders. "That would mean Melody's daughter would be almost thirty now." Her eyes cloud over, and I know without a doubt that in her mind she is back in the trailer park.

"This isn't your fault," I tell her quickly. "You didn't do any of this."

"But it's my fault this psychopath is after my daughter and that she killed an innocent girl in the process. She's doing it as payback for what I did all those years ago. If she is Melody's daughter then she's carrying out what Lacy started."

"That's where I think you're wrong," I say, shaking my head. "I think it was Lacy carrying out this girl's directions all along. Now, she's dying in prison and wants to set things right."

"Lacy is dying?"

I pause and remind myself that Lacy is still Madelyn-May's mother. "I'm sorry, that was thoughtless of me."

Madelyn-May shakes her head and looks lost in thought. "No, it's fine. I haven't seen her in so long. And after what she did..."

"From what I could tell when I went to see her she probably only has months left. My mother looked very much the same as her cancer progressed."

"And she wanted to help? You're sure?"

"She offered a safe place for Harlow to stay until this is resolved."

"In California."

"That's right."

"And you're sure she wasn't lying about wanting to make amends?"

I take a moment and center myself. "When my mother was dying, toward the end all she cared about was what she called '*crossing her I's and dotting her T's.* I think it helped her make peace with it all, knowing that everything had been said and settled and that there were no loose ends or regrets."

Madelyn-May clenches her jaw and looks me right in the eye. "I'm sure that's true, Sophie, but Lacy is not like other mothers. She doesn't have compassion or empathy, not that I ever saw anyway. I know you were trying to do the right thing, but there's every chance you just put my daughter on a bus straight to hell."

Chapter Sixty-Seven
VALENTINE

Sophie Miller. That's the name of the woman who has been helping Harlow. The day after I missed my shot at the prison this woman was hauled in by the FBI for questioning. It was the second story on last night's news bulletin. The first was the hunt for CJ Sinclaire the woman registered as staying in the room where FBI Special Agent Jasper Monroe's body was found.

Too bad for them CJ Sinclaire is a ghost. The truth is neither CJ nor any of my other aliases exist, simply because I don't exist. I have no birth certificate, no social security number, and no passport. My prints are not on file and I have never provided a DNA sample. Every identity I have is fake, and no one except Lacy knows my real name. Unlike regular people, my entire life has been lived under the radar. When they fingerprint the room, all they will find are dead ends.

Sophie, on the other hand, is a walking target. Within hours of her being taken to the FBI the media had reported her entire life story from losing her husband and child in a car crash to being a former book editor at Bastian Marozzi's publishing house. But the most helpful information of all was the part about her daughter. It seems Sophie has a terminally ill child who is receiving treatment at Maryland Harford Memorial.

When I arrive at the hospital, I look nothing like the woman Jasper claimed to have fallen in love with. My natural ebony hair is disguised by a blonde wig tied up in a ponytail and green contacts hide my bright blue eyes. At first glance, it would be impossible to link me to the grainy security camera images provided to the FBI by the hotel. So, it is with complete confidence that I stride into the hospital and search the directory for pediatric oncology. It's time to pay Sophie and her daughter a little visit.

Chapter Sixty-Eight
SOPHIE

"So, you'll go to see Lacy as soon as you get back to Philly?" I ask Madelyn-May as we walk back toward Poppy's room.

"Yes, as soon as I get on her approved visitor list. In the meantime, I'll organize a cancer specialist to go and see her. The minute she tells me where to find Harlow, Bastian and I will head out to California."

"Have you been back to California since everything happened?"

"No, I haven't," she says, "and it's not somewhere I ever planned on going again."

"I'm sorry I put her on that bus, Madelyn-May. I really was trying to do the right thing."

Madelyn-May nods but doesn't meet my eye. "Hopefully Lacy really was trying to make amends and Harlow will be safe. That's what I'm going to tell myself anyway. I'll know when I get to the prison. She never was a great liar."

"Well that's a good thing, right? Because she seemed genuine to me."

We walk the next few steps in silence and then Madelyn-May says something that causes my breath to catch. "He loves you, Sophie. Bastian, I mean."

"Oh... I..."

"He does and it's okay. It used to make me crazy thinking he would rather be with you. I was so jealous. But the truth is, our marriage was doomed from the start."

"But I know why you did those things," I tell her. "He must as well."

"He does," she says with a nod, "but it doesn't change the fact that he married a stranger."

Knowing I was involved in her lies makes it hard to find the right words, so I decide not to say anything at all.

"Sophie, do you recall when I said to you a long time ago that sometimes it's possible to measure our love by the secrets we keep?" she asks. "Well, I think there's also a freedom to be found in telling the truth. Not to another person but to yourself."

"I'm not sure I know what you mean?"

Madelyn-May stops in the corridor and turns to me. "For so long I blamed myself for everything that happened when I was a child. I told myself that I must have acted in a way that made my father think it was alright to touch me like that. I told myself that it was my fault Lacy didn't love me and that everything that happened after had to be my fault too because I'm the one who killed him. I blamed myself for the fact that Bastian and I's marriage fell apart because I kept things from him. But that wasn't the whole truth."

"No, what happened in your marriage was my fault too," I tell her. "I was part of it."

"No, that's exactly what I'm saying," she says. "I realized one day that what happened back in that trailer wasn't my fault. But for so many years I chose to believe that it was and do you know why?"

I shake my head.

"Because it hurt less than accepting the truth, that my parents didn't love me. Not like they were supposed to. It was easier, less painful, to tell myself that I was responsible because the real truth was something that I just couldn't bear to believe. It's the same with Bastian," she continues. "What I did was wrong, there are no two ways about that. But the truth I didn't want to tell myself was that if he really loved me, Sophie, it wouldn't have mattered how we had kids, or even if we had any at all. I would have been enough. But instead of facing that, I told myself it was the mistake I made that caused our marriage to fail. In many ways it was, but the real truth, the one I didn't want to tell myself, was that I never had his whole heart from the beginning. That's what broke us."

"Madelyn-May, he loves you. I'm sure he does." It's painful for me to say the words out loud and I wonder if I too have been unable to tell myself the truth - that I don't have his whole heart either.

"He does love me," she says. "But not like he loves you."

As we reach the door to Poppy's room, I look at Madelyn-May one last time and she holds my gaze. We don't say as much but I know in my heart that I will not see her again after this. As if reading my mind, she nods gently and steps inside the room to collect her phone. I follow her in and instantly we both stop where we are. A woman I have never seen before is sitting by Poppy's bed - and she has a knife in her hand.

Chapter Sixty-Nine

VALENTINE

"Well, isn't this quite the reunion," I say, as both Sophie, and to my surprise, Madelyn-May walk into the room.

"Who are you?" Sophie demands, her eyes moving quickly to the knife in my hand.

I move the blade closer and the little girl starts to cry.

"It's alright, sweetheart," Sophie coos, her arms outstretched toward her daughter. "Mommy's friend is just playing a little game. There's no need to be scared."

"Madelyn-May, this has been a long time coming," I say, unable to take my eyes off her as she stands there staring at me. I expected her to look terrified, like a fragile fawn frozen in the headlights but to my surprise, her eyes are hard, angry.

"You're Lacy's granddaughter?" she asks.

"That's right."

"And you've been hunting my daughter? Trying to kill her?"

"Two for two."

She takes a step toward me and I tighten my grip around the handle of the knife.

"Madelyn-May, no," Sophie whispers. "My daughter…"

Madelyn-May stops where she is and glares at me. "What do you want?"

"I want to know where precious little Harlow is," I tell her. "I want to finish this."

"Finish it?" Madelyn-May repeats. "You mean kill her."

"You catch on quick."

"I'm not responsible for your mother's death," Madelyn May says, her voice coming out as a hiss. "I know that's what this is about, but she was my sister. She was the only one who understood what it was like to live in that place, to have him come into our room every night. You have no idea what he did to us. I would never hurt her."

"But you did hurt her. You hurt her more than anyone," I tell her, "because you left her there to rot."

"No, we were both supposed to run."

"Well, she didn't."

"Then that was her choice," Madelyn-May spits, "and I hate her for making it because it killed her."

I can't believe the audacity. All these years I imagined meeting Madelyn-May, I pictured her cowering, remorseful, and afraid of me. Now the moment has arrived and instead she has the nerve to challenge me. "You made that choice for her when you abandoned her," I hiss. "You thought you were so much better than us like you deserved to be special, for the whole world to love you. But you're not special. You're nothing."

"That's not true. I loved my sister."

"No, you didn't," I hiss. "You wouldn't know the first thing about what it takes to be a good sister."

I watch as Madelyn-May struggles to fight back her tears. If she thinks I'm going to feel sorry for her she is greatly mistaken.

"It was Melody's idea to kill Daddy," she whispers. "When she found out she was pregnant with you she was so full of hate, so angry. She hated Daddy in a way that consumed her. She got the pills. She wanted to drug him and have me hold a pillow over his face. I wasn't sure at first but she was doing it with or without me. That much was clear."

"You're lying. She had nothing to do with it. It was you. It was all you."

"After he was drunk, he forced us both to join him in the bedroom," she continues, ignoring my accusations. He made me watch them together. I couldn't bear seeing him do those things to her and at some point, I just snapped. I was so sick of him betraying us and calling it love. When I picked up the hammer it just happened, like a dream."

"You're lying," I manage again, this time through clenched teeth. "That's not what happened." I search her face for any sign of anger, malice, or cruel intent but instead find only sadness.

"When Lacy came in and saw what I'd done she wanted to call the police, but your mom wouldn't have it," she continues. "She begged me to kill Lacy so we wouldn't go to prison. After that, she lit the fire and we ran. We thought they were both dead. It was only after we were out that we heard Lacy screaming."

"No, you're just trying to blame her for what you did."

"What we both did," she tells me through tear-stained eyes. "It was what we both did."

I breathe in through my nose, deep and long. My mother always told me that it was Madelyn-May who killed our daddy with the claw hammer and set the trailer alight. That's what I have always believed. It's what I need to believe because if what she is saying is true, I will be nothing more than a girl who has set fire to everything in her life.

"You're lying," I tell her with desperate conviction. "You're responsible for what happened and everything that came after. You need to say you did it. You need to be sorry."

"She never should have gone back there," Madelyn-May says, once again ignoring me. "That night was our one chance to get out and start over. To leave that filthy place behind."

"She was pregnant. Where was she supposed to go?"

"Anywhere!" Madelyn-May shouts suddenly, catching me off guard. "Anywhere but that abomination of a trailer park."

I want to kill her just to make her stop talking. "You're trying to trick me, just like you do to everyone."

"I can see you're confused," she says. "But please listen to me. Don't waste your life on a lie because it's easier than facing the truth. Your mom wanted him dead. I killed him. She set the trailer alight and then we ran. Those are the facts. I don't know why she chose to go back and more than anything I wish she didn't, but she did. So, believe me, when I tell you whatever happened as a result of that choice was not my fault and I will not let you harm my daughter because of it. This stops here. Today."

My mind is spinning. Jasper is dead and any second chance I might have had at life died along with him. If what Madelyn-May says is true then I killed him for nothing. I could have walked away at any time. If what she says is true then I have wasted my entire life fighting nothing more than shadows and ghosts.

"You have no idea what happened after you left," I manage, "or what I lost because of it."

"I know you lost your mom and I'm sorry for that."

"My mom," I say with a scoff. "Some mom she was. Always high. She never took care of me anyway."

She shakes her head and lets out a long breath. "I can only imagine how hard it was for her to go back there, but that doesn't justify you hurting innocent people. All these terrible things you're doing, you're just making yourself more and more like them."

I force a laugh and hope she cannot see any sign of the overwhelming fear beginning to swell in my chest. "I am them," I tell her. "And they are me. Every part of their pain and betrayal is in my blood. And if you don't tell me where Harlow is one of your daughters is going to die." I look at Sophie and push the knife hard enough to make the child cry. "You decide which one."

"Don't you tell her, Sophie," Madelyn-May warns.

I push the blade in just far enough to nick the tender skin on the child's neck. She cries harder and a rosebud of blood blooms up from the tip of my knife.

"Okay! Alright," Sophie cries. "I know where she is."

"Sophie, no." Madelyn-May spins around to face the other woman. "Don't tell her anything. You were right about Lacy. Harlow is safe. This psycho doesn't know where she is. Don't say a word."

When she says Lacy's name my ears prick up immediately. I refuse to let them see my surprise but the pain of knowing Lacy has betrayed me is like a knife in my chest.

"Just please put the knife down," Sophie tries again. "You don't have to do this."

I nod slowly and stroke Poppy's head with my free hand. "Sophie, do you know what happens when the blade of a knife slits someone's throat?"

"Just stop, please."

"First, the blade severs the trachea which is handy because it prevents the victim from being able to scream and shout. Second, it severs the carotid artery stopping their blood from circulating. Lastly, and my personal favorite, is that it severs the jugular which quickly drains all the existing blood from their brain. We are in a hospital which is in little Poppy's favor but in my experience, a victim has about thirty seconds, maybe a minute before they bleed out. So, what do you think, Sophie? You think they'll make it in time?"

As I wait for her to answer, I push the knife deeper, drawing a second drop of blood. "You could try screaming out for a doctor or nurse. They might get here in time. Little Poppy will never speak, or laugh, or sing a song again, but they might save her life."

"Sophie, don't you tell her a thing. She's bluffing you."

"Am I?" I grin. "I wasn't bluffing when I warned that girl in Philly to get out of my way or when Jasper tried to take me into the FBI."

"You killed the FBI agent?"

"Tell me where she is." I push the child's head to the right so Sophie can see the knife begin to slice her skin.

"Alright! San Diego. I put her on a bus to San Diego."

"Sophie!" Madelyn-May gasps and stares at her.

"I'm sorry, but it's an entire city. Harlow could be anywhere. She won't find her."

"But that's where you're wrong," I tell her. "There's only one place in San Diego that Lacy would send Harlow and I know exactly where it is."

Chapter Seventy
SOPHIE

The woman moves the knife away from Poppy's throat and I finally take a breath. What I have just done is a betrayal to Harlow and Madelyn-May but what choice did I have? This woman is clearly capable of murder and she was threatening my daughter.

"Don't bother trying anything clever," the woman warns, stepping away from the bed. "I'm walking out of here and neither of you is going to stop me."

But Madelyn-May steps in front of the door, her feet planted firmly in place. "Like hell you are."

The woman eyes us both, clearly assessing the situation. "Step aside Madelyn-May, I mean it."

"Do you really think I'm going to let you walk out of here so you can kill my daughter?"

"I do," she says, pulling a handgun from the back of her pants and pointing it at us. "Now move."

"Madelyn-May..." I breathe, "now what?"

"You think I'm not willing to die for my child?" Madelyn-May hisses. "Shoot me."

The woman hesitates and then smiles. "I'd love to but that's too easy."

"You're not walking out of here."

The woman turns her gaze to me and instead points the gun toward Poppy. "Tell her to move."

"Madelyn-May..." I whisper, "please don't let her shoot my baby."

It's a stand-off as we all wait for the other to make a move. I glance at Poppy. She's staring wide-eyed at the gun, clearly terrified. Since the day my son was killed, I blamed myself. I should have been in the car with him. I should have been there by the side of the road. I should have stopped him from going to soccer. I should have done a million things, but Madelyn-May's words ring in my mind and I wonder - was it really my fault, or is that something that's just easier to believe? If it was my fault, that means it was controllable, something I can understand. All these years, have I held onto that blame because despite the pain it brings, it's better than believing that the world is so dangerously random it can steal your child while you take an afternoon nap.

I look at Poppy and the woman holding a gun at her. I told myself Poppy's illness was my fault because it was caused by my cancer-prone genes, my geriatric body. I took the blame because it was easier than believing the truth, that the worst things in life are completely out of our control.

"Get that gun off my child," I say suddenly, in a voice that doesn't sound like my own.

"And what are you going to do about it?" the woman snaps. "I'll shoot her if you scream out. Right in the face. So, tell Madelyn-May to step aside."

I'm tired of taking the blame for things I cannot control. The world might be a terrifyingly random place, but I do have a choice. I can choose how to respond and as I look at this woman holding a gun at my child I choose to fight.

"You did this," I say, turning to Madelyn-May and hoping she understands what I'm doing. "All of this is your fault."

"Don't blame it on me," she says, stepping forward. "You wouldn't be involved in any of this if you'd just stayed out of our lives to begin with."

From the corner of my eye, I see the woman on the other side of the bed look from me to Madelyn-May and back again.

"You were the one who approached me in the park that day," I continue, opening my eyes a little wider to make sure she takes the hint. "Not the other way around."

"Oh, so it's my fault you slept with my husband?"

"Hey!" the woman shouts, but we keep going.

"He slept with *me*," I taunt her. "For years."

Madelyn-May suddenly lunges at me and we begin to struggle.

"Hey!" the woman shouts again before taking the gun off Poppy and pointing it at us.

Step One.

On our side of the room, we continue to struggle. I pull at Madelyn-May's hair and she pushes her elbow up into my face.

"I will shoot you!" the woman threatens.

Poppy starts to scream but I can't stop now.

"I hate you," I hiss at Madelyn-May. "I hate you."

Furious that we are no longer paying attention to her, the woman strides around the bed and tries to pull us apart.

Step two.

Catching her unaware, simultaneously Madelyn-May and I turn and throw all our weight against her and she stumbles back losing her balance. The gun falls free and Madelyn-May quickly kicks it to the other side of the room.

"I'm taking you to the FBI," I tell her, my voice unwavering, "then Harlow will finally be safe."

But to my surprise, the woman responds by suddenly screaming out. "Help me! They're trying to kill me!"

Madelyn-May and I exchange a surprised glance as a nurse appears in the doorway.

"Oh my God! What is going on?"

"Help me please," she cries out again. "They're attacking me!"

"She tried to kill my child," I shout over the top of her. "Get security."

When the security guard arrives red-faced and winded from running, he immediately pulls out a taser and points it at Madelyn-May and me. "Let the woman go!"

"She killed a girl in Philadelphia," I shout. "And she just tried to kill my daughter. You have to call the FBI. They're looking for the wrong person."

"They're lying," she cries. "They attacked me."

"Everyone just shut up!" he yells. "The police are on their way."

Step Three.

But from the corner of my eye, I see the woman reach for something in the side of her boot. "Madelyn-May lookout! The knife!"

She lunges and Madelyn-May leaps forward to avoid the blade. The guard shouts and fires his taser but Madelyn-May is in his line of sight and she goes down, instantly stunned.

"No! What did you do!" I cry out. "That woman has a knife."

But it's too late. She leaps to her feet and body slams the confused guard, quickly knocking him off balance. As he topples over, the woman pulls her knife on the nurse standing in the doorway who quickly steps out of the way. And just like that, she's gone.

Chapter Seventy-One

HARLOW

When the bus finally arrives in San Diego, I follow a line of tired, body-odor-riddled passengers down the aisle and out into the fresh air. It's the first time I've ever been to a coastal city and the scent of salt water immediately washes over me. Despite the crisp chill in the air, the sun is out and it would be easy to feel like this could be a new start. But deep down I know that I will never be able to start over. Not here or anywhere else. Not until this is finally over.

I walk out to the sidewalk and look around. Sophie said someone would be here to meet me but everyone is starting to disperse and I don't see anyone who looks like they might be waiting for me.

"You're Harlow, right?"

From behind me, a woman appears from nowhere causing me to jump. She looks to be in her late twenties and is extremely pretty with long black hair and striking blue eyes.

"Yes. Are you who I am supposed to meet?"

"I'm Casey-Jane," she tells me with a smile. "Lacy said you'd be coming."

I nod and shift my weight awkwardly from one foot to the other. "How do you know Lacy?"

"Don't worry about that right now," she tells me. "All that matters is getting you off the streets and away from prying eyes, if you know what I mean."

"So, you know why I'm here?"

"You're wanted by the FBI, Harlow, of course I know. Now come on. We can't stay out on the street."

She ushers me around the corner and into a white SUV parked just a few meters away. When we get inside, I notice right away the car smells brand new and there isn't a speck of dust anywhere to be seen. I glance around and see a rental car ad wrapped around the passenger side sun visor.

"I don't have a car," she says, noticing my confusion. "I hired this one so I could get you home without anyone seeing us."

I nod and put on my seat belt. Something doesn't feel right and an overwhelming urge to run scratches at my insides.

"How was the trip?" she asks.

"It was... long."

"I bet."

"Where are we going?" I ask, keen to settle my nerves.

"To my place. I live alone so you'll be safe there."

"Can I call my mom when we get there?"

"I don't think that's a good idea. They'll be tracing her calls for sure. Now that you've come all this way we can't go taking any chances now can we?"

Once again, I nod as the urge to run gets even stronger. I have no idea who this person is or why she's doing this and now that I think about it, it makes no sense. Why would a total stranger risk harboring someone wanted for murder?

"Casey-Jane, can I ask you -"

"Oh please, call me CJ."

"CJ..." I begin again, "why are you helping me? It seems like a big risk to take."

"Because I owe Lacy a favor. She saved my life once. Debts like that have to be paid back."

"She did?"

"Well, she didn't know it at the time but to me it still counts."

It feels like every question I ask only leaves me more confused. For the rest of the trip, we ride in silence, she watching the road ahead and me looking over my shoulder.

Chapter Seventy-Two

SOPHIE

When Madelyn-May shook off the effects of the taser, all she cared about was finding Harlow. Right now, she is on her way back to Philadelphia to meet Bastian and I'm headed back to the prison to see Lacy. I'm already on her visitor list so it's faster than waiting for reference checks and approval from the warden for Madelyn-May to get access.

The plan is for Madelyn-May and Bastian to get the first plane out of Philadelphia to San Diego. As soon as I have an address I will call and leave a voicemail so they have it the moment they land. There's just one problem. I lean in and turn up the car radio.

"Five states are bracing for wild weather as blizzard conditions move toward the east coast," the announcer says, as I turn up the volume. *"In the coming hours more than two feet of snow is expected to fall across New York, Philadelphia, and New Jersey, while to the south Delaware is also expected to receive heavy coverage accompanied by wild winds and dangerous ocean swells."*

The last time a spring blizzard battered the east coast all flights out of Philadelphia International, JFK, LaGuardia, and Newark were grounded. Hopefully, Madelyn-May and Bastian get to the airport before they start canceling flights.

I lean over the dash and peer up toward the sky. Ominous clouds have suffocated the sun and the world is growing dark. With a heavy feeling in my heart, I step on the gas and pray that Madelyn-May and Bastian make it onto a flight before it's too late.

Chapter Seventy-Three

HARLOW

After a fifteen-minute drive, CJ pulls into the driveway of a small bungalow-style house on a pretty tree-lined street. I have no idea what I was expecting but it wasn't this. Given her association with Lacy, I expected a small, dirty apartment or a place that felt transient. But this home has a colorful, well-maintained flower bed, and a quaint porch with cane loungers and a scattering of pot plants.

"This is your place?" I ask, as we climb out of the car and follow a curving path of stepping stones toward the front door.

"It is," she tells me. "I've been here for about five years now."

"By yourself?" I ask. "You must have a good job."

"I'm an art curator at a local gallery."

She opens the front door and I follow her in to find a warm living room decorated in pastel pinks and grays. There are house plants in cane pots and sprawling cream rugs across hardwood floors.

"This is really lovely," I tell her. "You're lucky to have a place that's so nice."

"Nothing to do with luck," she says with a smile. "Life hasn't always been easy, but I worked hard. Your room is the first door down the hall. Go and settle in. I'll make a pot of herbal tea to help you relax."

When I step into the bedroom it's just as welcoming as the rest of the home, full of pastel tones and pretty pot plants. I sit down on the edge of the bed and stare at the pillows with longing. The bus ride was so long and I'm so tired.

As if reading my mind, she appears in the doorway holding a towel and a pair of pajamas. "You look like you wear about the same size as me. Why don't you take a hot shower then you can rest."

"I would actually love that," I say. "Thank you so much, for everything."

The welcoming home and its soft furnishings have put my mind at ease. I still don't understand why she's helping me, but this is not the home of a criminal. It can't be.

"You're welcome, Harlow. Now go take a shower."

If it's possible I feel even more tired after the shower. The hot water has made my arms and legs feel heavy and I'm struggling to keep my eyes open.

"Your tea is ready," CJ calls, as I shuffle down the hall.

"I don't want to be ungrateful," I tell her, "but I'm not much of a tea drinker and I can hardly keep my eyes open."

"Here," she says, pushing the mug into my hand. "It will help you sleep."

"I really don't think I'll need any help."

"It's good for you. Go on, drink it."

She stares at me with an expectant look and I feel like it would be rude to say no. She has already done so much for me. So, I force a smile and to her obvious delight, begin to sip the tea.

"There you go," she says with a smile. "You'll be fast asleep in no time."

When I'm halfway through the cup, I notice a strange tingling begin to creep up my arms. I suddenly feel dizzy and struggle to focus my eyes. "What's... what's happening?"

"Come on," CJ says, taking my arm. "Let's go."

"Go where?"

She leads me up the hall toward the bedroom.

"What's happening?" I mumble. "What did you give me?"

She guides me down onto the bed and no matter how much I long to run, my body refuses to move.

"What did you do?" I say as best I can. "What... did... you...?"

My eyes close and my words slur. Within seconds I am out cold with no idea that CJ remains staring down at me.

Chapter Seventy-Four
SOPHIE

When at first Lacy didn't want to give me the address to the house in San Diego, I had a sinking feeling that I sent Harlow into harm's way. But Lacy was nothing if not a hustler and the promise that Madelyn-May had organized a visit from an oncologist soon had her sharing the address where Harlow would be staying.

I call Bastian's phone expecting to leave a message but to my surprise he answers.

"Why aren't you on the plane?"

"All flights in and out are delayed. This damned weather."

As he says the words, the first flurry of snow begins to fall across the prison parking lot. "Shit," I swear. "Now what?"

"This granddaughter, whoever she is, if she got an earlier flight she'll be there by now, Sophie. She's had too much of a head start for us to catch up."

"Bastian, I'm so sorry. She was threatening Poppy's life."

"It's an impossible situation," he says. "I feel like no matter what we do we lose."

The line falls silent as a snowflake flutters onto my arm and then quickly melts. Any hope of saving Poppy and Harlow is disappearing before our eyes and there's nothing we can do to stop it.

"All we can do is wait," he says. "They say maybe in a few hours if the front eases. If we take the car it's a forty-hour drive and that's if we don't stop and the roads are clear. Our only hope is the storm doesn't get as bad as they think and flights resume. Like I said, all we can do is wait."

I nod but forget to speak out loud. I have let everyone down. Now there's every chance both Poppy and Harlow will be lost to us forever.

Chapter Seventy-Five
VALENTINE

She looks so peaceful sound asleep in the bed. I watch her and wonder what she's dreaming but then realize I really don't care. All I care about is my own dream of slicing her open and watching her bleed out across these crisp white sheets. Then again, I could smother her instead. It would be quieter, and cleaner. She might not even wake up. It would be the compassionate thing to do, which is exactly why I dismiss the idea just as quickly as it comes. No one has ever shown me any compassion so why should I give her a peaceful death? I want Madelyn-May to read all the gory details, to know her daughter was sliced and diced, mutilated beyond recognition.

I turn the hunting knife over in my palm. Satisfaction is so close now. I watch the gentle rise and fall of her chest and feel my skin prickle with anticipation. I have longed for this moment. I have killed for it. All I have to do now is push my blade into her neck and watch it open up like a dark red rose.

I step forward and close my fingers tight around the knife. Madelyn-May was lying when she said what happened at the trailer park was my mother's idea. She almost had me but that's what Madelyn-May does. She tricks people into believing her. She did it to millions of women all over the world with that blog of hers but unlike them, I know who she is and what she's capable of. This kill is justified. It's right.

I tense my arm ready to slice Harlow open but before I have the chance to draw blood, behind me the door opens and for the first time since I was nine years old, I see her. My sister.

"Valentine." She is standing in the doorway, my name lingering on her lips as though it was inevitable.

"Hello, CJ."

Looking at her is like looking into a mirror. We share our father's bright blue eyes and Melody's long black hair. We are identical in every way and yet our lives could not be more different.

"You shouldn't be here, Valentine," she tells me, ignoring the knife in my hand. "You're not welcome in my home."

I glance at precious sleeping Harlow and nod. "I know that."

"And yet here you are."

I don't dare meet her eye in case her gaze causes me to falter. "I have to finish this. I have no choice."

At first, she doesn't respond and without looking I know she's staring at Harlow. "I'm not going to let you hurt her, Valentine. You must know that."

"And how do you plan on stopping me? You wouldn't have the first clue how to protect her from someone like me."

"I'll call the police."

"Come on, CJ, we both know they won't make it in time." Finally, our eyes meet and we stare at each other across the bed. I flip the knife over in my palm just for effect. "You know you can't stop me."

"I can try."

I chuckle and shake my head. "You're only brave because you know I won't hurt you."

"You've hurt me just by coming here," she says. "We've been over this. No matter how many times you invite me into your life I'm always going to say no. Pushing your way in and trying to hurt people only makes me more certain that it's the right decision."

I swallow the lump in my throat and focus all my strength on not letting her make me cry. "I don't want you in my life either, CJ, I got over that a long time ago." She nods but we both know it's a lie. "It must be nice to stand there judging me," I continue, a hiss creeping into my voice. "You weren't the one who was left behind."

Unlike me, CJ doesn't bother to hide her tears. She lets them fall freely over her cheeks and I marvel at her ability to show emotion so easily. Perhaps it comes from having a mom who loved you, even if she didn't carry you in her womb for nine months.

"Leaving wasn't my choice, Valentine," she tells me, her voice carrying the weight of weariness and frustration. "Lacy sold me to Denise when we were ten years old. I know you remember."

Memories instantly flood my mind of the afternoon CJ was taken by the hand of a woman wearing a blue floral dress and pink shoes and put into the back of a waiting sedan. When the car pulled away, I ran after it so fast I thought my lungs would explode. I ran and ran along the gravel road leading out of the trailer park until the car pulled onto the freeway and was swallowed up by the glare of the sun.

"You don't know everything about that day, CJ," I tell her. "I was a good sister."

She folds her arms across her chest and stares at me. "What are you talking about?"

"Lacy was going to send me with that lady. She wanted to be rid of me because I was too headstrong and always getting into trouble. But I begged her to send you instead. I told her I could make money for the trailer, that she needed me to stay."

"No, I remember what happened."

"No, CJ, you don't. That charmed life you had could have been mine but I stayed behind for you."

"Why?" she asks, with a shrug of her shoulders. "Why would you do that?"

"You really don't know?"

Silence finds its place between us and for a moment I allow myself to go back. From the moment we were born we were inseparable. In that trailer park with its rusty swings and constant smell of pot hanging in the air, we had been each other's salvation. Some afternoons we would go out to the dirt road and run as fast as we could, our fingers linked, our hair wild, shouting that we'd run away and never go back. We told each other stories of the house we'd live in together someday. A place with pretty gardens and comfortable beds. CJ said she'd be a model and I would be an actor in the movies. We were going to make our own rules, just she and I against the world.

"Because you're my sister," I tell her, pulling myself back to the present. She casts her eyes away, but I continue to stare, willing her to look at me. "Sending you away that day was the only good thing I've ever done."

"Well, that was your choice," she says, still not looking at me. "I never asked you to do that."

"You didn't have to. You wouldn't have survived the life I had there."

She finally looks at me through tear-stained eyes. "I know the things we said back then, Valentine, the things we promised each other. But it was so long ago. You can't expect me to be a part of... this." She gestures toward Harlow. "I know it must have been hard for you, but you need support. You need mental help."

"Oh, I need help?" I laugh. "You're the one pretending to be someone you're not. You grew up with the same dirt beneath your nails as I did, CJ. The only reason your life turned out different was because of the freedom I gave you. You have no idea what it was like for me there without you but I was never sorry. When things got really bad the only thing that kept me going was knowing that you were out there somewhere and that one day I'd find you and we could be together again."

"Valentine..."

"You and Madelyn-May are the same," I snap. "You think because you got out, you're better than the rest of us. Better than me."

She studies my face and takes a step back. "Is that what this is all about? You can't bring yourself to hurt me so you're taking everything out on Madelyn-May instead?"

"She did the same thing. She left mom and never came back for her. If she hadn't done that none of this would have happened."

"You thought I'd come back for you?" she asks. "I... Valentine, I thought you'd be long gone by the time we were grown. It never crossed my mind to go back there."

I nod and force back my tears. "No, I had to find you and even then you wanted nothing to do with me."

"It was too late," she tells me quietly. "Your life was... not something I could be a part of."

Once again, my mind pulls back to the day Lacy came home with a woman dressed to the nines driving a fancy car. I knew immediately what she had in mind. A child was a blank cheque and one she needed to cash. I also knew my sister would not survive life in the trailer park alone with Lacy.

I flip the knife over in my hand and silently scream at myself. "I saved you."

"Oh, Valentine," she says with a sigh, "we were just kids."

"But it was real," I tell her. "I meant all those things we said. Didn't you mean them too?"

She looks at me and all I see is sadness and pity. "Things change. We've changed. I paint now. I've spent the past month barely leaving the house so I could finish my work on an exhibit I have coming up. I have things I want to accomplish, Valentine, dreams and - "

"So?"

"So, you've killed people. You're a thief and a criminal. I can't have that in my life. I want something different than we had growing up."

"I had to do those things. I had no choice."

"I know it was tough there, believe me, I remember. But you didn't have to become..." once again she looks at the knife and shakes her head "...this. Please, just put down the knife and walk away. I won't say anything. You were never here. Just leave this poor girl and her mother in peace."

I consider what she's asking and wish that I could do it. The way she says *leave this poor girl and her mother in peace* makes me feel like a scourge bringing suffering to everyone around me. Under the weight of her gaze, I am a virus. An untreatable legacy of pain and suffering that refuses to go away. Every part of me wants to hand her the knife and leave. The child in me cries out to do what she wants, to try one last time to win her back. She is the only person I have ever loved and yet I can't make myself give in. Instead, I squeeze my eyes and feel my body tense with a self-hatred so strong it devours any chance of changing my mind. My fingers tighten on the blade and I decide to stop trying.

"I'm sorry, CJ, but I can't do that."

"Then I'm calling the police," she says. "You've left me no choice."

And with those words, I know that it is she who has left me no choice. She takes out her cell phone and starts to dial but I am around the bed and on her before she has a chance to complete the call.

"Valentine, no!" she screams, but it's too late. I already have my knife at her throat.

Chapter Seventy-Six

SOPHIE

I try Bastian's phone again and hope more than anything it goes to message bank, that he is on a plane, but to my dismay he picks up.

"Still no flights?" I ask, my hope sinking.

"They're starting up again now. There was one seat on the last flight out. Madelyn-May should be arriving in San Diego right about now."

"She went alone?"

"It was that or nothing," he says. "She wants to make things right with Harlow. She begged me to let her go. What was I supposed to do?"

"Tell her that you're going to save your daughter," I tell him with a little more judgment than I had intended.

"That's not fair, Sophie."

I immediately hate myself for blaming him. All three of us have done everything possible to try and save Harlow. I have no doubt that somewhere deep-down Madelyn-May blames herself and the fractured relationship she has with her daughter for the entire mess they're in. It makes sense she would want to be the one to make it right, but I know what we're up against. If there's a confrontation, Bastian would have had a better chance of overpowering that woman.

"You're right," I tell him gently. "I'm sorry. I shouldn't have said that."

He lets out a long sigh and I wait to see if he will let it go. "How's Poppy doing?"

And to my relief he does. "She's hanging in there. Hopefully we find a donor from the register in time otherwise..."

Neither of us elaborates or gives the sentence an ending. The thought is too painful.

"And how are *you* doing?"

Despite my earlier judgmental tone his voice is warm and caring. I feel his arms wrap around me. When I answer my voice is brittle, about to break. "I'm alright."

"Sophie..."

"I have to be," I tell him, desperate to find my own strength. "No matter what happens she needs me by her side. I have to be strong enough for the both of us."

"I'm sorry I can't be there with you."

"I know," I tell him. "We could get lucky. Maybe they'll catch this lunatic in time and Harlow will make it back to the hospital."

"If anyone deserves a miracle it's you, Soph," he says. "I'm going to do everything I can to save both our girls. I know I haven't met her yet but I do want to be Poppy's dad. I need you to know that."

Since Poppy was born, I have never allowed myself to imagine her with Bastian. The idea of him being present in her life, of her calling him Daddy and taking his hand is quicksand. If I take even one step the dream will devour me. But hearing him say that he wants to be her dad instantly tugs at my heart and it's impossible not to hope.

"She'd like that," I tell him. "I would too."

"Don't lose that hope, Soph," he tells me. "It's not over yet."

Chapter Seventy-Seven

HARLOW

Slowly I open my eyes and try to get my bearings. The room is unfamiliar and my face feels puffy and swollen with sleep. The bus trip. The woman who picked me up. The cup of tea. I try to think back. A distant memory plays over in my mind of two women arguing. Sisters and something about being left behind. Was there someone else in his room, I wonder. Or was it nothing more than a dream?

I pull myself up and try to clear my head. The clock on the bedside table reads four o'clock and from the filtered light falling in under the window shades I know it's afternoon.

Eventually, I let my legs fall over the side of the bed. My old clothes are where I left them bunched on a chair in the corner but when I pick them up the smell alone is enough for me to step out into the hall still wearing the pajamas CJ loaned me.

"Hello? Is anyone here?"

The house is still. I wander through the living room and out into the kitchen. Everything is in its place and the scent of lemon drifts up from the bench tops.

"CJ? Are you here?"

"You're up."

I spin around to find her standing behind me in the doorway. "Oh, you scared me," I say clutching at my chest. "I thought you must have gone out."

"Nope, I'm right here."

She doesn't say anything more. Instead, she stands staring at me, a grin on her face that doesn't reach her eyes.

"So, hey did you, like, put something in my tea before?" I ask. "I was out cold."

"Just a little something to help you rest."

I nod but feel uncomfortable about the idea of her putting something in my drink, especially given that was how this whole thing started. "Was someone else here before? I thought I heard someone."

"You were probably just dreaming," she says.

I take her in and try to put my finger on what's different about her. "Can we talk?" I ask. "I really don't know what I'm meant to do while the FBI finds this person who's trying to kill me. Do I just stay here in the house? I mean, how long do you think it will take?"

"Guess it depends on how clever the killer is."

The word killer and the way it hangs on her lips immediately sends a cold shiver down my spine. "What kind of person hunts teenagers anyway?" I ask. "She really needs some mental help."

"Maybe she feels like it's justified."

"Justified?" I sit down on the couch and shake my head. "What's justified about trying to kill me when I had nothing to do with anything? And what about poor Kempsey? What did she ever do other than being a bitch at school?"

CJ shrugs and walks over to the kitchen. "Maybe she just got in the killer's way. "

Coming here was a mistake and all I want to do is go home - if I had one. "So, do you think I could call my mom and dad? They'll be worried."

"No, it's too risky," she says. "I think it would be better if - "

"Harlow?" Suddenly someone is yelling and pounding on the front door. "Harlow, it's Mom. Are you in there?" I leap to my feet as CJ stops dead and stares in the direction of the front door.

"Harlow?" the voice calls again.

"Mom!" For all the times I've cursed and thought I hated her, I have never been so happy to hear her voice.

Before CJ can respond, I dash over to the front door and pull it open. Like always, my mom looks perfect dressed in nothing fancier than jeans and a windbreaker. I laugh out loud as I throw my arms around her. "I can't believe you're here."

I know my affection has taken her by surprise because it takes a moment for her to react. But then she quickly pulls me close and strokes the back of my head. "My God, Harlow, I've been worried sick, your dad too. He wanted to come but there's a snowstorm back on the east coast. I was lucky to get one seat on a flight out."

"Come inside," I tell her. "Come meet Lacy's friend CJ."

But the moment my mom steps inside and sees CJ she stops and pulls me in behind her. "Sweetheart, that's not Lacy's friend. It's her granddaughter."

I look out from behind my mom's back at the woman who has been giving me shelter.

"Stay away from my daughter," my mom threatens. "I swear to God I will kill you myself."

"Whoa, just calm down," CJ says, her arms stretched out before her, "I am Lacy's granddaughter, but I'm not her only granddaughter. There's also Valentine, my sister. That's who was trying to hurt Harlow, not me. We look alike. She's my twin."

"Mom, it's true," I say. "She hasn't tried to hurt me."

"Lacy asked me to protect Harlow until this is over and that's exactly what I've been doing," CJ says. "You have my word."

"And Valentine?" my mom asks. "Where is she?"

"I have no idea," CJ says with a shrug. "Hopefully somewhere far away from here."

"No, she was coming here to hurt Harlow. She told me herself."

But CJ just shakes her head. "I have no idea. I haven't seen my sister or any of my family since I was a kid."

"Then you must have got out," my mom says. "Away from the trailer park."

CJ thinks a moment and then says, "In a way you could say that. I didn't look back, let's put it that way. But now that you're here can I get you anything? Tea? Coffee?"

I can tell from my mom's face that she's still not convinced CJ and this house are safe.

"No, nothing for me," my mom says. "I'm just here to collect Harlow."

"Collect her?"

"You are?" I ask as hope swells in my chest.

"Do you have any things here?" my mom asks. "If you do go and get them and get dressed. You can't go out in pajamas."

I nod quickly and head up the hall to change back into my old clothes despite their smell. As I dress, I promise myself never to hate on my mom again. She has come all this way to find me and to help me. From now on, no matter what happens I'll try to be a better daughter. I'll try and make things right between us.

When I'm dressed and ready to go, I head out of the bedroom but stop when I hear a thumping sound coming from a room further up the hall. Unsure if I'm imagining it, I tilt my head to one side and listen again. Three thumps, then what sounds like a muffled voice.

"Hello?" I call out. "Is someone there?" I turn and slowly, one step at a time, make my way down the hall. When I reach the bedroom door furthest from the front of the house, the sound grows louder and there's no doubt in my mind that someone is inside.

"Hello?" I try again, turning the knob and finding it locked. "Who's in there?"

The sound of a frantic muffled scream comes from inside and I jump back so fast I almost lose my balance. "Mom! Mom, come quickly!"

I watch down the hall, but when my mom doesn't appear my stomach turns over. The voices I heard in the bedroom earlier were not part of a dream. There was someone else here. CJ's sister Valentine.

"Mom!" I call again, frantic this time as I suddenly realize the woman out in the living room with my mom is not CJ. Without thinking, I race down the hall and stop dead when I find Valentine standing behind my mom in the kitchen with a knife to her throat.

"No, don't!" I shout. "Please don't hurt her."

"Of course not," Valentine says with a smirk. "First she has to watch you die."

I look from Valentine to my mom and read her lips as she mouths the word *run*. I want to do what she says but I'm frozen to the spot. Again, my mom widens her eyes and mouths the word *run*. I hesitate but suddenly remember that CJ is locked in the bedroom at the end of the house. Knowing she is my only hope, I turn and run back down the hall. With no time to spare, I don't bother to slow down as I approach the door. Instead, I increase speed and throw all my weight against it, forcing it to crash open. Inside, CJ is down on the floor, gagged with her hands tied behind her back.

"CJ!" I shout. "Valentine has my mom. We need to help her." I quickly remove her gag and drag at the ties on her wrists and ankles until they come free. "She's going to kill her. You have to help me."

CJ nods and grabs a hands-free phone from its cradle on the bedside table. "I'm calling the police."

"I'm going back to help my mom."

"Harlow, no, wait -"

But before she finishes, I'm already halfway down the hall. I turn the corner into the living room but Valentine is already there to meet me. Her arm is still curled around my mom's shoulder, the knife pressing into her neck.

"You let her out didn't you," she says to me. "I really wish you hadn't done that."

"She did let me out and it ends here, Valentine," CJ says, coming up behind me. "Do you hear me, sister? This ends today."

I hear the sound of a bullet entering the chamber of a gun and turn to see CJ pointing a small silver pistol at her sister.

"Do you really think you have what it takes to shoot me?" Valentine goads. "You don't have it in you, CJ."

"Let Madelyn-May go," she commands. "We're your family for Christ's sake, Valentine. You don't have to do this."

"Neither of you is my family," Valentine spits back. "You're both deserters. You left my mom to die," she hisses into my mom's ear. "And, CJ, you never came back for me."

I watch as my mom and CJ make eye contact and seem to have a conversation that doesn't require words. Suddenly my mom stamps her foot into Valentine's shin. She gasps and momentarily lets her go. Behind me, CJ fires a warning shot. Valentine drops to the floor and I shriek, my hand flying up to my mouth. For a moment I think she is hit, but then she lunges across the room and manages to catch CJ's ankle toppling her to the ground. The gun slides out across the floor and without thinking I dive toward it.

"Harlow, no!" My mom shouts from the other side of the room, but I've already picked it up.

On the ground, Valentine and CJ wrestle. I point the gun at them and shout for Valentine to stop and move away but she ignores me. "I mean it!" I shout again. "Move away from her or I will shoot you."

Suddenly Valentine rises up and throws a punch that knocks CJ out cold. Then she turns her attention to me. "Give me that gun, kid."

"No way." The gun is visibly shaking in my hand, but I refuse to let go.

"I'm only going to take it from you anyway," she says, taking another step toward me, "you know that. So, make things easy on yourself and just give it to me."

"Shoot her, Harlow!"

My mom's cries catch me off guard and I glance over at her. Valentine takes the opportunity and lunges at me. As she grips me around the waist, I accidentally squeeze the trigger. A shot rings out before the gun comes free and Valentine's hands are around my throat. As she squeezes tighter and the air disappears from my lungs I stare into her eyes silently begging her to stop.

The room swims in and out of focus. I hear the muffled sound of my mom screaming. Something explodes behind me and Valentine falls backward, finally letting go. I clutch at my throat desperate for air. When I catch my breath, I turn to see my mom holding the gun. Valentine is on the floor, blood gushing from her shoulder.

"You bitch!" Valentine screams, grabbing at her shoulder. "You shot me."

In the distance, I hear sirens. Valentine is down and any moment the police will be here. I'm about to be free. My mom drops the gun onto the couch and rushes toward me. I move in close as she throws her arms around me. It's over.

My mom finally pulls back when we hear the sound of CJ starting to stir. Her left eye has already turned purple and she's rubbing at her jaw.

"CJ, are you alright?" my mom asks.

She looks around the room and surveys the carnage. I feel guilty that she has gone through so much trauma because of me. I am about to apologize but Valentine cuts me off.

"CJ," she calls. "Help me, please."

I expect CJ to tell Valentine that she's getting exactly what she deserves, but instead a look of confusion settles across her brow.

"I'm your sister," Valentine cries again. "We grew up together. You're the only person I've ever loved my entire life. You know that."

"CJ, no," my mom warns. "Don't let her trick you. The police are almost here. This is over."

"I saved you once," Valentine says with a hiss. "You owe me, CJ."

CJ looks back at Valentine and I follow her line of sight as she turns her attention to the gun lying on the couch.

"CJ," my mom warns again, "you know you can't help her."

But to our surprise, CJ pulls herself up and grabs the gun. She holds it on us as she reaches down and threads her arm under Valentine's shoulder.

"If you help her this will never be over," my mom tells her. "Please, she needs to go somewhere that she can get the help she needs. You know that."

"She's my sister," CJ whispers. "She saved me from that place but I never went back for her. You of all people must understand the guilt I feel about that, Madelyn-May."

"No," my mom tells her. "We all make our own choices, and right now, you're making the wrong one."

"Maybe, but it's the only choice I can live with."

With her free arm, CJ hoists Valentine up onto her feet. All we can do is watch as she balances Valentine against her shoulder and guides her out toward the garage.

"This will never be over," I whisper, as we watch them disappear from view. "Not ever."

Chapter Seventy-Eight
VALENTINE

I can feel the life draining out of me as we drive at top speed along a back road. I have no idea where we are or where we're going. All I know is that she saved me. Finally, my sister came back for me. "CJ," I manage, "you don't know what this means to me."

Outside the trees and sky blur together as I struggle to keep my eyes from closing.

"Don't talk," she says. "I'll find someone to help you."

"I don't feel so good."

"I know. Just rest."

Finally, my eyes flutter closed and the searing pain in my shoulder eases. I'm numb to everything but the fact she is by my side. It doesn't matter where she takes me because wherever it is, I will be home.

I don't know how long we drive, but when I eventually open my eyes the first thing I feel is the pain. The second is a biting cold that has settled in my bones. "CJ…"

"We're almost there," she tells me. "You've lost a lot of blood but try to hold on."

"Almost where?"

"Camarillo. I have a client from the gallery, a man. He has a plane. He's going to meet us at the airstrip."

Despite my pain, I grin. "That's the CJ I remember. Always ready for an adventure."

"It's not an adventure, Valentine. I'm trying to save your life."

I nod and look out the window. The sun has set, and shadows have swallowed the houses and buildings around us. I have no idea if I'm going to make it to this plane, but I'm at peace. I will either die here by her side or we'll have a chance to start over. Either way, I can finally let go. "How much longer?"

CJ begins to answer but from the corner of my eye, I see a dark shape suddenly dart forward. She swerves hard to the left and narrowly misses a dog that runs out from between two parked cars. The tires squeal and the seat belt cuts into my neck as she tries to correct the steering, but the car veers wildly to the right. The front wheel clips a small truck parked alongside the road and instantly the car spins out of control.

"Valentine!"

My sister's voice screaming my name is the last thing I hear before we crash into a telegraph pole and everything goes black.

Chapter Seventy-Nine

HARLOW

One Week Later

In a few minutes, the doctor will come and take me into theater where they will extract the bone marrow Poppy needs for her transfusion.

When the police and FBI arrived at CJ's house in San Diego, they found evidence of her communication with Lacy and enough images to identify her as the woman staying in the hotel room where special agent Jasper Monroe's body was found.

No matter how many times my mom and I tried to tell them there was another woman, her sister Valentine, they refused to believe us. Even Lacy kept her word, to a point. She offered to tell them all about who really killed Kempsey in return for walking free, but the FBI had already made up its mind. There was no point. They found DNA samples that belonged only to CJ in the house and the fingerprints of one other person beside us, which failed to match anyone in their system.

We begged and pleaded with them to look harder, to understand that CJ and Valentine were identical twins and shared the same DNA, but they put our story down to stress and the fact I still had Valerian, a herbal sleeping drug, in my system.

CJ had been at home working day and night on her exhibit when Valentine was recorded by the Philadelphian hotel's surveillance cameras so there was no one who could provide an alibi for her whereabouts. That meant as far as the FBI was concerned, CJ was now wanted for the murder of Kempsey Karrigan and the attempted murder of Sophie and my mom.

"Harlow, are you seeing this?" My mom's eyes are wide as she nudges me and points up to a television on the wall of the hospital waiting room. Beside her, my dad and Sophie are already staring up at the screen.

"The body of Casey-Jane Summers, wanted for the murder of FBI Special Agent Jasper Monroe, Philadelphian teenager Kempsey Karrigan, and the attempted murder of online celebrity Madelyn-May Marozzi and a second woman Sophie Miller, was found in a car wreck north of San Diego last night. It is believed the fugitive may have been heading to a private airstrip in Camarillo in an attempt to flee the country."

"Oh my God," I exclaim. "CJ is dead?"

"That poor woman," my mom says with a sigh. "All those years she managed to live a normal life and our past still managed to catch up with her."

We stare at the television as horrific images of the white SUV she picked me up in, now a twisted wreck, flash across the screen.

"Umm... I don't want to sound heartless here," Sophie says eventually, "and I know this is awful, but I think there's something else we all need to be concerned about." Together, we turn to her as she adds, "If CJ is dead, then where is Valentine?"

Chapter Eighty

SOPHIE

I tuck Poppy into bed and kiss her gently on the forehead. Behind me, Bastian is leaning against the door frame waiting to tell his daughter goodnight.

"How do you feel, sweetheart?" I ask still unable to believe the procedure is complete and she is at home with us.

"Mommy, you've asked me that a hundred times already." She rolls her eyes and pulls her favorite white bunny toy closer to her chest. "We're just fine."

I laugh gently and pull the blankets up around her. "Daddy is going to say goodnight now, alright."

"Alright, Mommy." She smiles and my heart quivers inside my chest. She is home and she is safe.

I step back as Bastian leans in and kisses her cheek. "Goodnight, little possum," he whispers. "Sweet dreams."

"Night, Daddy," she murmurs, her eyes already closing. "Sweet dreams..."

Downstairs we open a bottle of wine and collapse onto the couch, Miss Molly asleep at our feet. When Poppy's surgery was over, Harlow and Madelyn-May went back to Australia but Bastian stayed behind. I expected their separation to be traumatic for everyone, but it wasn't. Bastian and Madelyn-May had tried to make it work but they were both unhappy. In the end, she wished us well and I think she was happy just to have her daughter back and safe in her arms.

"I can't believe it's finally over," he says, handing me a glass of red. "I didn't want to say so at the time but there was a moment when I wasn't sure how all this would end."

"I'm just glad Poppy and Harlow are safe," I tell him. "And that things have worked out."

He smiles and pulls me in. "I always knew one way or another you and I would find our way back to each other."

I smile and my body warms at his words. "I hope Madelyn-May is alright. I know this is going to sound strange but I feel like she and I are almost like sisters. Always arguing and at each other's throats, but we've been through so much together. As much as I love you, I would never want to intentionally hurt her."

"Believe me, over the past few years Madelyn-May and I did our best to try and patch things up," he assures me. "We owed each other that much but it just wasn't working. If she wasn't alright with the idea of separating you'd know it. It was time. It's the best thing for everyone, including her."

I nod and sip my wine. "So, you and I, finally."

"Finally," he replies, "and inevitably."

I lean back into his embrace and let out a long breath. For so many years I have longed for this moment. Bastian and me at home on the couch, our daughter asleep upstairs and our clothes folded side by side in the closet. Through heartache, pain, and joy he has been my constant and as I glance at him through dream-lit eyes I can't wait to spend the rest of my life by his side.

"Mommy!"

From upstairs, Poppy cries out shattering my reverie. There is fear in her voice and I let out a long sigh. Since her surgery, she's been having nightmares. Doctor Yates said it's likely a lingering side-effect of the sedation and something that will eventually subside.

"You want me to go?" Bastian asks.

"No, she called for me. I'll soothe her back to sleep then we can start the movie." He nods and pats my bottom playfully as I get to my feet. "And maybe some of that," I add with a giggle.

As I make my way upstairs, Miss Molly remains at the bottom and begins to bark. I look back and pause when I notice the hair along her back standing up. "Miss Molly, what is it?"

For the first time since I brought her home from the shelter, she bares her teeth and growls. "Poppy's just having a nightmare," I tell her. "Everything's alright. Come and see for yourself."

I gesture for her to follow me, but she remains planted at the foot of the stairs, her lip pulling into a snarl. It's something I've never seen her do before and soon Bastian appears beside her.

"That's odd," I tell him. "I've never seen her do that."

He kneels down and gives her a scratch behind the ear. "You're alright, girl. Everything is alright."

"Let me sort out Poppy then I'll get her a snack," I tell Bastian. "That should calm her down. I won't be long."

I head up the stairs and into Poppy's room. I expect to find her staring at me wide-eyed with a sticky forehead, slick from the fear of whatever she was dreaming about but instead she is staring past me toward the space behind the bedroom door.

"Poppy?" I begin. "What is it, sweetheart?"

"Mommy, there's someone in my room."

"No, sweetheart, it was just a dream," I tell her, as I step inside. "We talked about this, remember?"

"No, Mommy, there's a lady." She lifts her arm to point and as I turn, suddenly the door slams into me and I topple sideways onto the end of my daughter's bed. Downstairs Miss Molly barks wildly and Bastian calls out asking if everything is alright. Before I can answer, Poppy screams and she is on me. Valentine. She grips me by the back of my hair and drags me across the room until we're by the window. Her hand is around my throat and no matter how hard I try to scream no sound comes out.

"What's going... Oh my God!" Bastian is in the doorway, his eyes wide as he takes in the scene before him. "Don't hurt her, please. Just tell me what you want. Anything. Money, whatever it is I'll get it for you. Just let her go."

"You think I need your money?" she snaps. "If I wanted it, I'd take it. That's not why I'm here."

I can feel the heat of her breath against my cheek. Her heart is pounding so hard I can feel it throbbing against my back as she presses herself against me.

"Mommy! I want my mommy!" Poppy screams, her little voice cracking with hysteria.

"Please, you're terrifying her," Bastian begs. "She just had surgery. I'll do anything you want. Just stop scaring her."

"Not my problem," Valentine hisses. "Now shut up."

She adjusts her position and I feel her reaching backward. Suddenly the chill of cold metal presses against my temple and I don't have to see it to know there's a gun at my head.

"You did this," she begins. "You helped Madelyn-May that day on the freeway and you helped her again by putting Harlow on the bus to San Diego. You keep putting your nose where it doesn't belong. Why?"

"I... Harlow was a donor match for my daughter. They're sisters. She needed bone marrow. She was going to die."

"Sisters?"

For a moment she is silent and I hold my breath waiting to see what she'll do next. Over in the corner by Poppy's bed, I see her little league baseball bat leaning up against the wall. It's child-sized but if I could get hold of it...

"You're the father of both girls?" she asks Bastian.

"I am."

Another long pause. "The freeway accident was too long ago. This kid wouldn't have even been born. Why did you help Madelyn-May back then, especially if you were fucking her husband?"

"I... I don't know," I manage.

"Yes, you do," she says, pressing the gun even harder against my temple. "Why?"

My entire body is trembling so hard that I don't know if I can continue to stand. Poppy is sobbing. Bastian is standing frozen to the spot staring at the gun pushed against my temple.

"Because... in many ways Harlow and Harry are my children too. "

"You gave birth to them?"

"No, but they came from my egg. I was protecting my children," I pause, "then and now."

Before she realizes what's happening, I gather all my remaining strength and throw myself back against the wall, the impact loosening her grip on my throat.

"Bastian, the bat!"

He follows my gaze to the baseball bat and grabs it up off the floor. "Here!"

As Valentine regains her balance, I grab the bat in both hands and swing it as hard as I can at her head. It connects with a sickening crack and she sways backward.

"Again!" Bastian shouts. "Sophie, you have to!"

I pull back the bat ready to swing, but Valentine raises her gun. As the bat connects with her head, she lets off a shot so close to my face that I feel a rush of air as the bullet screams past my cheek. I hit her again and again, and on the final blow she falls backward, smashing through the window and disappearing into the dark.

Breathless, I drop the blood-stained bat and turn to find Bastian slumped against the wall, his hands pressed tight against his chest. A dark stain is slowly seeping out between his fingers.

"Soph..."

"Bastian, no!" I rush across the room and throw myself down on the floor beside him. "No, oh my God, no! I'm calling an ambulance," I tell him frantically. "The phone is downstairs. Just hold on. I'll be straight back."

I take the stairs two at a time, grab my phone off the kitchen counter and dial 911. I ramble hysterically into the phone, then knowing the ambulance and police are on their way, I race back upstairs. Bastian is pale and covered in cold beads of sweat. "Just hold on my love," I whisper. "They're on their way."

"I love you, Soph," he whispers. "I always have."

"And you always will," I tell him, "because you're going to be fine. You have to be."

Downstairs Miss Molly barks, and I hear sirens getting closer. "They're almost here," I say with a sigh of relief. "Poppy, sweetheart I know this is scary," I tell her, "but Mommy needs you to stay in bed with bunny just till I go down and let the doctor in, alright?"

She nods but doesn't take her terrified eyes off Bastian as the blood stain seeps further across his shirt.

"Alright, I'll be right back. No one move."

Once again, I race down the stairs to let the paramedics and police in, but to my horror, standing on the landing is Valentine. Bloodied and bashed, the right-hand side of her head caved in. Pieces of bone are jutting out through sticky black hair like shards of broken glass.

"Oh... my God," I breathe, almost unable to look at what I've done.

Blood is pooling at her feet. Her arm is limp, but somehow, she is still managing to hold the gun.

"Valentine, stop. It's over," I tell her quietly. "The police are on their way. They're close, I can hear the sirens."

She lifts her arm as best she can and pulls the trigger but the bullet flies past me and lodges into the wall.

I duck and cover my head. "Valentine, stop."

"I won her back," she mumbles. "I won her back but I'm still alone."

"What are you talking about? "

"My sister."

Her injuries are grotesque, un-survivable, but I force myself to look at her.

"You're the one who messed everything up. I wanted to kill you, but..." she trails off as the red and blue lights of emergency service vehicles flash through my front window. "...I'm so tired."

"The police are here," I tell her, "and the ambulance."

With a vacant gaze, she stares out at the flashing lights. "It's over," she whispers.

"Yes, it is."

Valentine looks back at me. Our eyes meet and just for a moment, I feel all of her pain. I clutch at my chest as the weight of it tears at my heart. The anger, the sorrow. The heartache of being left behind.

"Valentine..."

"It's finally over," she whispers, then raises the gun to her temple and pulls the trigger.

Epilogue

Harlow throws the ball for Miss Molly and bests she can, my aging dog chases it across the grass. She's older now, and a little slower but she's not the only one. The past few months have taken a toll on all of us.

Bastian has a scar that creeps its way across his chest, a constant reminder of how close we came to losing him, and Poppy is still finding her way back from the transplant. Doctor Yates says her recovery is coming along well. It's early days and these things take time, but there's hope, and that's something I haven't dared to hold onto in a long time.

Above us, the sun is out. The sky is clear and the warm scent of spring is in the air. There's the promise of possibility, of life without fear or regret.

"Do you guys mind if I take off soon?" Harlow asks, checking her phone.

"Sweetheart, this was supposed to be a family picnic," Bastian reminds her. "You flew over here to spend your holidays with us."

"I know," she replies, looking awkward, "but Darcy said he'd come pick me up. It's just for a few hours, please?"

Bastian and I exchange a look and he grins. "Just for a few hours and not past dark."

"Dad, I'm in senior year."

"I don't care," he tells her. "After what we all went through, I want to make sure you're safe."

"Yeah, I get it," she says, "but Dad... it's *Darcy*."

"Go on," I tell her. "Have fun and tell him we say hi."

She beams as her fingers glide over the keyboard texting a message.

"You're too soft on her," Bastian whispers, nuzzling into my neck.

"Maybe I just remember what it feels like to need the person you love beside you."

"You think she actually loves him?" he asks.

I watch her fussing over her hair and checking her reflection in a small compact mirror. "I do," I tell him. "And I think he loves her."

"That's going to be complicated."

I smile and hold his gaze as beside us Poppy threads flowers through Miss Molly's collar. "Complicated yes, but not impossible. So long as they are honest with themselves about what it will take to make it work."

"That's very wise," he says with a grin.

"Someone once told me the most important truth is the one you tell yourself."

He searches my face and gently tucks a loose strand of hair back behind my ear. "And who told you that?"

"Just a friend." A smile tugs at my lip as I think of her and all we've been through. "More like a sister really."

Tell The World!

Loved The Secrets We Keep?

Your opinion matters! Without readers like you, authors like me would never have the privilege of doing the one thing we love most - writing.

If you enjoyed the book please leave a review to let other readers know that they might enjoy it too.

It only takes a minute and would mean the world to me.

Thank you!

About the Author

Nikki Lee Taylor is a long-time newspaper journalist turned fiction writer.

She is also a dreamer, a doer, a storyteller, coffee lover, and fur-mum to two golden retrievers Max and Sam.

She loves to write stories about women finding their inner strength and reminds herself every day that what we see as flaws, are really just the cracks that allow our light to shine even brighter.

Let's Stay In Touch

I love to hear from my readers and endeavor to answer all emails personally.

You can reach me at **nikki@nikkileetaylor.com**

- **Website**: nikkileetaylor.com

- **Insta**: @nikki.leetaylor

- **FB:** Nikki Lee Taylor

- **Goodreads**: Nikki Lee Taylor

Nikki Lee Taylor 💋

Made in United States
North Haven, CT
24 July 2024

55385233R00137